TWELVE
FINGERS

TWELVE FINGERS

Biography of an Anarchist

JÔ SOARES

Translated from the Portuguese
by Clifford E. Landers

Pantheon Books, New York

All rights reserved under International and Pan-American Copyright
Conventions. Published in the United States by Pantheon Books, a division
of Random House, Inc., New York, and simultaneously in Canada by
Random House of Canada Limited, Toronto. Originally published in
Brazil as *O homen que matou Getúlio Vargas* by Editora Schwarcz,
LTDA, São Paulo, 1999. Copyright © 1998 by Jô Soares.

Pantheon Books and colophon are registered
trademarks of Random House, Inc.

Grateful acknowledgment is made to Peer International Corporation for
permission to reprint lyrics from "Brazil" by Ary Barroso and S.K. Russell.
Copyright © 1939 by Irmaos Vitale. Copyright renewed. Administered by
Peer International Corporation for all countries of the world except Brazil,
Australia, New Zealand, and Mexico. International copyright secured.
All rights reserved. Reprinted by permission.

Library of Congress Cataloging-in-Publication Data

Soares, Jô.
[Homen que matou Getúlio Vargas. English]
Twelve fingers : biography of an anarchist / Jô Soares.
p. cm.
Includes bibliographical references.
ISBN 0-375-40893-2
I. Title: 12 fingers. II. Title.

PQ9698.29.0177 H6613 2001   863.3'42—dc21   00-051037

www.pantheonbooks.com

Printed in the United States of America
First American Edition
9 8 7 6 5 4 3 2 1

For my son Rafael

This book is also dedicated to
Fernando Morais, Rubem Fonseca,
and Hilton Marques,
the patient friends who, as always,
were kind enough to read this first.

I am grateful for the invaluable research help of Antônio Sérgio Ribeiro, a veritable walking archive on Getúlio Vargas, Carmen Miranda, and countless other figures, whom I consulted almost abusively during various hours of morning, noon, and night.

*Assassination has never changed
the history of the world.*
—BENJAMIN DISRAELI

*The figure of the gunman in the window was
inextricable from the victim and his history.*
—DON DELILLO

Honey, I forgot to duck.
—RONALD REAGAN

TWELVE
FINGERS

PROLOGUE

OURO PRÊTO, MINAS GERAIS, BRAZIL—1897

The capital of the state has maintained its political and cultural importance ever since the time of the Inconfidência uprising against Portuguese rule, that strangled cry of liberty when the city was still known as Vila Rica. Its sacred music is compared to that of Europe, and its famous School of Law, among the most traditional in Brazil, attracts students from every part of the country.

Rivalry among residents of the various "republics," as student boardinghouses are called, provokes the usual conflicts and arguments. Fights between students are common at Helena's Billiard Parlor, on Rua São José, one of the favorite spots of the young men studying in the city.

The night owls gathered there that rainy Monday evening, June 7, show no sign of the customary gaiety of bohemians. Leaning against the long bar worn smooth by the years, between drinks they comment in hushed tones that, despite being accustomed to the rowdiness of the young university students, they had never witnessed violence like that which had occurred the day before.

3

Late Sunday night, around one of the tables, three brothers from Rio Grande do Sul, sons of an influential general, snooker cues in hand, had started an argument with a student from Minas. Another law student, from São Paulo, seeing his colleague being humiliated, had come to his defense. His main target had been the youngest of the three brothers, a short, skinny lad who was studying Humanities, an indispensable prerequisite for later admission to the School of Law. The beardless youth had suffered a terrible beating. The other denizens of the establishment had finally managed to separate the combatants, but the harm had been done. As he limped out of the billiard parlor, leaning on his brothers' shoulders, he had vowed revenge.

A few yards away, at the exact moment that the habitués of Helena's were recalling the portentous incident, the youth from São Paulo who had been involved in the melee was returning calmly to his republic, walking along Rua Rosário. He attached no importance to the previous evening's fracas and found the brat's threats amusing. Concealed behind a wall, hidden by the darkness, the men from Rio Grande were waiting for him. He had no time to react. Cut down by nine revolver shots fired point-blank, he agonized for four days before dying.

His name was Carlos de Almeida Prado, Jr., the son of Carlos Vasconcelos de Almeida Prado, who had been a leading figure in the successful campaign to establish a republican form of government. The case rocked the nation. The Almeida Prado family traveled to Ouro Prêto, and Carlos was buried there.

To give some idea of the importance of the dead youth's family, it should be noted that one of the pallbearers was the governor of the state of Minas Gerais, Crispim Jacques Bias Fortes. Over four thousand people attended the funeral.

As for the brothers from Rio Grande involved in the sinister episode, Viriato, the oldest of the three at age eighteen, assumed responsibility for the shooting. Protásio, the middle brother, had turned sixteen a few months earlier. The youngest, the still beardless and diminutive boy who had sworn to avenge himself, was only fourteen. His name was Getúlio Dornelles Vargas.

ONE

A t the same instant that the tragedy was taking place in Ouro Preto, in the Bosnian city of Banja Luka, on the banks of the Vrbas River, Dimitri Borja Korozec was born. Dimitri's story is curious to say the least. His mother, Isabel, is a Brazilian contortionist born in São Borja, in the state of Rio Grande do Sul. Daughter of a beautiful black slave from the Bantu nation and an unknown father, she came into the world on September 28, 1871, born free of the fetters of slavery: as the pampas echoed her first cries, in Rio de Janeiro Princess Isabel was signing the Law of the Free Womb, declaring that all children born to slaves were free at birth. The girl was baptized with the name of her benefactress and that of her birthplace.

As was common in such cases, the evil tongues of the town swore that the little mixed-blood girl was the illegitimate fruit of a carnal rapture of the young lieutenant colonel Manuel do Nascimento Vargas, later to be the father of Getúlio. Manuel had distinguished himself as a military hero in the Paraguayan War and, still single at the age of twenty-six, had established himself in 1870 as a rancher in São Borja. The insinuation had been vehemently denied and discounted as gossip. Nevertheless, the surprising resemblance between the little girl and the rancher had fed this slander.

In 1890, Isabel had arrived in Bosnia as part of an Italian circus. At fifteen the young woman had run away from home with an acrobat-clown, one of the Brothers Temperani, when the famous troupe had toured Brazil in 1886. In her baggage were two gifts from her mother: a photograph of Princess Isabel and the novel *Mota Coqueiro,* by José do Patrocínio, the great black abolitionist hero.

In Doboj, the young woman deserts her juggling clown for Ivan Korozec, a Serbian linotypist who fell in love with the dark-skinned Brazilian woman and followed her throughout her Balkan tour. A hardened anarchist, Ivan is affiliated with the cabalistic Poluskopzi brotherhood. At that time there was an ancient secret Russian society, the Skopzi, or "the Castrati of Russia," whose adherents castrated themselves to attain spiritual wholeness. Those initiated into the Poluskopzi, or "Half Castrati," an ultraradical sect, practice the removal of just one of the testicles: the right one. The gesture is political, symbolizing that all of their descendants will perforce be of the left. The inflexible Poluskopzi boasts fewer than forty members.

Fate and Ivan's monotesticular libido decree that Isabel quickly becomes pregnant. A dedicated artist, she works until the very hour of delivery. When the circus appears in Banja Luka, after a nine-month tour, the public is astonished to see that lovely young woman contorting her enormous belly in the center ring. In the final days, Ivan Korozec begins to fear that the child will be born right there, twisted and amid lions and clowns. His fears are unfounded: Dimitri is born in the wagon of a Bulgarian trapeze artist with the bearded lady as midwife. He is a perfect creature except that he has an extra index finger on each hand.

This anomaly is neither shocking nor greatly noted, for the twelve fingers are totally symmetrical. The newborn is bathed at once in the waters of the Vrbas and seven days later, over Isabel's protests, as dictated by Poluskopzi ritual, his right testicle is removed and eaten by his father. If he were an adult, the excised gonad would be swallowed by the Grand Master of the order, Boris Kafelnikov, an obscure tailor from Vladivostok. To the amazement and pride of the semicastrati who participate in the ceremony, the baby does not cry.

From early on, Dimitri, or Dimo, as his parents call him, speaks not only Serbo-Croatian, his father's language, but also Portuguese, which his mother had taught him by reading and rereading José do Patricínio's book. Isabel tells him romanticized stories of the slaves' struggle for freedom. The legendary abolitionist takes on quasi-mystic proportions in the boy's fanciful imagination. He imagines him as a warrior saint lopping off the heads of slave traders. Dimo possesses an extraordinary aptitude for languages, and in the multilingual world of the circus he quickly learns German, French, English, Italian, Russian, Albanian, and Spanish. He speaks all of these tongues without accent.

By the age of eight one can see in him the handsome man he is to become. He has inherited his mother's dark, curly hair, his father's green eyes and snowy white complexion.

He knows nothing of his grandfather but takes pride in his grandmother's African blood. He becomes irritated when the clowns laugh at his statement that, inside his white body, he is as black as a Watusi prince. His lanky form and his unaffectedly elegant manners are enchanting to all. Later he would have what women call irresistible charm. He is intelligent and studious. His air of a vulnerable poet causes people to like him at first sight. He has a sole defect: stemming perhaps from the contortions undergone while still in his mother's womb, Dimo is extremely awkward. Not even his two extra fingers prevent objects from slipping out of his hands. Despite the rigor of the intensive training to which he dedicates himself, it becomes quickly apparent that he will never be a professional in the circus. He has an innate talent for climbing the pole that supports the tent or for ascending and descending the ropes to the trapeze, but he lacks the sense of balance needed for acrobatics. An anarchist from the cradle, with his father as mentor, by the age of twelve he has read Proudhon, Bakunin, and Kropotkin. He finds Proudhon overly theoretical and Bakunin practically a conservative. He prefers Kropotkin, who resigned as secretary-general of the Russian Geographic Society in favor of anarchism. Dimitri thinks, however, that he lacks a certain boldness. His tender age notwithstanding, he favors violent methods. He dreams of eliminating all the world's tyrants.

In 1912, Isabel is forced to give up the circus because of a dislocated vertebra. The unfortunate accident did not occur during her performance but on a picnic in the foothills of Mount Maglic. Dimitri tripped on a tree root while trying to open a bottle of wine, which flew out of his hands, hitting his mother in the lumbar region of the spine.

After months of fruitless treatment, Ivan Korozec moves his family to Sarajevo. Thanks to his contacts, he finds work at the print shop of a veteran anarchist, Nicolae Kulenovic. It is in the rear of that shop that, late at night, meet the adepts of the recently formed Ujedinjenje ili Smrt, "Union or Death," also known as the Black Hand, a secret terrorist society dedicated to unification of the Serbian people. To have an idea of the political climate that prevailed in Bosnia in that period, it is desirable to know something of the history of that organization and of its founder, who was to play a major role in Dimitri's future.

Union or Death, the Black Hand, was formed on May 9, 1911, by a group of ten men. Their objective: the creation of a unified Serbia that includes Bosnia and Herzegovina, free of Austro-Hungarian domination. The means for achieving those ends range from homicide to terrorism.

In merely a year, they already number over a thousand activists ready for anything. Several officers of the Serbian army belong to the group.

They use this seal (*right*) as their sign of identification.

Seal of the Black Hand.

The Black Hand trains its men in various methods of political sabotage and assassination. It is organized into cells of three or five members under the command of district committees, and their orders come from the Central Committee in Belgrade. To keep this hierarchy secret, its members know only what is necessary for carrying out their missions.

Upon being admitted, the initiates swear an oath at a solemn meeting: "I swear before God, on my honor and on my life, that I will obey orders and execute all missions without hesitation and without question. I also swear before God, on my honor and on my life, that I will take to the tomb the secrets of this organization."

The founder of the Ujedinjenje ili Smrt is the Serbian colonel Dragutin Dimitrijevic. Dragutin had become a specialist in coups d'état, conspiracies, and assassination. Recognizing the power of

Dragutin in dress
uniform.

information, the fervent patriot always remained behind the scenes of power, never revealing his true position. A friend connected to the court of the king of Serbia said of him, "He was never seen anywhere, yet we knew he was behind everything that happened."

Not all of Dragutin's conspiracies were successful. A year earlier, he had sent an assassin to Vienna to eliminate Emperor Franz Josef and the attempt had failed.

Husky and truculent, with an upward-pointing handlebar mustache, Dragutin Dimitrijevic wore his officer's uniform in impeccable fashion. If he were not such a powerful man, he would have been simply an object of ridicule. As an adolescent at the Belgrade Lycée, he had been a brilliant student. Indefatigable, possessed of limitless energy, popular with his peers, he acquired the nickname of Apis, the sacred bull of the ancient Egyptians. The sobriquet would accompany him for the rest of his life.

Ivan Korozec decides to enter this new sect. Dimitri's zeal and the almost fanatical admiration he feels for his father continue to grow. The latter reciprocates, fascinated by the intelligence and intellectual abilities of his son. Dimo appears older than his fifteen years. He stands almost six feet tall, and when he strolls through the streets of Sarajevo women turn their heads to watch him with hungry eyes.

On Friday, December 20, a snowstorm falls on the city. Yielding to his son's repeated entreaties, Ivan takes the youth to a secret meeting of Union or Death. The Bull is present, in violation of his own rules. He is looking for new talent for the ranks of the sect. Dimitri longs for this encounter. The atmosphere is one of excitement and civic fervor. Very near the end of the meeting, around 2 A.M., without being asked, Dimitri interrupts a speaker who was discoursing on the Austro-Hungarian Empire's dominion over Bosnia and makes an impassioned speech about the necessity for more action and less talk.

Apis is enchanted by the impetuous young man. Years before, in 1903, Dragutin had been the head of the conspiratorial officers who invaded the Royal Palace and assassinated the hated King Alexander Obrenovic and his wife, the former prostitute Draga. The colonel's charisma also does not escape the notice of Dimitri, who is pleased that both have almost the same name.

As professor of strategy and tactics at the Military Academy, Dimitrijevic exercises enormous influence on his students, who follow him to the death. Dragutin decides to make Dimo his protégé. He does not wish to see him gravitate toward the Mlada Bosna, the "Young Bosnia" movement that so enraptured university students at the time and has already cost him Gavrilo Princip, a student with a natural propensity for terrorism and a sharpshooter who he had sworn was his work of Pygmalion. Therefore, that night he initiates the following dialogue with Dimitri and Ivan Korozec:

"Ivan, is your son as bold as he seems, or are his words merely the echo from an empty head, as my grandfather used to say?" asks Dragutin, smiling.

"I don't know, comrade. I never met your grandfather."

"To tell the truth, I liked what he had to say."

Paying no further attention to the linotypist, the officer turns to Dimitri.

"How old are you?"

"Eighteen," Dimitri lies.

"Fifteen," Ivan corrects.

"When one fights for a cause, the younger the better," says the colonel with singular banality.

"Lack of age is the excuse of cowards," answers Dimitri, matching cliché for cliché.

Everyone is amused by the youth's brashness. The belligerent Apis helps himself to a pepper-flavored vodka, his favorite, and declares, "We'll see if you truly have the heart of a Serb. Have you heard of the Skola Atentatora?"

"The Assassins' School? Of course. I always thought it was a myth."

"Well, it isn't. It's located in an old abandoned convent near here, in Visoko. If your father agrees, beginning now I'll take charge of your education."

Ivan doesn't know what to say. He is divided between the pride of having his son as Dimitrijevic's protégé and the fear of Isabel's reaction. He knows his wife's temperament all too well. She has no desire to see her son involved in her husband's extremist causes. The elite admitted to the Skola Atentatora are trained in every technique of terrorism and assassination. There, nothing is simulated. Many lose their lives in the courses. Before Ivan can speak, Dimitri answers for him:

"Forgive me, Colonel, but my father has nothing to do with this decision." He raises his hands, displaying his four index fingers. "I was born with the mark of my destiny."

The group is astonished at that perfect imperfection. Even the unbending Apis is moved by the apparent presage.

"There is no further room for doubt. You are the Chosen One. The double trigger finger can only be the sign of the assassin." He raises his glass in an emotional toast: "Death to tyrants!"

The initiates present at this historic meeting hurl their glasses against Nicolae Kulenovic's worn printing press.

Returning home that night, Ivan Korozec fears that when she hears the news Isabel will rip out the only testicle he has left.

The year 1913 is a disturbing one for the Serbs, plunged into the first and second Balkan Wars, and one of great personal achievement for Dragutin Dimitrijevic. The officer is promoted to head of information for the General Staff, which affords him the opportunity to extend the claws of the Black Hand throughout the whole of Bosnia.

The Serbo-Croatian movement grows in the universities. The Bull observes everything. He has agents who have infiltrated among the students. Money pours in. There is no shortage of donations from anonymous sympathizers favoring a powerful, united Serbia achieved through violent action.

Dragutin diverts these moneys to a secret account at the Schweizerischer Glücksgeldbank in Zurich.

The Serbs quickly emerge victorious in both wars, the first against the Turks of the Ottoman Empire and the second against Bulgaria.

Meanwhile, far from these conflicts, Dimitri Borja Korozec spends the year cloistered in the old Dusa convent in Visoko. The monastery, surrounded by forest, occupies an area of 100,000 square meters a few kilometers from the small city. Razed by the Muslims in 1883, it had been rebuilt by the initiates using money from Union or Death and transformed into the Assassins' School. The convent's façade remains partially destroyed and the members who frequent it dress as friars. To avoid suspicion, the secret society had spread the word that the site was now a leprosarium run by Trappist monks. Still, anyone curious enough to venture inside the walls enclosing the monastery runs the risk of dying or being maimed by the land mines scattered throughout the gardens. A few careless students have also fallen victim to these snares.

The Skola Atentatora is overseen in implacable fashion by Major Tankosic, the Bull's adjutant. The exercises drive the initiates to the point of exhaustion. Even Gavrilo Princip, a youth with precarious health and the apple of Dragutin Dimitrijevic's eye, had left the school nine months earlier, unable to meet its rigorous training demands.

Dimo dedicates himself with intensity to his studies. He becomes familiar with the use of daggers and short knives among edged weapons. He learns fencing with foil, sword, and saber. During the training, his body is marked with several scars, the consequence of his innate clumsiness. He assimilates the craft of building and dismantling bombs and enthusiastically handles explosives such as dynamite and nitroglycerin. His bumbling becomes notorious among the other students, who avoid being present during these lessons. Those who know of the removal of his right testicle jokingly attribute his *gaucherie* to the Poluskopzi ritual. One of the instructors loses a hand while throwing one of the grenades prepared by him.

Despite his carelessness, Dimitri possesses unquestioned skill as a marksman. He can hit a cigarette in someone's lips at a distance of thirty meters. (As there are no volunteers for a demonstration, Dimo places the burning cigarette in the limbs of a far-off tree.) He learns how to prepare deadly potions like cyanide, arsenic, strychnine, and other lethal substances, but he despises poisons, considering them the tools of the craven. He wishes to meet the enemy face-to-face. He is equally distinguished in the martial arts, despite seldom finishing a class without dislocating something.

Thanks to his congenital inclination toward shooting, he specializes in firearms, primarily handguns. His favorite is the German semiautomatic Bergmann-Bayard, designed by Theodor Bergmann in 1901. The pistol was planned for military use under the name Mars. It is the first to employ 9 mm projectiles, bullets with high penetrating power. It measures 25 cm in length, weighs slightly more than two pounds, and has a four-inch barrel and a clip that holds six bullets. Its muzzle velocity is 305 meters per second. It has a formidable kick, which Dimitri finds anything but displeasing.

Bergmann-Bayard, 1901.

Schuler-Reform, 1904.

Besides the Mars, Dimitri always carries with him a small Schuler-Reform, 1904 model, with 6 mm ammunition, considered the masterpiece of the gunsmith August Schuler, a German from Suhl, the inventor of this gem conceived to fire either four consecutive rounds or all four at once. He carries it strapped to his leg.

In June, when he turns sixteen, he falls in love for

The famous painting *Guernica*, by Picasso. Mira Kosanovic
would be the woman on the left.

the first time. Ironically, the object of his affections is the instructor
of toxicology, a subject he holds in contempt. Mira Kosanovic is a
beautiful Serbo-Croatian woman of Albanian descent born in Dur-
rës, a port on the Adriatic. Her angular face, as if carved by a blade,
her prominent cheekbones, and her dark, sloe-eyed gaze give her a
feline, almost savage look. The loose-fitting, uncared-for clothing
that she wears in the convent cannot hide the sensuality of her body.
Comments are heard at the Skola Atentatora that Mira is even more
dangerous than is imagined. In the recently concluded First Balkan
War, she entered hand-to-hand combat against the Turks and, taking advantage of the shock she caused among the enemy, ripped out
their carotids with her teeth. She became known as Sabertooth. She
is eight years older than he, but Dimitri appears to be a young man
of twenty-one, with the pallor and dark circles under the eyes of the
classic image of the romantic poet. We have an idea of the brief and
overpowering passion that enveloped the two from a letter written
by Dimo shortly before leaving the Assassins' School, which Mira
Kosanovic still had next to her heart when she was found dead in

1937 in the rubble of the city of Guernica, bombed by the Germans during the Spanish Civil War. It is even said that the face of the woman to the left in Picasso's famous canvas is that of Mira. The painter is thought to have had an affair with the anarchist in 1923, in Paris.

The following is the full text of the letter.

Facsimile of the letter found on Mira Kosanovic.

My beloved,

When you find this missive, among the test tubes in your laboratory, I will be far away from here. Even before leaving, I already lament enormously the separation. Nonetheless, it is a decision without recourse.

I leave the Skola Atentatora prepared to follow my path. In keeping with the instructions from my tutor and protector, Dragutin Dimitrijevic, our leader, I cannot reveal even to you my first task. To tell the truth, nor should I even say good-bye to you, but I would not be able to go on living without this small disobedience. Knowing your revolutionary fervor, I am certain you will understand. I can only say that this mission will be vital for our cause and a mighty blow struck against the tyrannical Austro-Hungarian regime. If all goes as I hope, the Serbian people will remember me forever. More important than that is the assurance that you too will feel pride when you learn of the daring act of one whom you instructed.

I am not speaking of the lethal combination of chemicals

that you taught me with such patience. Me of all people, who hated poisons! You made me discover the romance of curare, the lyricism of an infusion of lily-of-the-valley, which in the correct dosage simply stops the heart from beating. The poetry of balm of rhododendron, so aromatic and yet so capable of inducing a lethal diarrhea in the victim.

I refer to more profound and personal teachings. I am speaking of love. Is it too bourgeois to speak of love?

You, the enchanted mistress of so many sleepless nights, revealed to me the intoxicating delights of sex, arousing pleasure in every centimeter of my body. Do you remember the first time? How awkward I was? The moment when you whispered in my ear that it was you, and not me, who should spread her legs? And how you laughed when I took your orgasm for an asthma attack . . . I can still feel the heat of your breasts marking indelibly the palms of my hands. I close my eyes and hear your voice inside me, telling me of the extraordinary rapture you experienced at being touched by my four index fingers. How can I forget that late afternoon in the monastery gardens when you pulled my head against the sweetness of your belly and, instead of your perfumed pubis, I eagerly kissed the grass?

Yes, more than the poisons, everything I know of life I owe to you. In this extraordinary year you, and not the classes, have transformed into a man the boy that dwelled in me.

I don't know if we'll see each other again, nor whether I will still be alive after the dangerous deed that awaits me. The risks are many. I know only, with the greatest of certainty, that I take with me the unforgettable memory of the brave and generous woman who taught me love.

Farewell,

Union or death!

Eternally yours,

Dimo

SARAJEVO—SUNDAY, JUNE 28, 1914

The most sacred date in the Serbs' historical calendar. It commemorates the Battle of Kosovo, which took place five centuries earlier and in which, according to Slavic myth, the flower of Balkan youth was slaughtered at the hands of Turkish barbarism. A cloudless sky over the city and the sun bathing the rooftops decorated with flowers and pennants. It is a feast day. Men and women sporting colorful clothes and folkloric costumes mark the occasion with dancing in the streets.

Whether through ignorance or stupidity, it is also the day that Archduke Franz Ferdinand, heir to the Austro-Hungarian throne, despised by the Serbian people, chooses for his visit to Sarajevo. The archduke has come to observe military maneuvers at the camp in Filipovic, at the invitation of the governor of Bosnia, General Oskar Potoirek. He is unaware that, spaced along the half-kilometer from the railway station to the city hall, where a ceremony is to be held, at least twenty-two armed conspirators from the Narodna

Odbrana, the "Nationalist Defense," are waiting for him. They are determined to eliminate this highly visible symbol of tyranny.

At 9 A.M., Dimitri Borja Korozec goes into the Café Zora on Franz Joseph Street, where he plans to get something to eat. Under his arm he carries the *Bosnische Post* from the previous evening, with the route to be followed by Archduke Ferdinand. He selects a table in back from which he can see the entire room. Since 5 A.M. he has been roaming the streets of Sarajevo, examining step by step the itinerary planned for the archduke and his entourage. He has never been so excited. Despite the heat, he is wearing a dark pea jacket and loose-fitting gray serge pants, for better concealment of the weapons he is carrying. The Bergmann-Bayard automatic stuck in his belt chafes his skin. Every few moments he pats his leg to make sure the other pistol, the Reform, is still secure inside his sock. If everything works out right, in less than two hours the deed will be done. According to his instructions, after the assassination he is to meet Dragutin in Belgrade. He mentally reviews the plan for the thousandth time. Nothing can go wrong.

Suddenly, two young men enter the café. Dimo recognizes the first: Vaso Cubrilovic. Like him, Vaso is seventeen. Quite thin, he wears a mustache to look older. He does not succeed: the sparse fuzz indicates only a boy attempting to appear more grown-up. The two go to the same secondary school, and Dimitri has not seen him since he entered the Skola Atentatora. Dimitri tries to hide behind his newspaper, but Cubrilovic has already spotted him. He comes over to the table, accompanied by a Muslim named Mohammed Mehmedbasic, from the Herzegovina province. In January, at the age of twenty-seven, Mohammed had been recruited by the Mlada Bosna, the "Young Bosnia" organization, to assassinate the military governor of Bosnia-Herzegovina, General Potoirek. To the general's good fortune, the police had carried out a routine inspection of the train taking him to the capital. Mehmedbasic threw his dagger and poison out the window and gave up on the assassination attempt. Dimitri senses that the two are nervous. Parts of the conversation among the trio were later written down by Mohammed and extracted from his *Notebook of a Muslim Anarchist,* discovered in a drawer upon his death, in 1940, in the house where he worked as a gardener:

"So, where've you been keeping yourself?" asked Cubrilovic, sitting down beside him.

I noticed immediately that the youth was bothered by our presence. He was almost a boy. He couldn't be any older than Vaso, who was seventeen.

"Oh, around," he answered, changing the subject.

I felt a certain apprehension in him. I pulled up a chair and sat down directly opposite him. Vaso introduced me:

"This is Mohammed Mehmedbasic. Mohammed, I'd like you to meet my friend Dimitri Borja Korozec. We're both students at the Gymnasium, and I can guarantee you he's the clumsiest person in the world," said Cubrilovic, laughing nervously, without hiding his agitation over what was about to happen.

Every few minutes he would glance at the door and check his watch. He wouldn't be able to keep the plan secret much longer. I tried to get him away from there, but it was too late. He told everything, looking Dimitri in the eye:

"In a short time we're going to assassinate Archduke Ferdinand."

Dimitri reacted as if he'd been punched in the stomach:

"We who?"

"The Narodna Odbrana, the Mlada Bosna! There are seven of us: Mohammed, Trifko, Ilic, Nedjelko, Popovic, and Gavrilo. Seven patriots ready for anything!" the chatterbox boasted, opening his coat and allowing a glimpse of the bomb he was carrying.

I thought Vaso was going too far and grabbed him by the arm, saying, "Shut up! Do you want to ruin everything?"

Vaso laughed. "Don't be silly. From the talks we had in class I know Dimitri sympathizes with our cause."

I studied the face of the youth across from me. His look was one of hatred, not of fear. The hatred wasn't directed at the archduke but at us, for he leapt to his feet, shouting and furiously raining blows on Vaso.

"How dare you? He's mine, understand? He's mine! Mine!"

I dragged the puzzled Cubrilovic away before the commotion brought the police.

As soon as the two leave the Zora, Dimitri senses the danger to which he has exposed himself. He is astonished at his reaction: he isn't given to such outbursts. He is generally of serene temperament. Everyone in the café turns to look at him, intrigued. If he now leaves abruptly it will appear even odder. Austrian secret agents are everywhere in the city. He must dissimulate, create some justification so that the pointless argument won't arouse suspicion. Remembering the phrase he shouted, he has a stroke of genius. He repeats it, this time in a querulous tone, giving a falsetto intonation to his voice:

"He's mine! I love him so much! O God, don't let him desert me!"

Feigning hysterical sobbing, he heads toward the men's bathroom with effeminate steps. As he passes, those present indignantly turn their heads and resume their discussions.

In the bathroom, as he washes his face and hands, Dimo reevaluates the situation. Nothing has been ruined. Not even the fact of there being other assassins lying in wait will stop him from being the first to open fire on the archduke. The only one he fears is Gavrilo Princip. He remembers the hollow-eyed, consumptive youth well from student meetings. He doesn't like him, for Princip has always disdained him as if Dimitri were a child trying to be a man, but he does respect his reputation. At the Skola Atentatora Gavrilo was known as a good shot. So what if he was? It would be enough for Dimitri to position himself in the best spot and the prey would be his. He had been trained for more difficult situations than this at the Assassins' School. He cannot weaken in the face of this obstacle. He knows exactly where to place himself to await the cortege, which is why he has chosen the Café Zora.

To arrive at City Hall the entourage will go along the Appel Quay on the banks of the Miljacka River, turn to the right onto the Lateiner Bridge at the Schiller market and take Franz Joseph Street. The Zora is located precisely at the next corner. Beside the Zora is an alleyway from which Dimo plans to fire his automatic. Standing before the sink, he checks the Bergmann-Bayard's clip, then cocks the weapon. He opens the bathroom door with renewed zeal and crosses the room toward the door. It's time to take his place at the site of the ambush. As he passes the counter, he sees his image

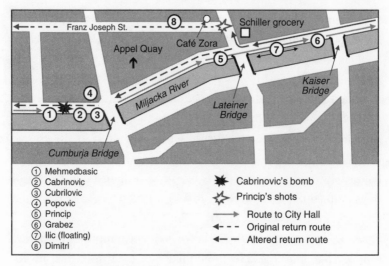

Sarajevo: positions of the assassins.

reflected in the large mirror behind the bar. In a rare gesture of vanity, the neglectful Dimitri runs his dozen fingers through his curly hair.

At ten o'clock, Archduke Ferdinand has just finished reviewing the troops and leaves for City Hall to attend the reception. His entourage consists of six automobiles. The mayor, Fehim Curcic, and the chief of police lead the cortege. Immediately behind them, with its top down and sporting the Hapsburgs' Austro-Hungarian banner, comes the car with Ferdinand, his wife, Sophia, and General Potoirek, sitting in the rear seat. The vehicle's owner, Count Harrach, sits beside the driver. The head of the archduke's military chancellery, the archduchess's lady-in-waiting, and Potoirek's adjutant, Lieutenant Colonel Merizzi, are in the third car. The fourth and fifth carry officers of Ferdinand's garrison, along with high-level Bosnian functionaries. No one is in the sixth automobile, which is merely a backup in case one of the others stalls.

The crowd, indifferent to political questions, amasses along the Appel Quay cheering the imperial couple. The seven assassins mingle with it. Princip and Grabez station themselves at the Kaiser Bridge. Ilic, who has no fixed position, moves along the avenue. Popovic remains a short distance away. Near the Cumburja Bridge are Cabrinovic, Cubrilovic, and Mohammed. Thanks to his position, Mohammed, the Muslim, is the first with a chance to attack. He grasps the grenade, but hesitates, fearful of wounding many innocent bystanders. While he is deciding whether or not to throw it, the cortege slowly drives past him.

A few meters further on, Vaso Cubrilovic, Dimitri's acquaintance, demonstrates that his rhetoric is more explosive than the gun he carries. He desists from the attack and retreats across the Lateiner Bridge. The next conspirator is more decisive. He is Nedjelko Cabrinovic, son of an old Austrian spy. An experienced agitator, Nedjelko has come from Belgrade to take part in the assassination and has no desire to waste the trip. As soon as the entourage passes, slowly descending the wide avenue, he takes the bomb from his coat pocket, breaks the percussion cap against a lamppost, and throws the smoking object toward Archduke Ferdinand.

In the short time the bomb takes to cover the distance between Cabrinovic's hand and the archduke's car, a small event drastically affects the terrorist's deadly act.

Upon hearing the hissing of the fuse being activated against the lamppost, Count Harrach, thinking that a tire has gone flat, orders the driver: "Stop the car. That's all we need! We have a flat," and starts getting out of the vehicle.

The driver, who unlike the count has seen the bomb approaching through the air, does exactly the opposite: he accelerates.

With the sudden movement of the automobile, the count is thrown backward into the seat, causing the device to pass over his head. Ferdinand, out of pure reflex, raises his arm and deflects the bomb, which explodes on the ground directly in the path of the third car. The explosion injures a dozen spectators and Lieutenant Colonel Merizzi suffers a neck wound. The principal target, however, is unharmed. The cortege continues toward City Hall at high speed.

When he discovers that the archduke has escaped unscathed, Cabrinovic swallows a vial of cyanide and throws himself into the Miljacka River. Futilely: the poison is old and the river is shallow. The frustrated assassin goes down in history as "the one who failed."

Archduke Ferdinand is furious when he enters City Hall. He says to the mayor, who struggles to keep up with his lengthy strides, "So, Mr. Mayor. I visit your city and am met with bombs? It's outrageous! Outrageous!"

The mayor, whether through nervousness or unconsciously, begins to spout the speech he had prepared previously, as if nothing had happened:

"Your Most Esteemed Imperial Highness, it fills our hearts with joy to receive such a noble dignitary . . ."

The absurdity of the situation serves to calm the archduke, and he concludes the ceremony by thanking his host for the cordial reception.

Meanwhile, the group of officers accompanying Ferdinand are discussing the need for an immediate change of plans. General Potoirek implores the archduke to leave the city by the shortest possible route. The heir to the Austro-Hungarian throne is braver than he appears. He refuses to interrupt the scheduled program: "Ridiculous. It takes more than an anarchist's bomb to frighten a Hapsburg!"

In addition to his courage, there is a secret known only to his closest advisers. Ferdinand is counting on a special kind of protection. He is wearing under his tunic a new bulletproof vest made of braided silk sewn in oblique strips. Overconfident, the archduke insists on attending the luncheon in the governor's residence and carrying out the scheduled visit to the museum. He thinks of his wife's safety:

"Sophia, it's not necessary for you to come with me. It's best that you leave immediately."

"My dear, if you think you can get away from me so easily, you're very mistaken," answers the duchess, looking at him with a mixture of apprehension and tenderness.

To understand the duchess's determination, it is necessary to know something about her situation vis-à-vis the Austrian court. The emperor had never approved of the marriage. Tradition demanded that Ferdinand marry a descendant of the House of Hapsburg or one of the reigning dynasties of Europe. Sophia does not meet the desired criteria. The union is accepted, but the marriage is morganatic, specifying the wife's inferior position.

Rigid imperial protocol did not allow her to sit in the carriage beside the archduke during ceremonies. Because the two were so much in love, they had both looked forward to the trip to Sarajevo, where, far from the court and the emperor's sight, they could appear together.

"All right. If that's what you want, so it shall be," agrees Ferdinand.

The couple descends the steps of City Hall and enters the waiting automobile.

Entering the car at City Hall.

Dimitri hears the thunderclap and the commotion brought about by the explosion. People are running in every direction. He sees policemen arguing and pointing toward the Cumburja Bridge. Despite his apprehension, he decides to wait before leaving the side street where he has positioned himself, concealed behind a stack of empty beer barrels. He has lost all notion of time. Finally, he can no longer contain his curiosity. He hides the automatic in his pocket and walks to Franz Joseph Street to try to find out what has happened. He deduces that one of the seven men of the Narodna Odbrana threw a bomb, but he doesn't know the outcome. He quickens his pace toward Appel Quay. When he arrives at the corner of the quay, across from the Schiller market, he bumps into a youth coming out of the market eating a sandwich. He recognizes him immediately. It's Gavrilo Princip. Feigning surprise, he says, "Gavrilo! It's been such a long time! What're you doing here?"

"I'm eating a sandwich."

"I can tell that. Don't treat me like a child."

"I guess there's no harm in telling you, since the attempt failed," Princip replies, with his mouth full.

"What attempt?" asks Dimitri, feigning ignorance.

"Against the tyrant's son who dares to defile our streets on the day of the Battle of Kosovo. Too bad the wretch got away."

"Got away how?"

"He brushed aside a bomb thrown by Cabrinovic. That idiot Cabrinovic couldn't hit an elephant lying down to sleep."

"Elephants don't lie down to sleep," Dimitri informs him absentmindedly, recalling the circus.

"Who cares? The fact is that now it's impossible to get him. The cowardly heir must have left Bosnia already hiding under his wife's skirts."

Dimitri is torn between sadness at the failure of the attack and joy at still having the opportunity to kill the archduke. "Maybe he's still in the city," he says hopefully.

"You're an optimist," replies Princip.

They fall silent, while Gavrilo finishes his sandwich and takes a grimy kerchief from his pocket to wipe his hands. When he opens his coat to put away the kerchief, Dimitri see a Browning pistol tucked into his waistband. Nonchalantly, Princip changes the subject, asking about a common friend they know from political discussions at the Café Zeatna Student, "The Thirsty Student."

"Have you seen Milosevic?"

"No."

"Neither have I. So, good-bye."

"Good-bye."

The two go their separate ways, walking in opposite directions. Dimitri Borja Korozec returns to his ambush spot in the alley, waiting for Franz Ferdinand to continue with the rest of his schedule, and Gavrilo Princip goes to meet his destiny.

Certain that the Austrian would never dare remain in Sarajevo, the other assassins disperse into the throng of people talking about what had happened.

Caring nothing about the opinion of the conspirators, the archduke resumes the parade with his entourage. There is a small detour from the original route. Before going to the museum, Franz Ferdinand plans to visit the people injured in the attack. But the individual responsible for these changes in itinerary is none other than Lieutenant Colonel Merizzi. Wounded by a fragment from the bomb, Merizzi is himself in the Centralna Bolnica, the hospital toward which the archduke is heading. Thus, none of the drivers has been advised of the altered plans. The procession once again moves down the lengthy avenue of the Appel Quay at high speed, but instead of continuing straight, following the Miljacka River to the hospital, it takes the original route, turning onto Franz Joseph moments after Dimitri and Gavrilo separated. When he notices the

Photo of Princip being taken into custody after the assassination. Arrow indicates the corner by which Dimitri made his escape.

Illustration of the assassination in *Le Petit Journal Illustré*. Dimo is hidden around the corner.

The bloodstained tunic of Archduke Franz Ferdinand.

Gavrilo Princip.

The weapon used in the crime: Browning model, 1900.

mistake, General Potoirek shouts to the driver: "This isn't the way! You have to take the Appel Quay!"

Startled, the driver slams on the brakes to begin backing up, and the archduke's vehicle stops directly across from the Schiller market.

Dimitri can't believe his eyes when he sees the tyrant's car motionless almost beside him. At that distance he can't miss. He takes the Bergmann-Bayard from his belt. To steady his aim, he rests his extended arm on one of the barrels in the alley where he has ensconced himself. His heart is in his throat. His excitement is comparable only to that which he experienced in the arms of Mira Kosanovic. He holds his breath and fires. The gun breech doesn't move. He fires again. Nothing happens. He has the impression that for some reason his finger has expanded and he can't squeeze the trigger. He examines the hand holding the weapon and sees to his horror what's wrong. Such was his will to assassinate the heir that, in the excitement of the moment, purely by reflex, he had inserted both forefingers on the trigger at the same time. He tries to pull them out by wetting his fingers with saliva and twisting the object as if it were a tight-fitting ring. No good. The automatic is stuck on his fingers. The anomaly that all had thought to be the mark of the assassin has occasioned the miscarriage of his mission. At the instant this occurs to him, Dimo hears two shots. He lifts his head in time to see an image that will haunt his nightmares forever: Archduke Franz Ferdinand, heir to the Austro-Hungarian empire, lying drenched in blood over the body of the dead duchess. Standing less than two meters away is Gavrilo Princip, the Browning still smoking in his hand.

On the trigger of the weapon, a single finger. The finger that unleashed the First World War.

The archduke's bulletproof vest was useless. Gavrilo's shot hit him in the neck, severing the jugular. It was impossible to remove the tunic to stanch the flow of blood because, to avoid wrinkles in the uniform, the vain heir to the throne had the habit of being sewn into the tunic beneath the gold buttons.

Despite being devastated by his failure, Dimitri Borja Korozec manages to escape the scene of the crime when the crowd hurls itself upon the young assassin. He gets rid of the Schuler-Reform pistol concealed in his sock. Hiding the other weapon, which is still welded to his fingers, in his coat pocket, he heads in the opposite direction along Franz Joseph Street. He has to get to his parents' house on Kralja Tomislava, not far from there. He must pick up his already packed suitcase and leave for Belgrade, where Dragutin, the Bull, is waiting for him. He can't imagine what the colonel's reaction will be, but he knows he cannot miss the appointed meeting.

At home, they believe Dimitri is responsible for the death of the archduke. He finds his mother in anguish and his father beaming. Clearing up the misunderstanding, Dimo reverses the situation: his mother is beaming and his father is in anguish.

"Why did you fail?" a saddened Ivan asks.

Without saying a word, Dimo takes the hand with the gun out of his pocket.

Isabel screams when she sees her son's purple fingers trapped in the trigger guard. Her maternal instinct surmounts her revulsion at that grotesque sight:

"Let's go to the kitchen. Butter should get that off your fingers."

They use butter, lard, and soap, but nothing succeeds in removing the automatic.

Dimitri's forefingers are becoming even more swollen. Isabel has an idea:

"Ice. You have to put ice on your fingers till the swelling goes down."

"I can't, Mother. I have to leave immediately. I just came to get my bag and say good-bye to both of you."

"You're only seventeen! I won't allow you to leave the house for any more of this craziness!" Isabel says indignantly.

"Well, I will, Isabel. His life no longer belongs to us; it belongs to the Black Hand, and, from the cradle, to the Poluskopzi!" states Ivan, ever faithful to the sect of the Half Castrati.

Without waiting for further discussion, Dimo goes quickly into his room and emerges carrying the small suitcase. He kisses his mother and father tenderly and heads for the door.

"Wait! You can't go out there hanging onto a pistol!" says Ivan, concerned.

The three say nothing as they ponder a solution. Then Dimo has an idea born of haste and desperation:

"Mother, I want you to make a bandage and wrap it around my hand and the gun."

"Are you crazy?"

"Not in the least. That way they'll think it's an injury of some kind. It'll even serve to divert suspicion from me. I know they're looking for students involved in the attack."

Ivan, his judgment clouded by the passion he nurtures for his son, thinks it an excellent idea. Much against her will, Isabel accedes to the youth's request. She brings bandages and wads of cotton from the bathroom. Skillfully, she transforms fist and weapon into a single large dressing. Dimo says good-bye to his parents and leaves for Belgrade. From the window, his mother waves a sad farewell. She doesn't know if she'll ever see him again. The last image she will have of the leave-taking is her son waving back, his arm extended and his right hand wrapped in what appears to be an enormous white boxing glove.

BOSNIA—BELGRADE—MONDAY, JUNE 29, 1914

Belgrade greets the morning smothered in a fog from the Danube. In a foretaste of the conflict that will shake the world, the fog spreads like a shroud to cover the White City. Dimitri Borja Korozec, in wrinkled clothes and fatigued from a sleepless night, heads for the park of the old palace of Princess Ljubice. The palace, a relic in the Balkan style, is near the Kalemegdan fort, constructed by the Celts atop a hill overlooking the junction of the Sava and Danube Rivers. It is there that Dimo is to meet Colonel Dragutin Dimitrijevic and receive his instructions. He is more confused than usual. He tells a curious taxi driver who asks about his bandages that he was mauled by a lion at the zoo. A nun, seeing him trip upon leaving the cab and noting the fatigue on his face and his apparent state of neglect, tries to take him to the Central Clinic on Pasterova Street so he can get his gigantic dressing changed. Dimo frees himself from that outpouring of compassion and with rapid steps closes the distance separating him from the entrance to the park.

Walking through the gardens, he finally spots the colonel sitting on a bench, under a tree. The Bull is not alone. Beside him, legs crossed and holding an umbrella, is Milan Ciganovic. He knows the old anarchist. Ciganovic is a supplier of arms and explosives to the Skola Atentatora. It was he who had given him the small Schuler-

Reform and the Bergmann-Bayard that was now an extension of his arm. The encounter is described in detail in a long letter from Ciganovic sent from Bucharest, in Romania, on August 29, 1914, to his half-sister Olga Krupa, a refugee in London and nurse at St. Mary's Dispensary at the New Hospital for Women:

[. . .] From a distance, the colonel gestured him to approach. Dimo gestured back with his padded hand. We were surprised at the youth's eccentric appearance. Dimitri seemed devastated:

"I failed, Colonel."

Dragutin stood up and slapped him forcefully in the face.

"Never use that word. Our men do not fail. You did not succeed, but Franz Ferdinand is dead. That's what matters." Looking at Dimitri's encased forearm, the colonel asked, "What are the bandages for? Did you injure your hand?"

Dimitri explained, abashed: "No, Colonel. It was what made me fa—— what prevented my hitting the archduke. I was in position, with the gun pointed, and when I went to shoot, perhaps from the excitement of the moment, I stuck the two index fingers of my right hand on the trigger."

"Good heavens! And you had to have an operation on your fingers?"

"No. The automatic is still caught there, hidden under the bandages. It was the only thing I could think of, since I needed to come to Belgrade at all costs. Wasn't it an ingenious solution?"

For a second I thought that Dragutin Dimitrijevic doubted the young terrorist's sanity. He finally declared it a creative solution, which made me doubt the colonel's sanity.

Dimitri Borja Korozec sat down beside us and recounted the assassination in minute detail. The colonel struck me as satisfied. I noticed that he harbored a special affection for this young man who was almost a boy. Dimitri was visibly disturbed. He inquired about the consequences of the incident. It was then that I was able to appreciate the colonel's capacity for political analysis. Exactly two months before, on June 29, his words had been prophetic. His eyes half-closed as if in a trance, Dragutin began to speak in a hoarse and distant voice:

"Now, what we have wanted above all else is going to happen. The emperor will send an ultimatum to Serbia. Even if the ultimatum is respected there will be war. Because of alliances, every country in Europe will soon be involved and we shall finally see the destruction of the Austro-Hungarian empire."

We listened, ecstatic, to the Bull's apocalyptic words. After a time, young Dimo broke the silence: "But what do I do till then?"

The colonel slapped him again:

Pound sterling in gold minted in 1911 with the likeness of King George V.

"How impatient youth is! It's a certainty that Major Tankosic and I will be accused of plotting the assassination. I probably will not live to see the realization of my dream. As for you, you will have to learn to make decisions on your own. There is an account in the Schweizerischer Glücksgeld-bank, in Zurich, in the name of Apis. I have left written instructions that you can make withdrawals and transfers using the password Nemesis."

I was astonished to see the Bull's confidence in the young man. Until then, only Tankosic and I had access to the code, and even then under the strict control of Dragutin. I used the money in Zurich for buying arms, and the major, for the expenses of the Skola Atentatora. No other member of the Black Hand knew of the existence in Switzerland of Apis. His subsequent gesture astounded me even more. Making sure that no one was coming through the gardens, he unbuttoned his uniform trousers and removed the secret belt he always wore next to his body, filled with gold coins. He handed Dimitri the leather belt with its clasp of galvanized steel made especially for him by a craftsman in Montenegro. Opening his tunic, he took out the cord with the key and placed it around the youth's neck:

Dimitri with his bandaged hand beside Ciganovic.

"Take it. It's a kind of life-preserver that I've had with me ever since the founding of our secret society. It contains two hundred gold pounds sterling, minted in 1911 and bearing the likeness of King George. You must use them only in case of extreme necessity."

While Dimo, with my help, put on the belt with a

certain degree of difficulty—his bandaged hand limited his movements—Dragutin Dimitrijevic took from his pocket a wallet and placed it in the young man's coat:

"You'll find some dinars, a thousand French francs, a passport in your name, and a ticket on the Orient Express to Paris. You travel this very night. It's best you go into hiding until things quiet down. As soon as you get there, look for Gérard Bouchedefeu. He's an anarchist friend who already knows you're coming and will put you up. The address is with the ticket."

Dimitri tried to demur: "But, Colonel, if there's war I want to be on the front lines!"

"Quiet!" shouted Dragutin, buffeting him again. "You have more important things to do. I didn't train you so you could waste your talents on conventional battles. Your function is to combat tyranny in any place, in any country. You are the whip of the Black Hand!"

I understood then that Colonel Dragutin Dimitrijevic, in an uncontrolled moment, had just modified the mission of the Union or Death. A man of unquestioned courage, sooner or later he would be condemned for his acts. Concealing the emotion gripping him, Dragutin took a camera from his briefcase: "I want a souvenir of you both."

He rose, backed up three steps, and took our photograph, of which I am enclosing a copy. From the framing, you will notice, as the nurse that you are, the severity of the colonel's emotional imbalance. After the photo, he kissed Dimitri paternally and ordered him to leave, as it was dangerous for us to be seen together. Dimo said good-bye to us, visibly nervous in the face of the uncertain future that awaited him. Before departing, he turned to Dragutin:

"Colonel, you're placing so much confidence in me; I don't know what to say."

"Then don't say anything," was the colonel's rejoinder, slapping him one last time.

I embraced Dimitri with great emotion. In a reflexive gesture, he extended his wrapped hand to Dragutin Dimitrijevic. Also without thinking, the colonel grasped the dressing forcefully. The pressure made the weapon covered by the bandages go off.

I barely heard the muffled sound of the automatic. The 9 mm bullet shattered the head of a statue of Diana the Huntress close behind us. I shall never forget the sight of Dimitri Borja Korozec staggering away through the park, shaking the arm with the smoking bandages . . .

TWO

In 1883, impressed by the trains he had seen in the United States, Georges Nagemackers, son of a wealthy Belgian banker from Liège and friend of King Leopold, decided to create the first transcontinental European railway. His enthusiasm spread to his family and to the king himself, who lent his support to the undertaking. Thus was born the Compagnie Internationale des Wagons-Lits et des Grands Express Européens. The new train traveled over more than three thousand kilometers of tracks linking Paris to Constantinople, with stops in Strasbourg, Karlsruhe, Munich, Vienna, Budapest, Bucharest, and Giurgiu, on the damp border of the Danube River between Romania and Bulgaria. From there, the passengers would be ferried across the river and continue in a more modest train to Varna on the Black Sea, where they would again transfer to arrive in Constantinople.

By 1914, the three-day trip had become more comfortable with the opening of new lines linking Budapest to Constantinople by way of Belgrade and Sophia. The cars are of the same type as those invented by George Mortimer Pullman in the United States. They were divided into sleeping cars, a dining car with excellent cuisine, a *wagon-fumoir* for the gentlemen, and a special car for the ladies that includes small compartments with basin and mirror so *les mesdames* can arrange their hair and makeup.

Each compartment is richly decorated in Art Nouveau style with Persian rugs, velvet curtains, mahogany panels, and overstuffed armchairs finished in Spanish leather. The lengthy journey attracts the elite of European society, including royalty.

It is precisely on the Orient Express that Dimitri Borja Korozec is to embark for his long trip to Paris. With quick step, avoiding the main thoroughfares, Dimo heads for the railway station. Nightfall

View of one of the cars on the Orient Express.

thickens the fog enveloping the city. En route, to disguise the hole blown in the false bandage by the bullet, Dimitri sticks into the opening a bouquet of wildflowers bought from a flower girl in the street, which gives the arrangement an even more bizarre appearance.

At the station, the kiosks are carrying special editions of the afternoon newspapers with the story of the archduke's assassination. Hundreds of passengers are vying for the few remaining papers to read about the tragedy. The platforms are alive with excited people, bumping into one another because they are walking with their eyes fixed on the news of the killing. From a distance, the crowd opening and closing the pages recalls the flight of white butterflies.

Dimitri pretends to be interested in the copy being read by a gentleman with gigantic sideburns who is walking beside him. When he notices the intrusion, the man folds his newspaper, hiding the information from the curious eyes of the busybody with the flowery bandage on his hand.

Dimo climbs onto the train and installs himself in the private, first-class cabin the colonel has reserved for him. He observes, almost compelled to do so, the place in which he finds himself. He is not the first to be intimated by the ostentatious luxury. Any of the more humble passengers who enter the cars for the first time, like the governesses and servants accompanying their millionaire masters, experience the same sensation. Later, the youth will relate to Bouchedefeu, in Paris, the shame he felt traveling surrounded by such luxury: "The money spent on a single car would feed the poorer districts of Sarajevo for months." Dragutin Dimitrijevic knew

Route on the Orient Express taken by Dimitri after leaving Belgrade.

what he was doing: no one would look for a young terrorist amid all that rolling ostentation.

The stationmaster, in a ritual repeated for several years, takes his watch from his vest pocket, blows his golden whistle, and the train pulls out at the appointed time. Steam from the locomotive envelops the people come to see the travelers off. The stationmaster observes with satisfaction the train slowly leaving Belgrade, rounding the *gare* like some immense brown-and-gold serpent creeping along the crossties. Another journey has begun for the legendary Orient Express.

On the departures platforms of the Hauptbahnhof in Munich, located near the Karlsplatz, a svelte woman, dressed in black and wearing a hat with a plume like a cavalry dragoon, waits impatiently for the train to arrive. She knows that the Orient Express left Salzburg at the expected time. The tulle veil concealing her face lends her an air of mystery. The oddness of the scene is enhanced by the Indian dwarf in a turban who carries her bags.

Supported by the diminutive man from the East, she rises on tiptoe, looking toward the horizon in search of the smoke that will indicate the locomotive's approach.

The woman's name is Margaretha Geertruida Zelle MacLeod, better known as Mata Hari. The reason for the pointless disguise is simple: Mata Hari is trying to travel incognito to Paris to meet an old lover, the French general Adolphe-Pierre Messimy. She does not want to arouse the suspicions of Lieutenant Alfred Kiepert, another former lover, connected to the German espionage service, with whom she still occasionally has relations. Kiepert, a man of means, had in several instances provided large sums of money for her to act as an occasional agent. He would take advantage of her tours through Europe to use her as a liaison. Since the dancer's return to Berlin, he has kept her under close surveillance.

In February, Mata Hari had taken lodging at the Hotel Cumberland, to appear at the Metropole Theatre in her show *Die Million-endieb*. The operetta, however, will not open until September, and the dancer has already exhausted almost all the money realized from the sale of the mansion in Neuilly, the horses, and the furniture.

Mata Hari doesn't look her age, but neither her beautiful, firm body nor her wrinkle-free face dispel the insecurity of a dancer who performs nude onstage at the age of thirty-eight. On impulse, she has decided to take this secret journey. Claiming to be suffering from a strong cold, she has interrupted rehearsals for several days, packed two of her forty-seven Louis Vuitton bags, and come to Munich to await the connection on the Orient Express to Paris. Her intuition tells her that the assassination in Sarajevo on the twenty-eighth can somehow improve her financial situation. Messimy is minister of war. Very soon, it's possible that the French will be interested in news about the German general staff. "And vice versa," thinks the dancer. She cannot know that she will become the most famous double agent in the Great War.

Margaretha Geertruida Zelle MacLeod's tempestuous life began in Holland, in Leeuwarden, where she was born in 1876. At nineteen, her beauty had not escaped the notice of Captain Rudolph MacLeod, a Dutchman of Scottish origin some twenty years her senior. MacLeod took pride in his lineage. He was a descendant of Olaf the Red, king of the Isle of Man. Despite the difference in age, they soon married and moved to The Hague. In 1897, MacLeod was transferred to Java. On the first of October the family embarked for the Dutch islands aboard the SS *Prinses Amalia*.

It soon became apparent that the vivacious nature of the young woman was not adjusting to the tranquil life of the island. The incompatibility of temperament between the pair became accentuated.

After five years, she separated from the captain and returned to her uncle's home in Nimeguen, Holland. A short time later she made her triumphant debut in Paris, following which she came to be sought after throughout the world.

From Java she brought Motilah, the Hindu dwarf who accompanied her everywhere; the secret of the island's sensuous dances; and the name Eye of the Morning. In Javanese, Mata Hari.

The drawn-out whistle of the locomotive warns the passengers on the platform that the Orient Express is entering the station.

ORIENT·EXPRESS

Mata Hari.

ORIENT·EXPRESS

ORIENT EXPRESS, FROM MUNICH TO PARIS

Having decided not to leave the train before arriving in Paris, Dimitri Borja Korozec observes the new passengers from the window of his compartment. His attention is drawn to the remarkable figure of the woman who is boarding the train escorted by her Lilliputian companion. The pair start to climb onto the car. First the lady in black and then, with some difficulty, the dwarf. He is so short that he can't reach the first step. He solves the problem by laying the Louis Vuitton on the ground and using the monogrammed luggage as a ladder. Rubbing his hands, he smiles contentedly at his mistress, happy at the solution he has found to board the car. The woman is less satisfied, as she is obliged to descend to the platform again to retrieve the baggage.

Despite his determination to stay in his compartment, Dimitri can't resist the impulse to take a closer look at his new traveling companions. He opens the doors and launches himself into the narrow passageway at the exact instant the two are approaching from the opposite direction. As a result, he trips over the dwarf and lands on top of Mata Hari. The veil falls from her face, and Dimo is mesmerized by the dancer's beautiful, enigmatic countenance. He extends his hands, babbling apologies, and assists her to her feet. Mata Hari is taken by the youth's air of helplessness. When she sees the enormous bandage from which the bouquet is sprouting, she takes the nosegay and says, "Thank you. I've never received flowers in such an original manner."

"And I've never seen a more beautiful woman in all my life," declares Dimitri, forgetting his passion for Mira Kosanovic.

The two stare intensely at each other as they remain there, forgotten by time, their bodies pressed together by the narrowness of the corridor. The magical moment is broken by a cavernous basso profundo voice. Dimitri is startled to note that the hollow sound is coming from the throat of the dwarf. Motilah is pointing, bowing as he does so.

"This is one of the compartments, *begum*," he advises, using the Urdu honorific for lady or mistress.

"Fantastic, right next to mine!" says Dimo, opening the door.

"If the begum prefers, she can use the other one, at the far end of the car. They are the same. I offered her mine because in the middle of the car one does not feel the shaking as much."

"No, no! I'll stay here," says Mata Hari, casting a sidelong look at Dimitri.

"As the begum wishes."

Dimo takes advantage of the occasion: "How rude of me! I haven't introduced myself: Dimitri Borja Korozec," he says, kissing the woman's hand.

"Mata Hari," she exclaims, forgetting her disguise.

From the lack of reaction on his part, Margaretha perceives that the youth has never heard of her. Looking down, the dancer introduces the little man: "This is Motilah, my faithful companion, secretary, chauffeur, butler, bodyguard—in short, my *homme à tout faire*."

Motilah acknowledges this with a nod of his head, bringing his hands together Indian-style.

Dimitri eyes the little man with indifference: "Bodyguard?"

"It's best not to underestimate him. Many men three times his size have paid dearly for doing so. Motilah is versed in the Hindu martial arts illustrated so well in the *kathakali* dance, one of my favorites. I don't know if you're aware of it, but *kathakali* dancers have such absolute control of their muscles that they can laugh with one side of their face and cry with the other."

Dimitri is enthralled by the stream of useless erudition: "You're a dancer!"

"An exotic ballerina."

"What a coincidence! My mother is a contortionist."

Mata Hari is amused at the comparison: "You've never heard of me?"

"I've just left the seminary," lies Dimitri. "I'm going to spend some time in Paris, at the home of a Dominican friend, to gain some contact with the outside world."

"Excellent! I'm going there also. Let's take advantage of the trip to get to know one another better," says the entertainer, squeezing his arm in a gesture replete with hidden intentions.

Flustered, Dimitri attempts to change the subject. Looking at the dwarf, he asks, "At that height, how can the little man act as your chauffeur?"

"He pushes back the front seat and drives standing up."

Dimitri is unsure whether to take this bizarre piece of information seriously. Mata Hari says good-bye, promising to meet him later: "We'll see each other in the dining car."

Dimitri returns to his compartment, still stunned by the encounter.

A slight jostling indicates that the train is leaving Munich. The ritual of the whistles is repeated. The locomotive slowly accelerates, imprinting on the tracks the monotonous sound that will accompany it throughout the journey.

ORIENT EXPRESS

In her compartment, Margaretha MacLeod, *nom de guerre* Mata Hari, prepares to make a conquest of the impetuous youth with the look of a poet, her most recent traveling companion. She wonders about Dimitri's age. "He can't be more than eighteen," she assumes, enchanted at the idea of seducing the young man. The trip to Paris is a long one, and longer still are the nights on board the train.

Nude, she examines herself in the tiny Venetian mirror in the cramped bathroom. She approves of the image the mirror affords her. The smooth face, the firm breasts with rosy nipples, the extremely white skin, the fleshy lips—in sum, the totality of the aura of sensuality that emanates from her body reaffirms her opinion of herself: no one would take her for over twenty-five. In an almost mechanical ritual, she opens her *nécessaire* and begins her toilet. First, with the tips of her fingers and using a dozen small moist cloths soaked in lavender, she cleanses her face, her underarms, her pubis, and every recess of her body. Then, with the stopper of the flask, she applies perfume to her neck, earlobes, and knees. She makes up only her eyes and mouth. She gets dressed again. She is ready to exercise once more the only art form in which she has no superior: the art of seduction.

ORIENT-EXPRESS

In the next compartment, Dimitri Borja Korozec awaits his time to be seduced.

ORIENT-EXPRESS

One passenger feels completely at ease in the confined quarters of the sleeping car: the Indian dwarf Motilah Bakash. To him the compartment is palatial in size. Except for the height of the sink in the bathroom, everything seems tailor-made to his measurements. Wearing a loincloth and turban, he assumes the lotus position. Eyes half closed, Motilah incessantly chants the secret mantra of the worshipers of Kali, the dark goddess of destruction. According to their doctrine, it was the infinite semen of Shiva, launched into her cosmic vagina, that generated the entire universe. Motilah Bakash has in front of him, surrounded by incense, a small statue of Kali. The image of the goddess is terrifying. Her disfigured face is covered in blood. Her mouth is open in a monstrous, repulsive grimace, showing her protuberant tongue and pointed teeth. Three of her four hands grasp a sword, a shield, and a noose. The fourth hand is extended in a gesture that her followers interpret as a blessing. Kali is nude and boasts a belt of human skulls and a garland of decapitated heads.

Little by little, Motilah goes into a trance. He attains *satori,* the interior enlightenment that leads to nirvana. He feels six feet tall. He is no longer the dancer's factotum but an omnipotent giant. No one knows that Motilah Bakash is a relic of the Thug sect. The terrible brotherhood of assassins had been exterminated in India by the English in 1837, but Bakash's parents managed to flee to the island of Java. The little man had been educated according to the tradition of the brotherhood, learning the Vamakara rites, the Tantrism of the left hand, in which its adepts attain the heights of pleasure by means of sexual practices. Several times, initiates achieve orgasm, without touching themselves, through the power of meditation. He studied *ramasi,* the Thug jargon, and the signs that members use to identify one another. These teachings now seem useless, as Motilah Bakash is probably the last of the Thugs.

Motilah has never renounced, however, the doctrine that made him into a master of strangulation. His weapon, which appears harmless, is the *roomal,* the sacred kerchief that he always wears around his neck. In his tiny fingers the smooth silk becomes a deadly garrote. In his hashish-induced deliriums, Motilah sees himself as a *Sistrurus miliarus,* the silent pygmy viper only thirty centimeters long but every bit as venomous as any other.

Admirers who approach Mata Hari are unaware of the risk they are taking, for the dwarf harbors a secret and obsessive passion for the dancer. Whenever the minuscule Asian judges that, for whatever reason, a suitor can be harmful to his mistress, he silently eliminates the luckless gallant. A trail of unsolved crimes in the cities where the entertainer has appeared speaks to Bakash's efficiency.

Unfortunately, Dimitri Borja Korozec has not fallen into the good graces of the small killer, who awaits the opportune moment to rid himself of that intruder. This is why he invokes the inspiration of Kali, the goddess of assassins. The cadence of the intoned mantra merges with the creaking of the locomotive.

ORIENT-EXPRESS

Ignorant of the danger he faces, Dimo, with the anxiety of adolescence, tries to make ready to rendezvous with the mysterious woman. He has never heard of Mata Hari, but he senses that she is a celebrity of some kind trying to travel without being recognized. He tells the attendant to bring him oil and a bucket with ice and soap. The servant does so without blinking, accustomed as he is to far more exotic requests on the Orient Express. Dimitri unrolls the false bandage and places his hand with the automatic inside the receptacle. A numbness climbs up his arm. He no longer feels the fingers that the ice has turned purple, but he notices that the two index fingers caught in the trigger guard are beginning to shrink. He takes the soap, applies a thick coating of foam, and massages the spot with oil. Then he secures the weapon behind the doorknob and, bracing his foot against the door, uses his leg as a lever, forcefully pushing himself backward. As a result, he pulls off the knob and falls on the floor. But he has achieved his objective: The Bergmann-Bayard finally comes off his fingers. Dimo massages his hand until the circulation is fully restored and then tosses the automatic out the window. He has no desire to take chances crossing the strict French border. He swears to himself that never again will he let the supplementary forefinger get in the way. "Not even if I have to amputate it," he thinks, drastically. He checks that the belt with the gold coins is still in place, touches the key over his shirt, and straightens his disheveled clothing.

A dining-car attendant comes down the corridor, announcing in French the last call: "Dernier service! Dernier service!"

Dimitri checks his appearance again and leaves excitedly for the appointed meeting.

ORIENT-EXPRESS

Dimo finds Mata Hari and Motilah Bakash already seated at the corner table in the luxurious dining car. He is impressed by the Limoges porcelain, the Baccarat crystal, and the fine linen tablecloths, all bearing the company monogram.

In the restaurant, the diners, appropriately dressed in formal wear, are discussing the dramatic events, excited at the prospect of a conflict.

"I've heard that there are highly placed Serbian officers involved!"

"Poor Sophia! What a horrible death; she was struck in the abdomen!"

"It seems the archduke's last words were 'Sophia, my love! Don't die! You have to live to take care of our children!' "

"I wonder if all the assassins have been caught?"

At one of the tables, a gentleman with a large mustache and wearing a dress uniform covered with medals is the center of attention. He is the Portuguese general Acácio Galhardo, aboard the Orient Express on a vacation trip. The general entered the reserves many years ago, but the uniform lends him the unquestioned status of expert in the art of war. Someone asks, "Well, General, will there be war?"

General Acácio pauses and replies with a serious expression, "If it happens, there will be. If not, it remains to be seen."

Under different circumstances, Dimitri would intervene heatedly in such discussions. But with the enthusiasm of the young, all he can think about at that moment is Mata Hari. He forgets the class struggle and the fact that he is one of those implicated in the conspiracy. He wants to take advantage of the journey with the extraordinary woman whom chance has placed on the same train. He approaches the table, smiling ecstatically. With Motilah at her side, she gestures for Dimo to take a seat across from her. They are drinking Kir Royale, and the dancer asks the waiter to bring one for Dimitri.

The dinner, taken with Cristal 1910 Champagne, the czar's favorite, begins with a Salade Aïda, a specialty of the chef. In a tureen with endive leaves, slices of green pepper form a kind of dome. Around the dome are interspersed segments of boiled egg, tomato slices, and artichoke hearts. Minced egg yolks complement the elegant dish. As the passengers watch, the maître d'hôtel stirs the dressing made from oil, vinegar, mustard, salt, and black pepper and sprinkles it over the salad. Mata Hari, Dimitri, and even the ascetic dwarf devour the first course and finish the initial bottle of Champagne. After the salad comes the famous Shrimp Cocktail à la Orient

Express, whose preparation has become one of the dining car's most charming rituals. And more Champagne. Next comes consommé, served in a soup tureen of English porcelain, over bread toasted in butter. And more Champagne. The *pièce de résistance* is Roast Beef avec de la Moutarde à la Menthe. Various gourmets have traveled on the train merely for the delight of tasting the unequalled flavor that the mint mustard imparts to the meat. To accompany the delicacy, they order another Cristal. And there is no way to decline the dessert, a light-as-air Crème de Thé, tea pudding served with purée of wild fruits. Only then is it time for Turkish coffee and liqueurs, but the trio sticks to Champagne.

ORIENT-EXPRESS

When the train leaves the station at Karlsruhe, the three are still in the dining car, quite intoxicated. Listless, Motilah Bakash, who has the morbid custom of collecting photographs of his victims, remains silent as he plans his attack. His tolerance for wine is propor-

Photo of Dimitri and Mata Hari taken by a drunken Motilah.
Point of view of the dwarf.

tional to his size. He feels his eyelids growing heavy, amid macabre alcohol-induced visions in which the fierce dark countenance of the goddess Kali merges with the alabaster features of Mata Hari.

Dimitri and the dancer, intimates by now, begin a lively conversation. A few passages were carefully recorded by Tartarin Charbonneau, a waiter with literary pretensions and the only one to recognize the entertainer. Charbonneau later attempted to peddle his notes to the press, but his jottings never gained credibility even in his family or among his fellow workers on the train. Following is the portion of dialogue overheard by Tartarin:

MATA HARI: Dimitri Borja Korozec. What a strange name you have! What is that *Borgia* doing in the middle of two Slavic names? It is Italian?

DIMITRI: It's not *Borgia,* it's *Borja.* My mother is Brazilian. Naturally, you don't know where Brazil is.

MATA HARI (*smiling*): That's where you're mistaken, my dear Dimitri. One of my most fervent admirers is a Brazilian whom I met last year in Paris. José do Patrocínio Filho. Do you know who he is?

DIMITRI (*startled*): I didn't know that José do Patrocínio had a son.

MATA HARI: Well, he does, and he loves to tell stories about his father. (*Curiously*) So you've heard of the Negro who helped overturn slavery in your mother's country?

[The youth stared at her and made a statement that I attributed to the wine, for it contrasted with the whiteness of his skin.]

DIMITRI: My mother owes her freedom to him. I'm the grandson of an African slave.

[Mata Hari gave me the impression that she was as incredulous as I, but she preferred not to go into details.]

MATA HARI: Well then, the son of this liberator is one of the most amusing men I've ever met. He's a journalist, writer, and attaché with the Brazilian consulate.

DIMITRI: I can understand your enthusiasm. Besides everything else, he must have inherited his father's striking good looks.

MATA HARI: Just the opposite! His charm and imagination are extraordinary, but he's short and skinny. Only a little bigger than Motilah.

[The drunken dwarf out of the *Thousand and One Nights* accompanying them emitted a slight grunt, probably from irritation at the comparison.]

MATA HARI: Sometimes he used to take advantage of his dark skin to pass as a Hindu prince. He once told me that he had secretly fought a duel over a woman, in the Bois de Boulogne, with King Albert of Belgium. I confess that I succumbed to the Latin charms of the fantasy-laden Brazilian. . . . But what about you? How did you come to end up in Europe?

DIMITRI: I've never been in my mother's homeland. I was born in Banja Luka, in Bosnia. Who knows? Maybe fate will take me to Brazil someday.

[For a few instants, the youth seemed lost in thought. Then he asked:]

DIMITRI: How did you meet him?

MATA HARI: Who, José? It was in the spring. I had the leading role in the musical comedy *Le minaret,* at the Théâtre de la Renaissance, with great success. Right away I noticed a small dark man ensconced every night in the front row who would throw me flowers at the end of the play. I changed vehicles in the summer. I went to the Folies-Bergère, doing a series of Spanish dances that won over both critics and the public. I saw the same little man who had attended me since opening night. Finally, my last night at the Folies, he came to my dressing room and invited me to dine with him. I couldn't refuse. That was the beginning of our friendship. We're still good friends even now.

[The youth named Dimitri, almost a boy, drew nearer to her.]

DIMITRI: I hope to meet him someday.

MATA HARI: If you spend any time in Paris and go to cafés, you're sure to run into him.

[That was when Mata Hari saw me out of the corner of her eye and realized I was listening to the conversation. She rose, dragging the youth by the hand.]

MATA HARI: It's getting late. We should go back to our compartments.

[I heard nothing more. They left, followed by the staggering, intoxicated dwarf.]

ORIENT-EXPRESS

Upon leaving the dining car, Dimitri Borja Korozec begins to feel the effect of the drinks more intensely. He is unaccustomed to ingesting such large quantities of alcohol. He leans against the dancer, slipping his hand around her waist. The trio make their way down the corridor: Dimo embracing Mata Hari, and Motilah Bakash behind them, sidling along the windows. He plans to wait for the dancer to go to bed and then follow Dimitri and silently strangle him in his compartment. Kali, the devourer, will once again have her hunger sated. But new developments show Motilah that he will have to modify his plans. When they arrive at Mata Hari's compartment, she pushes the youth inside and shuts the door. Bakash is perplexed. He has never seen the begum give herself to anyone at first meeting. No matter. He knows how to wait. Patience is a duty of the Thugs. He conceals his tiny body in the shadows of the car and begins to meditate, hands crossed over the *roomal* wrapped around his neck. In a few moments he is asleep standing up, as rigid as a blackamoor.

ORIENT EXPRESS

In the compartment, Mata Hari loses no time. She sucks Dimitri's lips in a prolonged kiss. Her experienced tongue explores the youth's mouth. Her hands, trained in the most perfected forms of caresses, traverse his shuddering body. She thrusts her powerful dancer's thighs against the youth's turgid member. He almost rips off her dress in his eagerness to stroke her firm breasts. He wets his fingers with his own saliva and lightly caresses her nipples. She nearly faints from pleasure. It has been years since she enjoyed so young a lover. She lies down on the berth and removes the rest of her clothing while Dimitri tosses aside his overcoat and slowly unbuttons his shirt. With his gaze he licks that dazzling nude woman offering herself to him. His eyes pause over her pubis, and Dimitri's head spins as in a whirlpool. Two, four, eight Mata Haris give themselves to him in an erotic kaleidoscope that he is unable to stop. Maybe he shouldn't have drunk so much. Suddenly, from his

stomach rises an overpowering sensation of nausea. To avoid breaking the mood of sensuality that envelops them, he pleads, "Wait, my
love! Don't move. I'm going into the bathroom to clean up for you."

She protests: "No! I want to smell all of you, just as you are! To
sniff your member like a bitch in heat!"

Too late. Dimitri has left the cabin and hurries down the corridor in search of the bathroom.

To be fair, the event that occurs immediately afterward owes
much more to the inexorable nausea caused by his intoxication than
to Dimo's intractable awkwardness. The bathrooms on the Orient
Express are located at the ends of the cars. He could have relieved
himself in the small basin in the compartment, but since his chamber is next to Mata Hari's, he wishes to spare the dancer the sounds
of his regurgitation. Overcome by nausea, Dimo dashes to the bathroom and opens the door. Seated impassively on the toilet, his
uniform impeccable and his trousers lowered, is General Acácio
Galhardo, who had forgotten to slide the bolt. The old soldier
looses an anguished battle cry: "Occupied! Occupied!"

Futile. Dimitri can no longer control his nausea.

"Can't you see it's occupied!" the outraged general continues to
bellow.

"Excuse me, General, excuse me!" replies Dimo, unable to control the gushing that spurts onto the gleaming medals.

Finally free of his nausea, he closes the door behind him and
dashes toward his compartment. He wants to clean up before meeting Mata Hari again. In the distance, the piercing cries of the hapless
vacationing general can still be heard: "But I told him it was occupied!"

ORIENT-EXPRESS

The noise awakens Motilah Bakash. Not understanding what is going on, he sees Dimitri hastily return to his compartment. Removing the scarf from his neck, Motilah approaches without a sound. Through the half-open door he observes Dimitri's movements. He holds the scarf between his fingers, preparing for the moment to strike.

Inside, Dimo leans out the window, letting the cool night air revitalize him. He feels better. He washes his face and gargles with water and a few drops of Dr. Pinot's dentrifice lotion. In a matter of seconds he will be back with Mata Hari. The thought excites him anew. As he is about to return to the arms of his beloved, he trips on the untied lace of his boot. He quickly kneels to knot the loose shoelaces. Exactly at that moment, Motilah Bakash lunges toward him to wrap the deadly lasso of the sacred scarf around his neck. The ensuing scene could have been choreographed by one of the acrobats of Isabel's old circus. As Motilah has not foreseen Dimitri's sudden ducking, he passes directly over the youth's back and disappears out the window. Unaware that he has almost been strangled, Dimo thinks that Bakash's gymnastic leap is the result of drunkenness and rushes to the window to see if it's still possible to help him. He thinks himself the victim of a hallucination, for Motilah Bakash is outside, hanging onto the side of the car. On closer examination Dimo sees that one end of the Indian's scarf is caught on a protuberance jutting from the car. Motilah is holding on for dear life to the other end. Dimitri leans out and begins to pull him inside. Bakash shows signs of weakening: "Don't give up! You're almost out of danger!" Dimo shouts, gathering in the scarf little by little.

He leans out further, putting his own life at risk, and grabs Motilah's outstretched hands. Just as he thinks he will manage to save him, his fingers slip from the sweat-dampened palms of the small assassin. The last words he hears from the dwarf are imprinted forever in his memory: "I'm going to fall."

Dimitri Borja Korozec silently watches the diminutive silhouette of Motilah Bakash vanish into the darkness, unaware that he has almost become one more victim of the last of the Thugs.

In shock, he has no idea how long he stands there looking out the window. The train's whistle brings him back to reality. The Orient Express has just arrived at the Strasbourg station.

ORIENT-EXPRESS

Once French, Strasbourg is now the last German city before the border. At this early-evening hour, the departures platform, illuminated by lamps, is unusually busy for that time. A young Hussar lieutenant and four German soldiers are talking to the stationmaster.

Out of breath, Dimitri enters Mata Hari's compartment. Not knowing how to inform the entertainer of Motilah's disappearance, he prefers to await a more opportune moment. Mata Hari, tired of waiting for the return of her new lover, has gotten dressed. She is visibly annoyed: "I thought you'd fallen off the train."

"Me?" replies Dimitri, giving an exaggerated guffaw.

He approaches her for a kiss. Mata Hari pushes him away impatiently. "Not now."

"Why?"

"It's better to wait till the train crosses the border. I'm eager for us to enter French territory."

The conversation is interrupted by a knock on the door. Dimitri moves away from her, startled. He imagines that the accident with the Indian dwarf has been discovered.

"Who is it?"

The door opens and the lieutenant who was on the platform comes in, addressing himself to Mata Hari.

"Madame Margaretha MacLeod?"

She tries to dissimulate: "There must be some mistake, my dear man. I don't know any such lady."

"My pardons, Madame, but we have express orders from Lieutenant Alfred Kiepert to invite you to leave the train and accompany us back to Berlin."

"I told you that's not who I am!" she insists, nervous at the prospect of being forced to interrupt the journey.

The young Hussar hesitates, in doubt over the impasse: "But we have reliable information, Madame, that you are indeed Margaretha MacLeod."

Wanting to help, Dimitri interjects: "I can assure you, Lieutenant, that this lady is not named Margaretha MacLeod. Her name is Mata Hari," he says emphatically, ruining everything.

The lieutenant turns elegantly to his beaten adversary. "Shall we go, Madame?"

Resigned, Mata Hari prepares to leave the train. "I need a few minutes to call my amanuensis. Where *is* Motilah?"

"I saw him leaving the car. He must be out there somewhere," stammers Dimitri in a half-truth.

"We haven't much time, Madame. The return train is waiting for us at the other platform," the Hussar says.

"Ah, servants. They're never around when we need them!" complains Margaretha. "Dimitri, if you see him, tell him to return to Berlin immediately. I can't wait for him."

The soldiers help her close her suitcases and carry out the luggage. Mata Hari kisses Dimo on the lips and says good-bye with an affectionate pat on the cheek: "*Quel dommage* . . . Who knows, perhaps someday our paths will cross again."

"I await that reencounter anxiously," states Dimitri, kissing her hand and still devastated by the gaffe he has committed.

She turns to the lieutenant: "I see that I underestimated the competence of the German secret service. I would merely ask that this unpleasant incident be kept in the strictest confidence. I would prefer this *escapade* not to become another scandal."

"You may rest assured of that, Madame. Lieutenant Kiepert gave orders for everything to be carried out with the utmost discretion. It will never be recorded that you attempted to travel incognito to Paris."

The small retinue leaves the car, escorting Margaretha Geertruida MacLeod, alias Mata Hari.

Dimo returns to his compartment, disconsolate. He can't forgive himself for having revealed the dancer's identity. If not for his ill-fated words, she would be in his arms now. He consoles himself with the thought that no one could imagine an exotic Mata Hari with such a prosaic name as Margaretha. Just who was that mysterious woman? What influence could she have on Germany's fate for her to be removed so peremptorily from the train? Had he put himself at risk in defending her? He sets aside these thoughts as a border guard comes to inspect his papers. After the routine examination, Dimitri lies down, exhausted, on the berth. He still has an eight-hour trip ahead and needs to arrive reinvigorated. He falls asleep quickly. He notes nothing when the Orient Express leaves Strasbourg to complete the last stage of the journey, heading for the Gare de l'Est.

THREE

Dimitri Borja Korozec falls in love with the city as soon as he glimpses the imposing iron structures of the Gare de l'Est. As happens with many travelers who disembark there for the first time, he has the clear impression that he has lived in Paris before. Met by Gérard Bouchedefeu, as had been arranged by Dragutin, Dimo installs himself in the mansard of 18, rue de l'Échiquier.

Bouchedefeu is seventy, but he has the vitality of a twenty-year-old. He still practices the delicate craft of taxidermy. As he works at home, the small apartment is a cross between residence and laboratory. Various stuffed animals like cats, dogs, birds, snakes, and

Gérard Bouchedefeu.

lizards—belonging to customers who failed to pay—decorate the locale. At the entrance, an owl with spread wings and eternally bulging eyes startles first-time visitors who venture into that inanimate zoo. Thin, almost six feet tall, with a long white beard, always dressed in black with his immutable beret on his head, Gérard Bouchedefeu is a living caricature of the old-time anarchist. An expert forger, a craft he had learned from an old fellow anarchist, Bouchedefeu creates for Dimitri documents with the prosaic name Jacques Dupont. He leaves his age as eighteen, the minimum for the youth to exercise the profession of taxi driver, a job that he gets thanks to the older man's connections. The first few days, Bouchedefeu accompanies the youth, maps in hand, to train Dimitri in his new profession. They go out early, driving through the streets in the classical dark red car, the traditional color of Paris taxis.

In two weeks, Dimitri has sufficient knowledge to attend to his customers, ready to brave any passenger's surliness. As he sometimes has to work late at night, he carries on the seat beside him an enormous stuffed Neapolitan mastiff, a veritable masterpiece executed by the old man in 1895. Bouchedefeu likes to joke saying that the dog is older than Dimitri. Within a short time Bouchedefeu has come to nurture a sincere affection for the youth. Dimo's enthusiasm for the cause reminds him of his own years as a young man, when he made the choice of the black flag of anarchy. He teaches him everything he can. At night, in the neighborhood bistros, the two hold long discussions with groups of anarchists and Serbian refugees.

The intense summer of the end of July heats up both people and events. As Colonel Apis had foreseen, on the twenty-third the Austro-Hungarian empire had sent an ultimatum to Serbia. All are aware that this is merely a pretext for the beginning of hostilities. Russia has already decreed the mobilization of thirteen battalions against Germany, and Kaiser Wilhelm II has declared *Kriegsgefahrzustand*—i.e., has placed the country in a state of "danger of conflagration." England, despite offering itself as a possible mediator, is ready to take action. Dimitri has been anxiously awaiting this moment. Like Dragutin, he naïvely believes that it is the only way to liberate Bosnia. France favors armed struggle, for it will thus have the opportunity to regain Alsace-Lorraine, taken by the Germans in 1871 after the Franco-Prussian war. It is time to even the score. In Paris, young students march down the boulevards shouting "On to Berlin! Death to the Kaiser!" and singing the *Marseillaise*. Newspapers like *Le Figaro* and *L'Écho de Paris* publish articles inciting the government to war: "[. . .] where everything is remade [. . .] it is necessary to embrace it in all its savage poetry . . ."

Throughout the nation a single voice is raised against the madness: that of the journalist and deputy Jean Jaurès. From the isolated trenches of *L'Humanité* he tries to arouse the good sense of his countrymen. In vain. However much the newspaper strives in its daily campaign in favor of peace, and despite his vehement speeches in Parliament demonstrating the absurdity of the approaching war, the French have made up their minds. They even go so far as to label the extraordinary socialist patriot a traitor.

In *Paris-midi*, Léon Daudet suggests in no uncertain terms: "[. . .] it is not our wish to encourage political assassination, but M. Jaurès should shudder before the possibility. His article is capable of provoking that desire in some fanatic."

In *Sociale*, Urbain Gohier writes these reckless words: "[. . .] If France had a leader, M. Jaurès would be nailed to the wall along with the notices of mobilization."

A steadfast pacifist, Jaurès remains unshaken by these attacks. The leader of the Socialist Party is a man of courage.

At the age of fifty-four, fat, sporting a beard that he grew not for style but so that he would not have to shave every day, Jean Jaurès is without a doubt the worst-dressed deputy in the Chamber. His absurd black clip-on tie purchased on sale at the Bon Marché looks more like a shiny old rag hung from his neck. In winter, over his old suit, he wears a dark overcoat whose color has become indefinable through use and which more often than not is buttoned in the wrong holes. A bowler hat, several times reblocked, completes his attire. In summer, his head is covered by a faded Panama hat that has seen better days. Jean Jaurès is not one for petty vanities.

His voracity is legendary. A member of his party once commented during a campaign, as they celebrated the Socialists' victory: "What an appetite our Jaurès has! He swallowed a large soup, half a goose, a whole paté, and an omelet, then patted his stomach saying, 'How I enjoy these between-meal snacks!' "

If gluttony is his only vice, his life is *L'Humanité,* which he founded in 1904. When he received 25,000 francs in 1911 for a series of lectures in South America, he used the entire amount to relieve the paper's financial problems. Despite the apprehensions of his wife, his daughter, and his friends, who fear for his life, he has never yielded an inch in his indefatigable campaign for peace. If it is up to him, there will be no war.

It becomes obvious to Dimitri Borja Korozec that Jean Jaurès must be eliminated. Bouchedefeu disagrees. He tries to convince the youth of the futility of the gesture. He attempts to explain to Dimo that a conflict of those proportions will plunge the world into a bloodbath of unprecedented scope and that, in any case, the assassination of Jaurès would be unlikely to hasten events. They converse for hours on end, until early morning, but Dimitri does not yield to the old anarchist's arguments. Methodically, he follows the outspoken politician till he establishes his routine. Jaurès is a man of simple habits. Early each morning, he leaves his residence on rue de la Tour, stopping at the newsstand, where he exchanges a few words with the vendor before buying the *Daily Mail* to learn the news from England. As he has no automobile, he takes the Metro to the offices of *L'Humanité* at 142, rue Montmartre. At lunch he likes to go to the Coq d'Or along with friends, but he is a more assiduous frequenter of the Café du Croissant, because of its location—right beside the newspaper. In the afternoon he goes to Parliament and, following his fiery speeches, returns to the journal.

On one occasion, Dimo had the opportunity to take him in his taxi, but he resisted the temptation. By the last week of the month, he is ready. He knows exactly how he will eliminate the intransigent pacifist. If all goes well, Jaurès, craftsman of such a bellicose peace, will never celebrate his next birthday.

PARIS—RUE DE L'ÉCHIQUIER—FRIDAY, JULY 31—3 P.M.

As he wanders around the tiny mansard, Dimitri Borja Korozec gathers the few accessories needed for his undertaking. The scheme is a simple one. He has studied the Café du Croissant in minute detail and knows the location of the rear entrance used by purveyors. With the aid of a wax mold, made after closing in the late hours of night, he has fashioned a key that will give him access to the spot at the opportune moment. He takes the key from the mouth of a mummified lizard and puts it in his pocket, alongside the fake beard and mustache acquired in a store selling theatrical items on rue Lepic, near the Moulin Rouge. He lays out the white apron, the vest, and the black jacket that will complete the disguise.

He will have no difficulty entering the restaurant under the guise of a waiter and then approaching the deputy's table. Only then will he release the homemade weapon painstakingly manufactured in his bedroom. It is not the conventional bomb of anarchists, but a delicious chocolate *bombe,* a poisoned one. In the classes in poisons taught by Mira Kosanovic at the Skola Atentatora, he learned to transmogrify common household cleaning materials into lethal weapons. He knows, for example, that naphthalene, used everywhere to kill moths, if administered in the correct dose can be as toxic and fatal as cyanide. Its crystals destroy the red blood cells, causing irreversible damage and inducing coma. The symptoms, such as nausea, fever, and hematuria, begin no later than twenty minutes after ingestion of the substance, but it is preferable that the victim not die at once, or that he have any idea what is happening. Using a pharmacist's pestle, Dimitri grinds fifty of the white spheres until he transforms them into a powder as fine as sugar.

With a stiletto, he opens the sweet bought in an elegant *pâtisserie* on rue de Rivoli and mixes the poison in with the delectable cream of the filling. He recloses the *bombe,* disguising the cut with an extra layer of chocolate, which he has prepared in Bouchedefeu's kitchen. For a few seconds he observes the culinary work of art that he plans to serve Jaurès that evening. Glutton that he is, the fat tribune will never resist the temptation. He will wolf it down in a single bite, without even noticing its taste.

Seated before him, Bouchedefeu grumbles disapprovingly as he busies himself stuffing straw into the belly of an Angora cat with blue eyes made of glass. Dimo pays no attention to him. He smiles as he thinks of the irony of what is to happen in a few hours. "Since he's known for his brilliant oratory and his insatiable appetite, Jean Jaurès will die as he lived: by his mouth."

PARIS—RUE D'ASSAS—FRIDAY, JULY 31—3 P.M.

What Dimo does not know is that he is not the only one who so fervently desires the journalist's death. In a stuffy room in a hotel on rue d'Assas, Raoul Villain, a young man with blond hair, a student of Egyptology at the Louvre, slightly older than Dimitri, collapses onto the old bed next to the wall. The springs, worn from the pressure of the bodies of hundreds of guests over the years, creak under his weight. His arms crossed behind his head, he contemplates the black revolvers resting on the dresser. He plans to use them soon as tools to extirpate from the nation the infamous Judas named Jean Jaurès.

There is a fundamental difference between the two young assassins. Unlike Dimitri, who sees the elimination of Jaurès as merely a job to be done, Villain has developed an almost pathological enmity toward the deputy. He has never read a line the journalist wrote; he detests him without knowing him. He blindly hates the man and everything he represents.

Son of a mentally ill mother and an alcoholic father, Raoul left his family in his early youth and joined the Association of Friends of Alsace-Lorraine. It was there that he learned to execrate Jaurès.

On a trip to the border, he dreams of killing the Kaiser. As the dream turns out to be impossible, he will have to settle for killing the traitor. The previous evening, while watching the entrance of *L'Hu-*

manité, he saw five men leaving the newspaper. A passerby commented to a friend, "Look, it's Jaurès!"

Villain asked, "Excuse me, gentlemen. Could you tell me which one he is?"

The two stared at Raoul in astonishment, not believing there could be anyone in Paris who didn't recognize the celebrated advocate of peace: "The one in the middle, of course!"

Raoul thanked them and followed the group to the Café du Croissant. Pretending to be a socialist, he asked the manager, "Does Citizen Jaurès come here often?"

"Almost every night, after the newspaper closes," the manager answered proudly. That was when Villain decided that the last day of the month would also be the last day of Jean Jaurès's life.

Raoul Villain rolls over in bed and takes from the nightstand a book worn from use. It is Maeterlinck's *The Blue Bird.* He doesn't know just why, but when he reads the Belgian writer's play about the quest for happiness in the world, he always feels as calm as a Zen monk.

PARIS—PLACE DU PANTHÉON—FRIDAY, JULY 31—3 P.M.

Built in 1764 on Mount Sainte-Geneviève, in the fifth arrondissement, the monument had initially been conceived as a church dedicated to the patron saint of Paris. Later, the French Revolution had transformed the construction into a majestic mausoleum to house the mortal remains of illustrious men, changing its name to the Panthéon. With the return of the monarchy and the Second

Empire, the edifice was hurriedly altered once again, becoming a church.

Nineteen years later, Léon Gambetta proclaimed the Third Republic. Political changes demand symbolic changes. The Panthéon became the final resting place of the notables of France. It was now necessary to reinaugurate it with full pomp. An occasion presented itself in 1885 with the death of one of the most famous writers in the world: Victor Hugo. Exiled for defending republican ideals, Hugo is more than a man of letters. He is a symbol. His ashes are taken to the Panthéon in a funeral cortege that moves the nation.

It is beside this tomb that two men, whispering, carry out a secret conversation. One is the chief of the Municipal Police, Xavier Guichard; the other, a tenacious inspector first class named Victorien Javert. Tall, with a chiseled face and wide jaw, a forelock falling across his brow, a flat nose with wide nostrils, and a cold, penetrating gaze, Javert is at thirty-two the spit and image of his grandfather.

The latter, also a policeman, was a veritable legend in the French police force for the persistence with which he dedicated his life to the pursuit of one Jean Valjean. It was said of him: "When serious, he looks like a hunting dog; when he smiles, a tiger."

The same description would fit his grandson. Despite his father's insistence that he take up the profession of telegrapher, from childhood Javert has had a powerful fixation on his grandfather. His name opened the doors of the Police Academy to him, and it soon became clear that the resemblance between the old inspector and the present one is more than merely physical. The grandson had also inherited from him his almost fanatical dedication and tenacity. Victorien Javert asks the chief:

"Forgive the impertinence, *monsieur le directeur,* but could you explain to me the reason for so much secrecy and the purpose of this meeting in such a remote location?"

Guichard looks around him to make sure that the two are not being observed. "The reason is simple, my dear Victorien. I want to assign you to an unpopular case. Not even my superiors know of what I'm about to ask of you."

"At your orders, *monsieur le directeur,*" agrees Javert without hesitation.

Guichard lights his pipe and explains, "You must have noticed the revolt that Deputy Jean Jaurès is stirring up in the populace with his antiwar statements."

"Certainly, *monsieur le directeur,*" replies Javert, though he does not read *L'Humanité* and takes no interest in politics.

"Well then, I fear that some extremist may make an attempt on his life. There are constant threats. We must avoid a catastrophe. That's why I'm ordering you to follow Jaurès like a bloodhound, without his becoming aware of it, and to protect his life at all costs."

Javert becomes pensive for a moment. "*Monsieur le directeur,* your confidence is of course a great honor, but why me? My precinct is the Châtelet; wouldn't it be better to use someone from the rue du Mail, in the second arrondissement?"

"That's what I wish to avoid. Jaurès knows all the policemen in the district. As soon as he notices he's being followed, he'll be furious. The man has stubbornly refused any form of protection."

"If that is what *monsieur le directeur* desires, so it shall be," Javert concludes.

Xavier Guichard relights his pipe and places his arm paternally around the inspector's shoulder. "Excellent. You should know that the choice was not made arbitrarily. I know your persistence and from whom you inherited it. When I was just a young gendarme they spoke to me with admiration of old Javert. A shame he died so tragically."

"Thank you, *monsieur le directeur,*" the policeman says, embarrassed; he does not like to be reminded of his grandfather's suicide.

Guichard resumes his tone of command: "Leave at once for the Chamber of Deputies. That's where you'll find him. Starting now, I want Javert to become Jaurès's very shadow."

The inspector first class moves away with long strides, resolved to fulfill the mission entrusted to him or die in the attempt.

PARIS—OFFICE OF *L'HUMANITÉ*—FRIDAY, JULY 31—7:30 P.M.

At the newspaper on rue Montmartre, the nervousness is almost palpable. Recalling Zola, Jaurès decides to write a formal charge in the style of *J'accuse.* Production assistants go by carrying files of earlier articles. Circulating among the various desks, the deputy, who held forth most of the afternoon inveighing against war, asks the editor if there is any news about England's position.

"For the moment, no. Prime Minister Asquith is scheduled to make a statement in the House of Commons."

"We'll not know anything interesting before nine. Asquith's speech may have tremendous influence. I'm going to wait. I don't want to start writing without knowing about it."

An editor says, "Then how about having dinner first? It looks like a long night."

Someone suggests, "At the Coq d'Or?"

"No. There they have music, women, lots of distractions. It's better to have something to eat next door, at the Croissant," Jaurès decides. He examines the notes scribbled on various pieces of crumpled paper scattered in his pockets. "Let's go, gentlemen. It promises to be a most dramatic night."

PARIS—CHEZ POCCARDI—FRIDAY, JULY 31—7:30 P.M.

Nearby, sitting at a table next to the restaurant's window, Raoul Villain caresses the knot of his *lavallière* necktie. A fixed smile is on his lips. He has selected the most expensive dish on the menu. He has chosen a bottle of Chianti to accompany the food, despite the sommelier having wrinkled his nose. Upon finishing the meal, he orders coffee and brandy. He rarely allows himself the luxury of such an expensive meal. The allowance of 120 francs that he receives from his father, a court clerk in Reims, does not permit such extravagances. The alcohol and the weight of the two revolvers that he carries in the inside pockets of his coat give him a seldom-felt sense of confidence. He thinks that the role of vigilante fits him like a glove.

Finishing the drink, he pays seven francs for the meal, leaving the waiter a generous tip, and heads toward the bathroom. He carefully combs his blond hair, washes his hands—not like Pilate—and leaves down the rue de Richelieu toward the Boulevard Montmartre. He feels as light as an angel. An exterminating angel. Villain will kill the villain.

PARIS—RUE DE L'ÉCHIQUIER—FRIDAY, JULY 31—7:30 P.M.

Alone in the mansard, dressed as a waiter, Dimitri Borja Korozec puts the finishing touches on his disguise. He applies the mustache and goatee, then examines himself in the mirror. The result isn't great. The fake hair contrasts with his youthful face. He places no importance on the fact. Avoiding pedestrians, he plans to slip along the streets, head lowered, until he reaches the Croissant. The café is not far from where he is. He has already chosen his itinerary: he will follow rue d'Hauteville as far as Boulevard Poissonnière, go down rue du Sentier, and turn right at Jeûneurs, making his way quickly to Montmartre.

He places the poisoned chocolate *bombe* on a dessert dish, which he wraps in thin pink paper, being careful not to crush the pastry. Gérard Bouchedefeu, annoyed at the project since its inception, has left to play chess with a Basque friend in Pigalle. Dimitri is unconcerned; he actually prefers being alone during the final preparations. He is certain the old man would make a jest about his disguise. He checks to see that the key to the restaurant's rear door is safely in his pocket, then leaves, carrying death in his hands.

PARIS—142, RUE MONTMARTRE—FRIDAY, JULY 31—7:30 P.M.

Ever since Jaurès returned to the newspaper office, Inspector Javert has been in position, discreetly, near the entrance to the building. Obeying Guichard's instructions, he has followed the journalist from Parliament, taking care not to be spotted. He is skilled in the art of spying without being seen. At the kiosk on the corner he buys, for the first time, a copy of *L'Humanité*. He has never been interested in the socialists and their progressive ideas. To him, any movement seeking to change the existing order is nothing but subversion. Like his grandfather, whom he never met, he guides his life by two simple sentiments: hatred for rebellion in any form, and an unshakable respect for authority.

His enormous hands leaf through the newspaper, which he uses to hide himself from the passersby. He is horrified at what he reads. How can the government allow such absurdities on the newsstands, within the reach of anyone? His indignation grows with each page. Almost two hours go by without his noticing.

Suddenly, his attention is drawn to a young waiter who passes by him carefully holding a package wrapped in pink. By the awkward way he's carrying it, he lacks much practice in balancing trays. Javert's bird-dog instinct tells him there is something strange about the youth's face. The mustache and the goatee don't go together. They make him look like the jack of spades. He ponders whether he should stop him for questioning, but he doesn't want to lose focus on the task entrusted to him.

While he hesitates, a noisy group comes out of the building, turning to the left on rue Montmartre. Among them, talking louder than the others, is Jean Jaurès. The youth turns around and, seeing the men walking toward the corner, increases his pace. Javert detects a certain nervousness in the gaze of that inexperienced individual. He leaves his post and follows Jaurès, without losing sight of the youth with the goatee.

The young man turns into a dark alleyway, and the journalists continue to the café on the corner. Javert reads the name on its front: "Café Restaurant du Croissant." For a moment he hesitates. Should he follow the waiter or stick with Jaurès as expressly ordered? Blind obedience inculcated during years of service speaks louder: Inspector First Class Javert sticks the paper in his pocket and goes into the restaurant behind Jean Jaurès.

PARIS—RECEPTION AREA OF *L'HUMANITÉ*—FRIDAY, JULY 31—9:20 P.M.

A well-mannered blond young man wearing a *lavallière* tie comes up to Mme. Dubois, the receptionist at the newspaper. Smiling at the elderly lady, he removes his hat and asks respectfully, "Pardon me, madam. Is Deputy Jaurès in?"

Accustomed to the lack of manners of the personnel of the newspaper, she is charmed by the young man's politeness: "No, monsieur. They all went to dinner near here, on the corner."

"Thank you, madam. Sorry to bother you."

"My pleasure, monsieur."

Raoul Villain puts his hat back on, pats the two revolvers inside his coat, and walks serenely toward Le Croissant.

PARIS—LE CROISSANT—FRIDAY, JULY 31—9:30 P.M.

There are no empty tables at the Café Restaurant du Croissant. Waiters and waitresses thread their way amid the usual happy excitement, dexterously placing plates of food in front of the customers. The heat increases the diners' thirst even more. At the bar, draft beer is served with machinelike precision. The glasses pass beneath the tap like parts on a factory assembly line. Albert, the manager, supervises everything with his customary ill humor.

The personnel of *L'Humanité* and the directors of the Socialist Party occupy three tables in the rear, to the left of the entrance. Jaurès is eating and taking part in the animated conversation. Often, the group is obliged to shout to be heard by the journalists from the *Bonnet Rouge,* seated some distance away. The topic, naturally, is the possibility of war. Someone argues that *L'Humanité* has missed a good opportunity to take up a popular cause by not demanding the return of Alsace-Lorraine to French hands. His mouth full, Jaurès replies, "If we've put up with the situation for forty years to keep the peace, I don't see why we should get into this fight because of Serbia."

Various acquaintances pass by the group and stop for a moment to exchange views. The journalists finish the main dish. Some, like Jaurès, choose to have dessert; others, in a hurry to get back to the newspaper, order only coffee.

Standing at the door, Inspector Javert pretends to be waiting for a table, never taking his eyes off Jaurès. He doesn't notice a blond young man passing in front of him, bumping against his shoulder. The man excuses himself and heads for the bar. Javert doesn't reply.

His gaze continues fixed on the journalist. Suddenly, from the rear of the room, the same waiter with mustache and goatee whom he had glimpsed a short time earlier in the street enters his field of vision. He approaches Jaurès carrying a plate with a chocolate *bombe*. The inspector's instinct tells him that something is wrong. At a glance he realizes what it is: the sweat caused by the intense heat is beginning to loosen the appliqués on the waiter's face. "They're false!" Javert thinks. The mustache is almost falling off, dangling from his upper lip, and the goatee is inching down his chin. The youth appears unaware that his disguise is melting. He approaches Jaurès, holding out the plate. Javert rushes to intercept him, but the two are several steps apart. He pushes his way past a couple saying good-bye to the manager and nearly trips over a waitress. The inspector must prevent the young man from reaching Jaurès. He smells an assassination attempt, senses that the journalist's life is in danger. Before he can move, he hears the deafening roar of a gunshot, and a bullet grazes his ear. Jean Jaurès is mortally wounded, his face down on the table. Javert has difficulty understanding what has just happened. Where did the shot come from? He hadn't seen the awkward waiter with the chocolate *bombe* take out a weapon. Only then does he turn around to see the blond young man who had just gone past, a smoking revolver in his hand, being overpowered by the other journalists. Astonishment overwhelms his reason.

Someone rushes out into the street screaming, "Jaurès's been killed! Jaurès's been killed!"

Dimitri Borja Korozec, the fake beard hanging from his chin, can't believe what has happened. Livid, he stares at the polemicist's bloodstained body as if hypnotized. Someone calls for a doctor. A pharmacist dining at the restaurant takes the socialist's pulse. He shakes his head in dismay. Her back against the counter by the entrance, a small flower girl sobs convulsively. Dimo can't take his eyes off the corpse. He is lost in thoughts of frustration and defeat. After all his preparation, someone had usurped his right to liquidate the enemy. Stupefied, he holds the *bombe* he had so painstakingly prepared, while Jaurès's friends push him aside. One of them unintentionally bumps into his elbow. The motion rams the deadly dessert into Dimitri's open mouth. He inadvertently bites into the poisoned tidbit.

The acrid taste of naphthalene instantly brings the clumsy terrorist back to reality. He feels the poison searing his throat and stomach. He curses his absentmindedness. If he doesn't get to a hospital within minutes, he will surely die. Overcome with horror, he throws the rest of the sweet on the floor and staggers toward the exit.

Inspector Javert recovers from his shock. Driven by intense hate, he follows Dimitri's steps. If not for him, he would have saved Jaurès's life. It was the clumsy waiter who diverted his attention. For the first time in his life, the inspector first class has failed in his duty. And in a mission ordered by the head of the Municipal Police! He will never forgive himself. He picks up the remains of the pastry. A single sniff reveals that it has been poisoned. He wraps the rest of the éclair in his handkerchief and puts it in his pocket. Several gendarmes from the vicinity have surrounded the assassin. Raoul Villain, his expression serene, says with the solemnity of the stupid, "What I did, I did for my country."

Javert can do nothing further for Jaurès, but he knows he will not rest until he brings to justice the other young man, the quasi-murderer. Could he be an accomplice? Absorbed in his *idée fixe,* he crosses the kitchen, knocking over pans, and takes up Dimitri's trail like a man possessed.

Door of the Croissant just after the assassination.

Making his way once again to rue Montmartre, Dimo begins to feel the first symptoms of the poison coursing through his insides.

He rips off the rest of the disguise that still hangs from his face and runs down the sidewalk, shoving aside the pedestrians who block his path.

He knows of a nearby clinic, the Hôpital Lachaparde, at the corner of rue de Paradis and d'Hauteville. He crosses a busy street, dodging the cars, and runs along rue de Trévise. He comes to rue Richer, across from the Folies-Bergère.

He thinks he must be the victim of some delirium brought about by the naphthalene: at the door of the theater, the seminude figure of

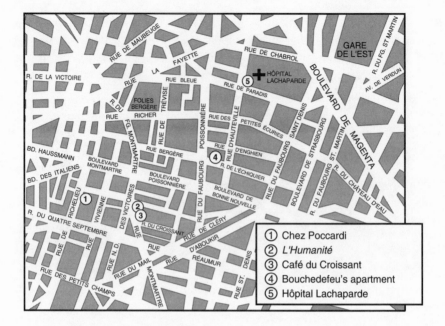

① Chez Poccardi
② L'*Humanité*
③ Café du Croissant
④ Bouchedefeu's apartment
⑤ Hôpital Lachaparde

Mata Hari dances before his eyes. He shakes his head and realizes that he isn't suffering from a delusion. What he sees is the poster from the previous summer when the entertainer appeared at the Folies in her Spanish-dance show.

He moves away and turns onto rue des Petites Écuries. Stumbling and supporting himself against the buildings, Dimitri finally arrives at rue de Paradis and faints, babbling, into the arms of a woman in front of the Hôpital Lachaparde.

Two blocks away, panting from the effort, Inspector Javert sees in the distance his prey being carried into the hospital by two orderlies.

Passage from the incomplete notebook of Dimitri Borja Korozec entitled *Memories and Lapses: Notes for an Autobiography*, discovered in November 1954 in one of the hiding places of the Muslim Brotherhood sect in Alexandria, Egypt.

PARIS—FRIDAY, JULY 31, 1914—NIGHTTIME IN THE HÔPITAL LACHAPARDE

I awoke on the first floor of an empty infirmary. Beside me, only one other bed was occupied by a patient, who was sedated and awaiting a procedure of some kind. The news of Jaurès's death had spread rapidly through the establishment. Interns and attendants whispered nervously in corners, and the corridors were more agitated than usual. I regained consciousness, far from that bustle. At first, I didn't know for certain whether I was waking up or had arrived in heaven: the lovely and serene face of a lady was looking down

Dimitri's notebook, found in Alexandria, Egypt.

at me gently, standing out from the white walls of the room. She appeared to be in her middle years and was dressed discreetly. She was wearing a long gray pleated skirt and a white blouse with a high collar, fastened at the neck by a wide ribbon of black velvet displaying a cameo. Her curly chestnut hair was entwined in a casual bun. I remember thinking that the image on the cameo resembled my mother. A soft smile lighted her lips. What impressed me most was her eyes. Eyes that penetrated into me with an expression of intense curiosity. She was directing her gaze toward my fingers wrapped around her wrist. Only then did I realize that I was firmly holding the woman's hand between my own. I tried to get up, but she stopped me, sitting on the bed and saying firmly, "Easy, young man. You're still quite weak. You've already given the orderlies enough work with the pump."

"Pump?" I said, startled.

"The stomach pump. Don't you remember? Before you fainted, you told me you had swallowed naphthalene. They pumped your stomach with sodium bicarbonate and gave you a diuretic to protect your kidneys. You're out of danger. Could I have my hand back?"

I relaxed the pressure of my fingers and asked, "Are you a doctor?"

The woman smiled, enigmatically. "No, but let's say my work is connected to medicine."

"I know, a nurse," I said stupidly.

Amused, the young matron replied, "You're not very far from right. I'm Marie Curie."

Even though I knew history and politics like few young men of my age, my culture in other matters still left much to be desired. I confess that until then I had never heard of the scientist, who had already won two Nobel Prizes: the first for physics, in 1903, and the second for chemistry, in 1911. Disguising my brutish ignorance, I kissed her hand frantically. "Madame, I owe you my life."

Madame Marie Curie was amused by my rapture. "You owe me nothing. It was mere chance that made you collapse in my arms as I was leaving the hospital."

My encounter with the famous physicist could not have been more fortuitous. Marie Curie told me she had come to the hospital that evening to speak to Professor Aristides Grimot, head of surgery at Lachaparde.

She told me that Grimot, a member of the Academy of Sciences, had become better known for his extraordinary research in the area of organ transplants. In his laboratory, a Pyrenees hen had survived for more than twenty minutes with the heart of a Leghorn rooster. He kept in close contact with Alexis Carrel, who had carried out the first heart operation on a dog, at the Rockefeller Institute for Medical Research, in New York.

Concerned about the imminent war, Madame Curie wanted Grimot's support along with that of the manufacturers of radiological materials in order to create x-ray stations in every hospital in the Paris area. She had made available the entire equipment in her laboratory. She also wished to recruit, from among professors and technicians, specialized volunteers to operate the equipment.

As the professor had been delayed owing to several emergency surgeries, fate would have it that Madame Curie's path crossed mine, as she was leaving after her meeting with Grimot. Even unconscious, I hadn't let go of her hand since my arrival there; moved, Marie had overseen the treatment, giving instructions to the two orderlies with her characteristic efficiency. If not for the respect that her position commanded, I would surely not have been attended to so quickly and would have died.

Perhaps to spare me, at first she had not said a word about the assassination of Jaurès. She could never have imagined that she had just saved the life of a frustrated assassin. Despite being very weak, I knew I had to get out of there right away.

"Madame, I have to return home. My mother must be worried," I lied.

"It's not advisable for you to leave in this condition; there's a crowd in the streets."

"A crowd, at this hour? Why?" I asked, playing the innocent.

In order to spare me greater shock, she hesitated between telling me the truth and making up some story. She concluded that one so young as I would not be interested in political events: "You don't know yet, but Jaurès has been killed. All France is in mourning. It will no longer be possible to stop the warmongers," she said unhappily, her thoughts probably filled with visions of death. She could never imagine that war was what I desired above all.

I tried to convince her to let me leave: "I live nearby, Madame. Don't worry."

Madame Curie ignored me. Changing the subject, she asked, "You haven't told me yet how you managed to swallow naphthalene."

"It was a joke by my younger brother. He put mothballs inside the chocolate bonbons," I fabricated.

"What's your name?"

"Jacques, Jacques Dupont," I lied again.

"Very well, Jacques. Do you promise you won't leave here before you get a good night's sleep?"

"I promise," I said, lying once more.

I knew I would have to flee that hospital and that I couldn't do so until she left. I yawned widely and pretended to go to sleep.

A few instants later, I saw through half-closed eyes that she was tiptoeing toward the exit. Like a beneficent shadow, she made her way to the corridor and closed the door behind her. That was the last I saw of my savior, the discoverer of radioactivity, Madame Marie Curie.

PARIS—RUE DE PARADIS—FRIDAY, JULY 31—11 P.M.

With the patience of vultures, a form clad in black waits in the shadows at the entrance to the Hôpital Lachaparde. Inspector Javert is in no hurry. He saw Dimitri Borja Korozec being taken to the hospital. His angle of vision allows him to observe the side entrances as well, so he knows that the suspicious youth has no way to escape. He would have gone after him if not for the inopportune appearance of Madame Curie and all the excitement that ensued. "Women," he thinks, "they should stay home instead of snooping around laboratories. Before long they're going to want to enter the police force. . . ." He regrets the irreverent thought almost at once. Javert harbors an almost morbid respect for institutions, and Madame Curie is after all an institution. All he has to do is wait. "He went into the hospital and, in accordance with the laws of physics, whatever goes in must come out," concludes Javert humorlessly. Suddenly, startled, he spots Madame Curie at the door to the building. Dare he interrogate her? He approaches, drawn by his deep sense of duty. Obsequiously, hat in hand, the gaunt figure goes up to the Nobel Prize winner.

"Madame Curie?"

"Yes?"

"Inspector First Class Javert. Forgive me for taking the liberty, Madame, but I should like some information about the young man that you were kind enough to assist."

Marie becomes irritated. From an early age, back in Poland, she has always rebelled against arbitrariness.

"By whose authority?"

"By authority of the investigation I'm conducting of the death of Deputy Jaurès."

"It seems to me that your investigation is rather tardy. I've heard that the assassin was caught red-handed."

"I am aware of that, Madame. However, my intuition tells me that perhaps the young man is involved in the crime. I should like to—"

She interrupts: "Your intuition is ridiculous, my friend. He's just a boy. He doesn't even have a beard."

"Ah, but he *had* one. It fell off," states Javert, taking from his pocket the false beard that he had picked up en route.

Marie Curie is surprised at the pile of hair in the inspector's hand. She is unsure whether she is standing before a policeman or a degenerate. Recomposing herself, she says, her voice rising, "I have no explanations to give you. Get out of my way. I've never seen such a thing! Involving a child in this tragedy. You may be assured that I shall report your impertinence to the Minister of Justice! Good evening, monsieur."

Madame Curie walks toward the car awaiting her, while Javert, perspiring heavily, babbles apologies, trying to rid himself of the false goatee that sweat has stuck to the palm of his hand.

Dimitri Borja Korozec waits a few minutes to make sure that his unexpected benefactress isn't coming back. He hears no movement in the corridor. He gets up to retrieve his clothes, tossed over the back of a chair. Marie Curie was right: he has no notion of how weak he still is. As soon as he takes two steps, he feels his head spinning. He tries to go back and lie down, but he faints onto the bed of the unconscious patient, the only other person in the room, knocking him to the floor.

The momentum of his fall causes the poor devil to roll under the other bed. In an almost synchronized movement, as soon as the man disappears under the bed, two orderlies rush in, carrying a stretcher.

"Let's take care of this right away. Dr. Grimot and his team are waiting," the first one says.

"I don't know what's got into the man today. Three operations in a row," the second orderly comments.

"It's none of your business. They're cases that can't wait," the first one says.

Picking up Dimo by his extremities, they throw him onto the stretcher. The second orderly looks at Dimitri's face. "That's funny, when we brought him here he seemed a lot older. Don't you think so?"

The other man answers distractedly, "How should I know?

Maybe it's the effect of the disease. What do you know about medicine? Anyway, it has to be him. You see anybody else here? Enough talk. You know Professor Grimot hates to be kept waiting."

The two leave quickly, carrying the unconscious Dimitri to the operating room.

Dimo comes to under the intense light of the surgical theater, surrounded by men and woman wearing rubber gloves and dressed in white. He sees only their eyes, as a rectangular piece of cloth covers their mouths and noses. He asks anxiously, "What happened? Where am I?"

Dr. Grimot, the head of the surgical team, attempts to calm him:

"Take it easy, young man. There's no need for concern. Soon you'll be asleep."

"Asleep?"

"Obviously. Or did you think we were going to remove your kidney with you awake?"

An abyssal terror overwhelms Dimitri and he tries to rise, but three members of the group hold him firmly. "There's nothing wrong with my kidney!"

"You think you know more than doctors?" asks Grimot, turning to a nurse who holds a rubber mask containing a pad soaked in ether through which the nitrous oxide will pass. "Let's have the anesthesia."

Before Dimitri can say anything, his nose is covered with the mask and the nurse opens the tubes permitting the flow of gas. Grimot continues: "Despite being indigent, you're fortunate enough to have the benefit of the latest thing in anesthetics, ether combined with nitrous oxide, better known to laymen as laughing gas."

The effect of the mixture is almost immediate. Dimo tries to explain the misunderstanding, but what emerges from his mouth is a huge guffaw. His words are intermingled with hysterical laughter: "You're going to take out my kidney? Ha! Ha! Ha! Ha! Instead of twelve fingers I should have been born with four kidneys! Ha! Ha! Ha! Ha! I swear to you that you're mistaken! My kidney is fine! Ha! Ha! Ha! Ha!"

After this grotesque delirium, Dimitri Borja Korozec loses consciousness under the doctors' puzzled gaze.

"What you have witnessed was merely a mild delusion brought on by the nitrous oxide. Despite this side effect observed in some patients, it is much more efficient than chloroform," pontificates Professor Grimot to his students as he expertly makes a long incision in Dimitri's unconscious body.

Even the patience of vultures has limits. Tired of waiting, Inspector Javert decides to continue the search inside the hospital. He knocks at the door of the building and the night attendant appears: "Can I help you?" he asks sleepily.

"Inspector Javert," he says, showing his identification. "I'm looking for a young man who was admitted here approximately two hours ago."

"Name?"

"I already told you. Inspector Javert."

"The young man's name," the attendant explains.

"I don't know, but he was the last person brought in. I saw it when he fainted at the door and was helped by Madame Curie and two orderlies."

"That must be the young man who was poisoned. He's resting in the infirmary on the second floor, but visiting hours are over. If you come back tomorrow morn——"

"I'm here on an official investigation," Javert interrupts brusquely, waving his police identification again. "Where on the second floor?"

"Second door on the right in the corridor," the orderly replies.

Javert shoves him aside and bounds up the stairs.

The sedated patient who had been awaiting surgery wakes up under the bed where he had rolled after being pushed by Dimitri. He has no idea of what has happened. Still woozy, he returns to his bed with difficulty, pulling the sheets over his head, just as Javert enters the room. In the shadow, the inspector sees only a form lying in the bed and throws himself upon it.

"You don't fool me! I know very well you were after Jaurès! But your accomplice was faster! Come now, confess!" bellows Javert wildly, shaking the poor wretch by the throat.

With great effort, the patient manages to pull away the sheet covering his face. When he sees the sinister figure in black who is nearly throttling him, a stifled scream emerges from his throat: "Help!"

Javert realizes his error and jumps from the bed, startled.

"Sorry, monsieur. I thought you were a poisoner."

Terrorized, the hapless patient still has the strength to ring the bell to summon the nurse before collapsing with a heart attack. Now it is Javert's turn to panic. His long experience tells him the man is dead. If he is found there, he will surely be charged with homicide. It was all a regrettable error, but he knows perfectly well that his position as inspector first class admits of no mistakes. He goes into the corridor, slipping into the shadows, runs to the first window he sees, and leaps out, making his way to the street and vanishing into the darkness.

PARIS—SATURDAY, AUGUST 1

For the first time in his career, Javert feels completely disoriented. Confused, he is torn between duty and shame. As an impeccable professional he knows his obligation is to turn himself in and confess the monstrous blunder that led to an innocent person's death. At the same time, he could never bear the humiliation and disgrace that would result from his precipitous act. The name Javert, almost an institution among the police of France thanks to his grandfather's legendary career, would be tarnished forever. Lacerated by doubt, he wanders for hours in the streets of Paris, lost in terrifying thoughts, far away in time and space.

Around four in the afternoon, he circles the Place du Châtelet, across from his precinct house. When he sees before him the building that to him symbolizes absolute respect for authority, he finally comes to a decision: he enters and heads like an automaton for his desk, not even acknowledging the salute by the sergeant on duty. He sits erectly, takes pen and paper, and writes in a firm hand:

To the illustrious M. Xavier Guichard,
Commissioner of the Municipal Police

Facsimile of Javert's letter.

Dear Sir:

I am obliged to inform you, with immense regret, that I have been unable to carry out successfully the task you were generous enough to assign to me.

My inattention led to two irreparable tragedies, the first culminating in the assassination of Deputy Jaurès, whom I should have protected with my own life, and the second redounding in the unfortunate passing of an innocent in the Hôpital Lachaparde, who died of fright as a result of my reckless action.

Fully aware that a member of the police force does not have the right to make mistakes, much less twice, I ask you to accept my unconditional resignation so that the unforgivable acts of the grandson will not come to stain the irreproachable name of the grandfather.

Respectfully,
Inspector First Class Victorien Javert,
assigned to the Châtelet
Paris, August 1, 1914

He carefully places the folded letter in an envelope. He goes to the sergeant and tells him to deliver it personally to the commissioner the following morning.

He leaves the precinct house and crosses the square till he arrives at the quay. He leans over the parapet and gazes at the turbulent waters of the river. There, currents beneath the surface create deadly whirlpools. He removes his hat and lays it on the edge of the parapet. Then, in a nimble leap, he throws himself into the Seine, disappearing at the same spot where his idolized grandfather had committed suicide exactly eighty-two years before.

At the beginning of September, just a month after the outbreak of war, the German army is advancing in French territory like an avalanche. Paris is bracing for invasion. At eleven o'clock on the night of the second, the government withdraws to Bordeaux by way of the Quai d'Orsay to avoid falling into the hands of the enemy, who is dangerously close. The cabinet ministers fear an aerial attack. The Undersecretary for Fine Arts is carrying with him the Crown jewels, usually on display in the Apollo Gallery at the Louvre. Dozens of trucks leave the capital, transporting to safe locations gold from the Bank of France, the most important works from the museums, and the state archives.

President Poincaré has already left in a special train from the Gare d'Auteuil-ceinture. Along with the exodus of officials, many Parisians are deserting the capital in every train departing for the south of the country. Some weeks before, General Joseph Gallieni, a hero of the Franco-Prussian War, was called to defend the city. Gallieni comes out of the reserves to assume the thankless task. A warrior of great ingenuity, the new commander is ready to carry out his orders at any cost. Before the highest ranks of the government leave for Bordeaux, he says firmly to Millerand, the new minister of war:

"Do you know what this means, Minister? Perhaps the destruction of the Eiffel Tower, of the important factories and industries, of every bridge in Paris, including the Concorde, so that nothing can fall into the power of the Germans."

"Do whatever must be done," the minister replies before departing.

Upon leaving the hospital five pounds heavier and one kidney lighter, Dimitri Borja Korozec encounters a climate of despondency and gloom. The loss of the organ had been compensated for by healthy food and regular meals, benefits that he hadn't enjoyed since leaving his parents' home. During the long recovery period his appearance of a helpless young lad had won the hearts of all the nurses, who had pampered him with tidbits.

Professor Grimot had not admitted his mistake vis-à-vis the needless operation and would visit him as if he had saved his life, bringing students with him and discoursing about the case. Dimo had resigned himself to his fate.

As soon as he could receive visitors, he sent a message to Bouchedefeu, who was upset because he had had no news of Dimitri for several days.

Abominating government of any kind, Gérard had come to believe that Dimitri had been arrested secretly at the time of the assassination and tortured to death in the cellars of the Sûreté.

Bouchedefeu spent his afternoons at the hospital, speaking about his new passion: the study of bidets over time and their influence on the liberation of the working class. According to the old man, the bidet was the symbol of decadence and responsible, sooner or later, for the weakening of the ruling class. He explained enthusiastically, "Although there is mention of similar instruments in the Middle Ages, it was during the reign of Louis XV, in 1736, that the ebonist Rémy Pèverie created the first specifically designed for intimate hygiene. The name bidet comes from the verb *bider,* which is archaic French for 'to trot,' because of the horseman's position that the person assumed in using it."

"I thought that 'trot' came from *trottoir,*" Dimitri jested.

Bouchedefeu pretended not to hear.

"In 1743, Petri, an obscure Florentine poet, even composed a sonnet that called prostitutes 'Le amazzone del bidet,' the Amazons of the bidet. It proved an immediate success at court. Madame Du Barry even owned one with morocco-lined edges."

"Was that why King Louis fell in love?" interrupted Dimitri, mockingly.

Bouchedefeu continued: "In 1748, Voltaire himself ordered one for Abbot Moussinot, who took care of his finances, saying in a letter, 'My ass, envious of the beauty of my furniture, demands a lovely perforated seat with great reserve basins.' "

"And what does that have to do with the weakening of the ruling classes?" Dimitri asked, amused.

"Don't you see?" retorted Bouchedefeu, furious. "This hygienic comfort leads to idleness and decadence. To me, the bidet was the great factor responsible for the French Revolution and, later, the decline of that same revolution. Marat himself died stabbed to death on the bidet."

"It was in the bathtub," Dimitri corrected.

"That's what the history books say. To me, the truth is different . . ." hinted the anarchist, with the air of one possessing secret information.

Finally, thirty-four days after having been admitted to the Hôpital Lachaparde, Dimitri is once again circulating in the nearly empty streets of Paris in his taxi belonging to the Kermina-Métropole

Company. He cannot imagine that he will soon be involved in the war that he so desired.

On the third of September, when the troops of the First German Army, commanded by General Heinrich von Kluck, are only thirty kilometers from Paris, an act of disobedience changes history.

Instead of invading the city, the general moves toward Meaux, in the region of the Ourcq and Marne Rivers. By this maneuver he hopes to take advantage of the territory vacated by the retreating English troops and attack all of General Joffre's armies from behind. His aim is to annihilate them in a single, definitive battle. The unprotected City of Light can wait.

What von Kluck doesn't know is that Gallieni has managed to regroup the Sixth Army in Paris under the command of General Maunoury. Not expecting any attack from that direction, von Kluck leaves his right flank, made up of the Fourth German Regiment, completely exposed.

In three days of unbroken successes, Maunoury arrives at the Marne.

It is then the situation takes on a different complexion. Despite facing a counteroffensive from the south by Joffre's armies, von Kluck abandons his strategy of taking on the entire French army and turns his full force toward helping his men. Thwarting Gallieni's plan becomes a personal challenge for him.

Maunoury resists but is in desperate need of reinforcements to save Paris. Such reinforcements exist: the men of the Seventh Colonial Division, under General Trentinian, who have come to the capital from Verdun. They are exhausted but ready to do whatever it takes to stop von Kluck's advance.

There's just one problem, apparently insoluble: there aren't enough military transports to get the six thousand soldiers to the Marne.

At nine o'clock on the night of September 6, in the office of the Lycée Victor-Duruy where he has set up his headquarters, the creative General Gallieni has an unusual idea. He quickly summons Captain Jacquot, the requisitions officer. The young captain has total confidence in his commander, for whom he feels an almost filial affection. He enters the room and stands at attention: "At your orders, General."

"Jacquot, I think I've found a way to transport the troops to the battlefront," the general tells him, his eyes glowing with excitement.

The captain is heartened by the prospect. He hasn't slept for two days, imagining his beautiful city invaded by the Boche. "I was sure the general would find a solution."

Gallieni rises from the desk and approaches Jacquot. "I want you to requisition every taxi in Paris."

Jacquot thinks he has heard wrong. "Taxis?"

"Yes, the taxis and their drivers."

The captain is surprised. "But, General, the taxi drivers are civilians."

"So?"

"Civilians have never participated in military operations."

"There's a first time for everything. Or would you prefer that Paris fall into the hands of the Germans?"

Jacquot immediately regains his composure. "Of course not, General. Anything is better than that. Even going to war in a taxi."

"Well then, get to work. The first caravan has to leave tonight. And don't forget that everything must be done with absolute confidentiality."

Captain Jacquot salutes enthusiastically and departs to carry out the unusual mission. He must enlist every policeman in the city as well as the Republican Guard. From his room, he calls the Préfecture de Police, bellowing into the telephone: "That's what I said! Taxis! All the taxis and all the drivers! By order of the military governor, General Joseph Gallieni!"

And thus, with six hundred taxis, Gallieni will make possible the French victory at the Battle of the Marne and introduce to history automotive transport of infantry troops.

In the apartment on rue de l'Échiquier, Dimitri Borja Korozec is drinking wine and playing backgammon with Gérard Bouchedefeu, totally unaware that at that same moment someone has moved the pieces in another game in which he will be one of the pawns: the game of war.

The evening of September 8, Dimitri is driving his cab through the streets of Paris looking for passengers, who are becoming ever more scarce. When he turns onto the rue de Rivoli near the Place de la Concorde, a policeman signals for him to stop. Dimo pulls his taxi over, bothered by the interruption. He has already learned the irritated tone of Parisian taxi drivers: "Now what? What did I do wrong?"

"Nothing, young man. Just that you and your jalopy have been requisitioned."

"Who by?"

"By the military governor, General Gallieni."

"And may I ask why?"

"To take troops to Meaux," answers the policeman, getting in the car. "Let's get moving. There's a detachment leaving in a few minutes from the Esplanade des Invalides."

"But I have to stop by my place and change clothes!"

"What you're wearing is fine. This is no time to worry about fashion."

When they arrive at Invalides, a immense line of taxis filled with soldiers is pulling away from the locale. A lieutenant approaches them: "Lieutenant Alexandre Lefas, Division of Transport. How many you think will fit in this heap?"

"However many you want," replies Dimo, already caught up in the adventure.

"Around six, if we squeeze them," the lieutenant judges.

"If we really squeeze them, eight," says Dimitri, exaggerating.

"Too many. I don't want you breaking down on the way," says Lefas, ordering a group of infantrymen into the vehicle. He hands Dimitri a map. "Take this. The route to Meaux is marked, leaving through the porte de la Villette."

"Don't worry, Lieutenant. I know the way to go very well."

"In any case, you can't miss it. Just follow the car in front of you. Good luck," says the busy lieutenant, heading for another taxi.

Essaying a jest, Dimo turns to his uniformed passengers squeezed into the cab, lowers the flag on the taximeter, and says, "Where to, gentlemen?"

The soldiers reply in unison, "To the Marne!"

Dimitri puts the car in gear and joins the armed convoy leaving for the front.

"To the Marne!" The last taxi is Dimitri's.

Around eight o'clock that evening, fate once again intervenes in Dimitri's troubled life.

As he drives over a hole hidden in shadow, the car's left front tire blows. The soldiers get out to help, as they watch the line of the other cars ahead of them disappear into the darkness. In the time it takes to change the tire they find themselves alone, cut off from the column. The brave infantrymen are concerned: they don't want to miss the battle. Dimitri says soothingly: "Don't worry. I know this area like the back of my hand. Just up the road there's a shortcut that will allow us to make up for lost time. Meaux is less than twenty kilometers from here."

They get back in the taxi and Dimitri turns onto a trail to the right of the main roadway.

Three hours go by before Dimo confesses that he's completely lost.

After traveling in circles, examining the map, and running over a cow, they finally approach a city. The darkness is total and the silence is oppressive. No one is moving in the streets. They get out of the taxi, stretch their legs, and try to get their bearings. Dimitri says, "That's it. We've arrived."

The six soldiers look at one another as if standing before an idiot. One of them, Corporal Fouchard, a short, stocky man with few friends, inquires, "Obviously we've arrived, but where?"

"At Meaux, of course," Dimitri assures him.

Bernadet, another one of the passengers, a man with a large mustache, states nervously, "It's not Meaux. I've been to Meaux. This place is bigger than Meaux."

"Then where are we?" asks Delesserd, the tallest of the men.

"Anywhere but Meaux," concludes Bernadet.

Picardin, a bicycle mechanic in civilian life and the most practical among them, suggests, "The best thing to do's to go into the city and ask."

They get back in the taxi and cautiously approach the central area. Poirot and Balardin, who as raw recruits have yet to make their views known, shout simultaneously, pointing to a corner house with the light of an oil lamp flickering in one of its windows: "Look, the Auberge du Vieux Cochon!"

Dimitri brakes abruptly, throwing the passengers in the rear to the floor. He parks the car and they all head toward the inn. Fouchard, with the authority his rank of corporal bestows on him, rings the bell. A fat lady opens the door, startled.

"Who's there?"

"The French army!" says Fouchard, exaggerating.

"What a scare! I thought it was the Prussians," says the woman, unburdening. "Come in, come in. What are you doing here at this hour? The whole city's asleep."

"We were on our way to Meaux and got off the road," Delesserd explains.

"And how you got off it! Meaux is fifty kilometers to the north."

"Then this isn't Meaux?" insists Dimitri, under the furious glare of the soldiers.

"Of course not. You went to the right instead of continuing to the left," the innkeeper replies.

Disconsolate and exhausted, the men sit down at a table in the corner of the room.

"And just what city is this?" Balardin asks.

"Melun."

"Melun? But that's where they make the best brie in the world!" says Poirot, who dreams of one day becoming head chef in a large restaurant.

Bernadet runs his hands over his mustache with the authority of a connoisseur: "Oh no! The best brie in the world is precisely the brie from Meaux. There's no comparison between Melun brie and Meaux brie."

"Only somebody who's never tasted Melun brie could believe such idiocy," insists Poirot.

"The crust of Meaux brie is more uniform. The mold formed by the fungus makes Meaux brie much creamier," pontificates Bernadet.

"But it takes away the flavor," retorts Poirot. "That doesn't happen with Melun brie, which ripens in three days, unlike Meaux brie, which takes four days."

"Hearsay," scoffs Bernadet.

"I prefer the Pont-l'Évêque," Fouchard injects.

"Did anyone ask you?" Bernadet says cuttingly.

"No, but I have a right to my opinion. I've been in the army longer than you have. Or are you forgetting that I'm the corporal?"

Balardin decides to get into the discussion: "I agree with Fouchard. I was brought up in Normandy, and the Pont-l'Évêque is incomparable. It's a small cheese, but its aroma makes your mouth water."

"If you want to talk about aroma, I'll go with Bleu d'Auvergne," grumbles Picardin, getting into the argument.

"What about Roquefort? Isn't anyone going to defend Roquefort? The cheese of kings and popes, the favorite of Charlemagne?" shouts Delesserd indignantly.

Balardin, who has been quiet, turns to Dimitri. "And you, what do you think?"

"I'm a civilian. If it's cheese, I eat it," Dimo answers, not wishing to take sides.

Poirot claims the floor again. "I'm not interested right now in the taste of other cheeses. What I said was that Melun brie is better than Meaux brie. Actually, it's easy to prove what I'm saying." Turning to the proprietor, he asks, "My pardon, Madame, what is your name?"

"Marguerite Bourdon, and I agree with you. Our brie is much better."

"Well, so as to put an end to any doubt, bring us some of your delicious cheese and a bottle of red wine," Poirot orders.

"Bring two," Dimitri says. "I'm dying of thirst."

Twelve bottles and four cheeses later, Dimitri, the six soldiers, and the fat innkeeper are still arguing, drinking, and eating, without reaching any conclusion.

Photo of the six taken by Madame Bourdon.
Seated: Poirot and Bernadet. Dimitri
had gone to get more wine.

At the same time, fifty kilometers away, the French army wins the battle by surprising the Germans in a devastating night attack. Of Gallieni's taxis, only one failed to arrive: Dimitri Borja Korozec's.

The next morning, all of them are still asleep, under the table, their arms around one another. A rooster's crowing rouses Corporal Fouchard, his mouth dry and his eyes wild. He wakes Dimo, who is sleeping like an angel on Madame Bourdon's immense lap.

"Know what I think, kid?" says Fouchard, his voice hoarse and groggy from sleep and wine.

"Haven't the slightest idea," replies Dimitri, yawning and rubbing his eyes.

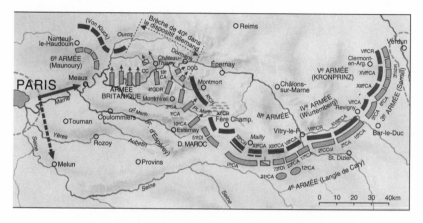

→ Correct route for the taxi convoy
⇒ Route taken by Dimitri

"We'll never get to the Marne," he concludes. Then he belches and goes back to sleeping the sleep of the just.

Prussian medal coined
prematurely to
commemorate the
German troops' taking
of Paris.

Passage from the incomplete notebook of Dimitri Borja
Korozec entitled *Memories and Lapses: Notes for
an Autobiography*, discovered in November 1954 in one
of the hiding places of the Muslim Brotherhood sect
in Alexandria, Egypt.

PARIS—JUNE 7, 1917

Today I am twenty. I make use of the calm of this rainy
afternoon to record the anxieties that besiege my mind. In
the living room, Bouchedefeu is finishing stuffing a mouse
caught in our rat trap. He plans to make me a present of the
delicate animal on this date. The quiet of evening is in contrast to the uncontrolled slaughter of the battlefields. The
war, which both sides foresaw as short and without many
casualties, has already gone on for almost three years. After
the Battle of the Marne, from which I found myself excluded
by circumstances contrary to my will, both the Germans and
the Allies dug winding lines of trenches protected by barbed
wire. These trenches extend for a thousand kilometers, from
Switzerland to the North Sea, and resemble nothing so
much as giant anthills. The soldiers have come to lead a sub-
terranean life. Veritable cities have been built underground,
with command posts, supply depots, infirmaries, kitchens,
and latrines. The lines are equipped with strategic emplace-
ments of machine guns to ward off enemy attacks, and with

underground shelters to protect the men from aerial bombardment. In some areas these shelters are more than fifty meters deep. I learned from a letter from Poirot, who became a friend of mine, that Corporal Fouchard was killed by a bomb. The weapon didn't even explode, but by chance it fell directly on his head.

In the bathroom, where I always go when I need to meditate, I sit on the toilet and carefully record these thoughts. Surveying my life as an assassin trained by the Union or Death, I recognize that my talents have yet to be fully utilized. I hope, nevertheless, not to waste the expertise acquired at the Skola Atentatora. Perhaps the future has greater projects in store for me. Even so, I feel frustrated to think that at my age Alexander of Macedonia had already conquered Persia.

Two pieces of news especially depress me. The first came in a letter from my father. In Salonica the trial of the Black Hand is being held, and a death sentence for Colonel Dragutin is considered a foregone conclusion. I know I shall miss the Bull's counsel. What should a single assassin do in wartime, when thousands die every day, and tyrants command the bloodbath far from the front, in safety? The second is on the front page of the newspapers: Mata Hari was arrested as a spy and awaits trial before the Third Council of War in the prison at Vincennes. She will surely be shot.

My mother wrote also. She seems worried about developments and, based on her way of expressing herself, I fear she has the idea that I will never see her again. For the first time, she made a point of revealing to me the name of my Brazilian grandfather, a certain General Manuel do Nascimento Vargas, whose bastard daughter she would be. That was always a closely guarded secret, which to me never made the least sense. What importance could knowing that name ever have to my life? I take much more pride in the African blood of my grandmother. She also wants me to take a solemn vow to one day visit her native land. Whenever she writes she mentions the subject. That desire is becoming a veritable obsession. Well, that's how mothers are.

I read that Madame Curie, my savior, had created mobile radiological units with moneys raised by the Union des Femmes de France. The French affectionately call the vans that she equipped "Les Petites Curies." I even volunteered to drive one of the vehicles but failed the physical examination because of my fingers. The narrow-minded military doctors thought that my insignificant anomaly might impair my performance as a driver.

The Americans have entered the war. France is getting ready to receive them. The first contingents should arrive next week. Despite the conflict, Paris has resumed its artistic and cultural activities. Theaters have reopened. Books and plays exalt the courage of the soldiers.

In some cases, attitudes border on exaggerated chauvinism. *La Parisienne,* by Henry Becque, closed despite sold-out houses merely because it tells the story of a married woman with two lovers. They don't want to give the enemy the chance to use it to denigrate the image of French women. Silly jingoism. In Sarajevo there was a woman from Berlin, a German teacher, who had four.

I interrupt my reflections here because Gérard is knocking at the door wanting to use the bathroom. Later we are going out to celebrate my birthday. Bouchedefeu has acquired from an anarchist friend, the prompter at the Casino de Paris, two invitations to the new review *Laisse-les tomber.* The prospect of seeing beautiful chorus girls prancing nude on-stage, behind feathered boas, excites me. Afterward, we'll have dinner at the Brasserie Lipp, where the flower of the city's artistic, political, and intellectual circles meet.

Who knows if, upon reaching the age of twenty, I may find something there that will change my life? The night is promising and life is an unexpected guest.

The Brasserie Lipp is packed despite the lateness of the hour. The smell of high-quality Havanas impregnates the air. Famous for its beer, sausage, and sauerkraut, the brasserie was founded by Léonard Lipp in 1870 and still preserves the charm of the Belle Époque. The Art Nouveau mirrors on the walls double the size of the rooms.

In one corner of the restaurant, drinking bottles of Brouilly in a happy tumult, are Pablo Picasso, the poet Guillaume Apollinaire, Jean Cocteau, the composer Erik Satie, and Modigliani, a young Italian plastic artist much loved by the group. The discussion centers on the criticism published by Jean Poueigh in the *Carnet de la Semaine* about the ballet *Parade,* staged by Cocteau with music by Satie and sets and costumes by Picasso. Apollinaire wrote an introduction for the program. Grandiloquently, Modigliani reads aloud the almost offensive text:

"'Despite the propaganda and the hubbub surrounding the name Picasso, the plot and music of the ballet *Parade* have, in equally grave measure, the idiocy of the former and the banality of the latter. Laying bare their imagination, MM. Jean Cocteau and Erik Satie clearly demonstrate this for us. It is at times amusing to confirm for oneself the levels that incompetence can achieve.'" With a sneer, the young painter folds the newspaper clipping and continues, "What do my friends plan to do about this ignominy? If it happened to me, I would go to the newspaper and make the worm eat the entire page."

"You're a hot-blooded Italian. Adults don't respond to children," states Cocteau, phlegmatic as ever.

Deep down, everyone is amused at the reaction they have provoked. It was precisely what they had planned. *Parade* was done with the goal of shaking conventions, ruffling conservative feathers. Nothing beats scandalizing the petit bourgeoisie.

Apollinaire, who even though excluded from combat because of a head wound still wears his artillery officer uniform, takes from the pocket of his tunic a crumpled envelope and turns to Picasso.

"I also have news. I hadn't told you, but the high command has decided to follow your advice."

"What advice?" asks the painter.

"If I may, allow me to read this to the others. This is the letter our dear Pablo sent me on February 7, 1915."

Removing the wrinkled sheet from the envelope, he begins reading in a pseudo-pompous inflection: "'I'm going to give you an excellent suggestion for the artillery. Even when painted gray, the artillery, the cannons, can be seen by aeroplanes, because they keep their same shape. Instead of that, they should be painted in very bright colors, some parts in red, yellow, gray, blue, white, like a harlequin.'"

Cocteau comments facetiously, "Fantastic, you even managed to take your obsession with harlequins to the battlefront! You should propose the same mixture for the soldiers' uniforms. Generals could dress as Pierrot and nurses as Columbine."

Erik Satie picks up on the cue. "Excellent idea. Thus war will become transformed into one great *commedia dell'arte.*"

The group dissolves into laughter. Turning to Picasso, Apollinaire continues in the same tone: "One never knows how the minds of the military work. Maybe you've unwittingly invented a new type of disguise."

Modigliani rises to his feet solemnly, glass in hand: "I salute Pablo Picasso, inventor of the art of camouflage!"

All stand and sip their drinks, laughing uproariously at the absurdity.

As he and Gérard Bouchedefeu enter the Lipp after the extraordinary review at the Casino de Paris, what catches Dimitri's attention is the same little dark-skinned man who was shouting enthusiastic bravos from the first row of the theater during the rehearsal. He is seated at the table opposite a group of bohemians, probably artists, who have just proposed a toast to someone.

The slightly built man reminds him of an elf from the fairy tales that peopled his childhood. Despite his strange appearance, he possesses an indisputable charm. He is smoking a cigarette in a long ebony holder and is punctiliously dressed. He carries a walking stick with a knob at its top and is wearing gloves and spats. A polka-dot bow tie stands out above his turned-down collar. It is obvious that his clothes have seen better days. Nevertheless, his threadbare cuffs subtract nothing from his aristocratic pose. Just the opposite: they confer upon him a romantic air of faded nobility. The beautiful women in his company seem fascinated by him. Dimo recognizes the young women, still heavily made up. They are three of the most beautiful chorus girls from the show they have just seen: a blonde, a redhead, and a brunette. They drink champagne and talk excitedly.

Drawn to this unusual personality, Dimitri gestures for Bouchedefeu to take the table nearest them. They order beer, pigs' feet, and fried potatoes. When the waiter leaves, Dimo begins listening to the story that the elf with the cigarette holder is telling the dancers, in a French almost without accent:

"At that period I was spending some time in the Amazon region and had trained a pair of parrots to say 'Viva José do Patrocínio Filho!' as loud as they could. One day, the birds flew away, which quite annoyed me. I forgot the incident and embarked for Europe. Years later, I returned and was again hunting in that same jungle. After bringing down two enormous jaguars, I sat on a tree trunk beside the river to rest. I was almost asleep when I heard a great commotion coming from overhead. I looked up and saw that the sky was literally covered in a cloud of parrots. They were flying in a flock around me and repeating like a chorus, 'Viva José do Patrocínio Filho! Viva José do Patrocínio Filho!' They had learned the phrase from my two runaway parrots."

Upon hearing the name, Dimitri butts into the conversation, speaking in Portuguese. "Pardon my boldness, sir. But the coincidence is simply too much. Can it be that I have the honor to be addressing the son of the great José do Patrocínio?"

The little man is surprised and responds in the same language. "Exactly, young man. Zeca himself. Or Zeca Pato to his friends." He switches to French, out of consideration for the chorus girls and Bouchedefeu. "But how is it that you know about my father?"

Dimitri quickly narrates his story and his origins. He speaks with pride of his black grandmother and of how much the elder

Patrocínio meant to his mother. Zeca is surprised, for Dimo's white skin in no way reveals the race he is so proud of. He avoids only any mention of his activities as an anarchist and concludes by relating his unforgettable encounter with Mata Hari and what the sacred dancer of the Hindu ritual had said about him, Patrocínio.

Patrocínio Filho, confesses softly, "What a woman! You know, young man, because of her a fellow could even get enmeshed in the world of espionage . . ." he adds mysteriously, taking a long puff on his cigarette holder.

The redhead leans on his shoulder. "José! Don't tell me you're a spy?"

"I'm not saying I am and I'm not saying I'm not . . . In any case, I left my post at the consulate in Amsterdam for a few days to try to sneak past the guards at Vincennes and visit Mata Hari in prison. Maybe organize an escape, I don't know . . . All in the name of what once was . . ."

"And it would be worth the risk?" asks Dimitri.

"What is risk for a man like me, who fought a duel in the Bois de Boulogne with King Albert of Belgium over the love of a woman?"

"You did that?"

"Of course! But I spared his life. I didn't have the heart to deprive Belgium of her sovereign. George told me confidentially that he still bears on his hand the scar I gave him when I sent his foil flying with a short thrust."

"George who?" asks Bouchedefeu.

"George V of England."

Bouchedefeu appears skeptical about those deeds: "Be that as it may, Mata Hari must be very closely guarded."

Patrocínio waxes enthusiastic once more, remembering the dancer. "What a woman! Unfortunately, it was an untenable situation. I knew that someone was paying for her luxuries and whims because I had no means myself to shoulder such debts. Therefore, I sometimes became jealous and disgusted with myself and would insult her. I'd raise my fists to crush her, and she would smile, come toward me like a kitten, and murmur, 'Baby . . .' "

"Baby?" repeats Bouchedefeu, sizing up the elf.

"That's just what she called me. Baby . . . There was a Hindu dwarf who always accompanied her. I don't know where he can be these days, now that Maty's under arrest."

"Maty?" inquires Bouchedefeu, almost aggressively.

"An affectionate nickname I gave her. It was Maty, Baby, Baby, Maty . . ."

Dimitri lowers his head, uncomfortable at the memory of Motilah Bakash flying out the window of the Orient Express.

The Brasserie Lipp. Arrow indicates the table occupied by Dimitri and Bouchedefeu.

Patrocínio looks dreamily at the three chorus girls and serves another round of the drink. Bouchedefeu still has doubts about the veracity of the story.

"Are we talking about the same Mata Hari?"

"The one and only! Once, wild with jealousy, I threw her against a sofa and slapped her insanely."

Excitedly, the brunette asks, "And did she strike back?"

"Just the opposite. All she did was hold out her arms in supplication and repeat, 'Baby . . . Baby . . .' I rolled on the floor with her, like a madman, possessing her again. What an insatiable woman! It was seven, eight times a night."

"All of them with you?" asks Bouchedefeu, incredulous and half drunk.

Patrocínio Filho casts him a disdainful glance and, turning to Dimitri, changes the subject: "You have to visit Brazil."

"That's what my mother never tires of repeating. Maybe after the war."

"If you want some advice, leave here now. Don't become part of this conflict. Brazil is the country of the future; there, everything is still to be done. How old are you?"

"I'm twenty today."

Zeca raises his glass: "Then, viva! You're too young to be wasting time here."

"Too young and too nice," adds the beautiful blonde girl, aroused by the champagne and the stories, as she kisses Dimo on the cheek.

"What's your name?" Dimitri asks, suddenly interested and returning the kiss.

"Annette. I'm no Mata Hari, but I think you deserve a little pampering for your birthday . . ."

She gets up, dragging Dimo by the arm before he can react.

"Judging by the boy's appearance, it looks to me as if you're the one who's getting a present," says Patrocínio, laughing. He takes a *carte-de-visite* from his vest pocket, scribbles a name, and hands it to Dimitri. "If you do decide to go to Brazil, this is the name of a good friend at Lloyd Brasileiro. He's just been named captain of his own ship and should be coming to Marseilles soon. If you wish to, just look him up."

"Thank you, sir. I can't express the honor and the privilege I consider it to meet you."

"Perish the thought! Happy birthday. Annette, take good care of the boy. Poor me! Tonight I'll have to make do with two . . ." declares the heir of the great abolitionist.

And thus it was that Dimitri Borja Korozec became aware of the existence of José do Patrocínio Filho, a tall-tale–telling mulatto of incontrovertible talent, polyglot, consular official, poet, and journal-

Photo of Patrocínio Filho without lighting effect.

Photo of Patrocínio Filho with lighting effect.

Dimitri's portrait by
Picasso, done on a napkin
at the Brasserie Lipp.

ist, whose mythomania nearly got him hanged in London, months later, as a spy.

Though completely intoxicated, Gérard Bouchedefeu notices that Dimitri is about to retire. Resentful like all drunks, he grumbles, "At least don't forget the present I made for you with such affection." Sticking his hand in his coat, he tosses Dimo the stuffed mouse.

The youth fails to catch the small animal, which falls onto the neighboring table, into the lap of Jean Cocteau. Cocteau shrieks and climbs onto the chair: "A rat!"

Pandemonium sweeps the restaurant. The women scream, the men complain, the waiters dash about helter-skelter. Dimitri takes advantage of the confusion to pick up the small stuffed gift, which had come to rest in Modigliani's empty glass. He apologizes, embarrassed, and leaves in haste, dragging the blonde Annette by the hand. Apollinaire and Satie attend the poet, who is in a state of near-shock, while Picasso rolls on the floor clutching his sides in laughter.

Years later, the painter would still laugh when he recalled the episode and that confused young man leaving the Lipp, holding a small dead rat by the tail.

PARIS—MONDAY, OCTOBER 15, 1917

Despite the French euphoria over the victory at Verdun, for the first time in his life Dimitri Borja Korozec finds himself in a deep depression. As he had foreseen, Dragutin was shot as a traitor, and the execution of Mata Hari had just taken place at Vincennes, that morning; the Third Council of War had denied her final appeal. Dimo spends a sleepless night thinking about the dancer's unhappy end. The Bolsheviks' triumph in the Russian Revolution troubles his thoughts even more. Was political terrorism the correct option, or had all his training been futile and merely made him an assassin without victims? He spends entire days in his room, not getting out of bed, immersed in his books, rereading Bakunin and Kropotkin.

Gérard Bouchedefeu comes upon him in this mood, exactly five hours after the death of Mata Hari. The somber message that the old anarchist brings through the intermediary of a comrade just arrived from Sarajevo will deepen his young companion's melancholy even more. Dimitri's parents have died in a typhus epidemic. Even having spent his life dealing with death, the taxidermist doesn't know how to announce a misfortune of such magnitude. He remembers that in antiquity the rulers would order the bearers of bad news killed. He goes to Dimitri and yanks aside the blanket covering him.

"I've been thinking. There's no reason to be so unhappy. I want to tell you a Japanese fable that's sure to raise your spirits."

Dimo leans back in bed, curious, and Bouchedefeu sits down beside him.

"A monk returned to the monastery after years of wandering. As soon as entered the gates, he saw that the barbarians had burned down the temple and destroyed the gardens. In despair, the poor man threw himself to the ground, rending his garments and shouting to the heavens, 'I go off in search of wisdom and resignation, and when I return this is what I find? What is the meaning of this affliction?' At that moment, another monk, old and blind, approached and said, 'So, has your journey meant nothing? Did you not learn that, however great one's misfortune, something worse could always have happened?' The young monk replied impatiently, 'Don't be foolish, you blind old man. What could have happened to make me more unhappy than this?' And the old man replied, 'It is you who are foolish. For you are crying over the plants in the garden and the stones of the temple when your father and mother died of typhus.' "

Dimitri looks at Bouchedefeu for an instant and bursts into laughter. "Gérard, you're crazier than that blind old man. What do monks and monasteries have to do with me?"

"Nothing. But your father and mother did die of typhus."

It takes Dimo a moment to realize the enormity of what he has just heard. "What are you saying?"

"Just that. Your father and your mother died of typhus. I'm sorry, boy. If it's any consolation, I'm an orphan myself."

Dimitri Borja Korozec weeps silently over the irreparable loss. He feels alone and unprotected. Bouchedefeu, in anguish, doesn't know what to say. "You'll see. One day this suffering, which you feel to be unbearable, will end. As the proverb says, 'The greater the pain, the greater the consolation.' "

Dimitri, who has never heard such a stupid proverb, continues his convulsive sobbing. Bouchedefeu awkwardly strokes the young man's cheek, then leaves, closing the door behind him. Solace is not the chief virtue of old anarchists.

After a cold shower and a light lunch eaten quickly, Dimitri Borja Korozec leaves the apartment at two in the afternoon determined to make a radical change in his life. The shock of losing his parents awakens him from his lethargy. He will keep the promise made to his mother; it is time to act. He will leave for Brazil on the first available ship. He doesn't even think about using the card offered him by José do Patrocínio Filho. He won't travel for free. He has at his disposal the funds of the Black Hand, on deposit at the Schweizerischer Glücksgeldbank in Zurich, in the name of Apis. To get them, he has only to use the password given him by Dragutin. Till that moment he has never made use of that resource, but he thinks the time has come. Enough of apathy. Enough of this miserable way of life. He has to learn, among other things, how to spend money. The French branch of the Glücksgeldbank is on rue Tronchet. He decides not to take the Métro to the bank. He gestures toward a taxi parked in front of his building. It doesn't move. Nor can it; it's his. In a gesture of rebellion, he also decides he won't drive to his destination and signals to a colleague on rue de l'Échiquier: "Taxi!"

To him, the common shout has the special savor of freedom.

"I'm very sorry, sir, but this account was closed in September 1914, just after the start of the war," the teller wearing pince-nez, his hair parted down the middle, explains once again.

"There must be some mistake," Dimitri insists. "Maybe I didn't write the access code correctly. It's Nemesis. Could you check again?"

"We've checked it five times. Don't you want to speak to the manager? He would like to see you."

Dimo is taken to the presence of M. La Fortune. The immense room has a somber décor befitting a Swiss banker. La Fortune, tall, with an athletic physique, rises when the young man enters. He appears to have been apprised of the situation. He speaks between clenched teeth, not from lack of courtesy but from discretion.

"I am sorry, my dear sir, but I can only repeat what my employee told you. Unfortunately, for us as well, the Apis account, access code Nemesis, was closed three years ago. I asked to see you because I have here the copy of a document that was sent to all our branches. We have instructions to give it to the person who comes to activate the account."

Dimo receives in trembling hands a manila envelope and departs, stunned, leaving the manager with his hand outstretched.

As soon as he leaves the bank, Dimitri goes into a café on rue Auber. He orders a pastis and reads the faded copy of the text, translated some years before by a Portuguese monk in the São Bento monastery at Viana do Castelo:

To Whom It May Concern:

I write these lines in August of the Year of Our Lord 1914 as testimony to His infinite goodness and mercy. It was the Almighty's will to make me the instrument of His goodness, through the intermediary of my brother Milan Ciganovic, a notorious anarchist who must have committed many evils against his fellowman, for from an early age he displayed a tendency toward destruction. As his half-sister, it is with regret that I acknowledge that malignancy and, several times in London after my conversion, I meditated on the Heavenly Will to bring me into the world in the midst of a family so little God-fearing. I nevertheless knew that it all must be part of the plan of the Great Architect of the Universe.

Upon receiving, last month, a letter from Ciganovic, the compassionate divine plan finally became patent before my eyes with the undeniable clarity of a miracle. Without knowing that I had had the "Revelation" through the sisters of the St. Mary's Dispensary, Milan told me of a meeting with the infamous Colonel Dragutin, whose soul will surely burn in Hell, and he inadvertently indicated to me the name of the code, of the account and the bank where the large sums were deposited that financed his bloody murderous activities. Thus I was able to take control of these funds for the creation of an enlightened institution of charity that will raise to even greater heights the name of the Creator: The Home of the Milliner Unwed and Abandoned Mother Olga Krupa. I hope that the Lord does not take as vanity my having joined my humble name to this work of divine inspiration.

Hosanna in the highest! Mysterious are the ways of the Lord, for He writes straight with crooked lines.

I know that the person who now reads these words, whom I already consider the patron and benefactor of our foundation, will join me in shouting to the heavens: Thanks be to God! Thanks be to God! Thanks be to God!

> Sister Olga Krupa
> Founder and President of
> The Home of the Milliner
> Unwed and Abandoned
> Mother Olga Krupa
> London, 15 August 1914

Dimitri folds the sheet and puts it in his coat pocket. He calls the waiter and orders another pastis. He is determined not to allow himself to be defeated by events. He still has the belt with the gold coins, but he decides to keep it for greater emergencies. He will go to Brazil. Patrocínio Filho was right: there is nothing to keep him in the Old World. He looks upon his reversal of fortunes as a challenge. He examines the *carte-de-visite* the Brazilian gave him and decides to leave that very night for Marseilles. The waiter returns with the drink. Dimo's thoughts are so far away that, without realizing it, he thanks him in Portuguese: "Obrigado."

He downs the greenish liquid in a single gulp.

RIO GRANDE DO SUL, BRAZIL—SÃO BORJA, OCTOBER 1917

Holding a *maté* gourd in one hand, the man in gaucho trousers settles into the hammock on the porch. He is small in stature, but his calm appearance transmits unusual self-confidence. One senses in him the strength and charisma of the born leader. His young daughter follows him and sits on the floor beside him. She doesn't take her eyes off her father, whom she truly idolizes. The two remain silent, watching the onset of twilight. Venus appears in the sky and the sun begins to sink below the horizon, coloring the rooftops orange. The man is weary. A state deputy for the Republican Party since 1909, he is there as part of his campaign for reelection to a third term. He is always moved when he visits the old ranch where he grew up among the peasants. He misses the long horseback rides through the open plains and the barbecues over an improvised fire. He still has his first long knife, a gift from an old overseer.

The man is intrigued with a letter that was waiting for him at the ranch. The missive comes from afar, from Sarajevo, cradle of the conflict that has rocked Europe for the last three years. He takes from his pocket the envelope worn from so much handling. He again looks at the text written in a trembling hand, as if by one lacking the strength to hold the pen. The woman who wrote it relates that she is dying from typhus and has only a few days to live. In her delirium, she claims to be his natural sister, born when their father, the old general, was still single. She speaks of a son born in Bosnia, who would be his nephew and therefore their father's grandson.

She claims to have left Brazil with an Italian circus and that she married a Serbian anarchist. She fears for her son's life, as the young man appears to be following the uncertain path of the terrorist. The story is too convoluted to be true. It describes events in distant lands that he knows only through newspaper accounts. The man attributes that almost incoherent narrative to the hallucinations of fever. He decides the episode warrants no further attention. "Probably just one more poor woman who lost her mind because of the war," he thinks. He has a campaign to worry about. His reelection is considered a certainty, but in politics today's sure thing can be tomorrow's defeat.

The man takes out a match and sets fire to the letter. He lights a long Santa Damiana cigar. His daughter, who watches his every gesture in fascination, asks, "What's that paper?"

"It's nothing, Alzira," replies the man, Getúlio Vargas, patting her head and taking a long puff on his cigar.

FOUR

MARSEILLES—OCTOBER 1917

After checking into in an old hotel near the station, Dimitri walks down La Canebière, the long avenue that descends to the ancient port of the city. The Lloyd office is not far from the docks. He heads there in search of the person mentioned to him by Patrocínio.

Autumn is usually a time of rains in Marseilles, but today it is hot and sunny, a contrast with the dead leaves that dot the street.

He goes up the Quai des Belges and the Quai du Port as far as rue de la Coutellerie, and after walking for some time more he glimpses at the corner the small building of the shipping company. On its front, in faded letters, appears the name of the firm: Lloyd Brasileiro. The door is shut, but through the window he sees a man in his sixties leaning against the counter. The old employee is eating bouillabaisse from a plate placed inside a drawer as he reads a back issue of the *Jornal do Commercio*. Dimitri knocks on the glass and says to the man in Portuguese, "Could you please help me?"

The man raises his eyes and shouts, "We're closed. Today's an optional workday."

Dimitri has a perfect command of the language, but he has never heard that expression before. "What kind of workday?"

"Optional. It's like a holiday."

"Here?"

"No. In Brazil. It's National Bookkeepers Day."

"Please, sir. All I need is some information."

With great reluctance, the aged employee comes to the door and lets Dimitri in. He returns to the counter, visibly annoyed at the interruption, and closes the drawer with the plate. He takes the stub of a pencil from behind his ear and picks his teeth with it. He yawns and asks, "What's so urgent?"

"I'm looking for Captain Saturnino Furtado de Mendonça. Is he in Marseilles?"

The old man puts aside his newspaper. "Who wants to know?"

"The captain doesn't know me. My name is Dimitri Borja Korozec, and I was sent by a mutual friend," he explains, showing the card given him by Patrocínio.

The man scratches his head with the pencil-toothpick and returns the card with his thumb imprinted in grease: "He came in yesterday and leaves for Rio de Janeiro tonight commanding the freighter SS *Macau.*"

"And how can I find him?"

"No idea. If you want, you can look for him at the docks."

The weary public servant considers the matter closed. He goes back to reading his newspaper and, opening the drawer, spears with a blackened fork a fish head from the bouillabaisse and sucks it noisily, while grumbling between his few remaining teeth, "They don't even respect an optional workday anymore. That's the limit!"

Document found in the inactive files of the Imperial
German Navy attached to the log of the SS *Macau*.

SS Macau–*17 October 1917*

We set out from Marseilles at 20 hours on Tuesday, on
the high tide, for the port of Leixões, Portugal, first stop
on our return to Rio de Janeiro. At the request of the esteemed José do Patrocínio Filho, the distinguished consular attaché of Brazil in Amsterdam, I took aboard as
passenger a young man by the name of Dimitri Borja
Korozec, who is said to be a refugee, a citizen of Bosnia
whose mother was Brazilian. Given his credentials, I saw
nothing untoward in granting the request of such an illustrious civil servant, especially in light of the belligerency
taking place on the European continent.

The young man appears to possess an excellent education and speaks several languages fluently, including Portuguese, which, as he explained to me, he learned from his
mother.

He is in perfect health, but I have doubts about his adap-
tation to life on the ship during the crossing. I assume that
he must have had his physical equilibrium shaken by the
dislocations of embarking, for in short order he succeeded
in breaking, in my cabin, a magnificent sextant given me by
my father when I graduated from Merchant Marine School,
a solid instrument that had survived various storms.

He also broke three plates and a serving dish in the
mess, where he also accidentally injured, with his fork, the
right hand of First Pilot Magalhães; then he split the rail

on the quarterdeck, almost falling into the ocean, and, on a brief visit to the bridge, would have shattered with his elbow the glass dome that protects the magnetic compass if not for the prompt intervention of First Mate Rodrigues. He most certainly does not possess, as the French nautical jargon puts it, "sea legs." He is probably less awkward on terra firma.

We crossed the Strait of Gibraltar with relative tranquillity and continued on calm seas under a starry sky, at a speed of nine knots.

There is some apprehension among the crew members because of the sinking of the vessels Tijuca, Paraná, and Lapa in disregard of our declared state of neutrality, which has led to the severing of relations with the Kaiser's empire. Any further aggression against our fleet will doubtlessly cause Brazil to enter the war on the side of the Allies.

Actually, Officer of the Watch Souza and Steward Santos have told me in confidence that they feel uneasy about the fact of this freighter formerly being the Palatia, taken from the Germans while anchored in our ports. Besides this, they told me based on news gathered in Marseilles that the area was infested with German submarines. I do not know whether to give credence to this information or to consider it superstition, like the legend of sirens glimpsed by mariners of old.

As for me, I believe we shall make the port of Leixões tomorrow, in early evening, without major inconvenience.

Saturnino Furtado de Mendonça
Captain

The next day, some two hundred miles off Cape Finisterre, in Spain, Captain Wilhelm Kurz, of U-boat 932 of the imperial fleet, feels a pang in his heart when he sees the 3,557-ton prey clearly outlined in his periscope. Born in Bremen, the son of a shipbuilder and fascinated by the navy since childhood, he was at dockside when the freighter was launched in 1914. His sadness is even greater because his father had helped construct that vessel. It doesn't matter that the Brazilians renamed her; to him she would always be the SS *Palatia*. Wilhelm puts aside these sentimental memories and concentrates on the target. After all, such nostalgic thoughts are inappropriate for one of the most decorated officers in the Imperial Navy. At twenty-three, he has already sent twelve freighters and five cruisers to the bottom.

Pale and drawn from long periods confined in the U-boat, he appears older than he is. Submarines are designed exclusively for efficiency in combat, making no concessions to comfort.

The crew sleep beside torpedoes, in work clothes that have not been changed since the journey began. The bunks are narrower than cots in a convent. The men go for weeks without taking a bath, as water is reserved for drinking. They use gasoline to remove the eternal grease that envelops every part of the submarine, setting aside a small amount of water to clean their faces and hands.

In the battle zone it's impossible to use the toilets, for the noise of discharge can be detected by the enemy. After twelve hours, the air becomes almost unbreathable and, to save oxygen, not even the most addicted dare light a cigarette.

All of this contributes to reinforcing the sense of solidarity among the men. More than rank, it is personal values that define leadership. At times, the small space of that metal shark takes the tension of relations among comrades to the limits of the humanly possible. Even so, neither Wilhelm nor his men would choose any other way of life. Stealthily approaching the game under the water and catching it by surprise in mid-ocean is his greatest passion. From time to time he thinks, abashedly, that the pleasure of sinking the enemy is greater than that which he finds in a woman's arms.

This sensation seizes him now, as he orders Berminhaus, one of his officers, to launch the torpedoes. The twin weapons leave the firing tube and streak silently toward their target.

Leaning on the bulwarks of the upper deck, Dimitri looks at the sea. Following the orders of the captain, who fears another accident, an officer watches him from a distance, leaning against the second mast. Suddenly, Dimo turns to him, pointing at the waves: "Look how pretty! Two dolphins swimming underwater toward us. Incredible how fast they are and how they manage to stay the same distance apart. It looks like it's choreographed."

The officer comes over and leans on the bulwarks beside him.

"Isn't it a dazzling show of nature?" asks Dimitri, absorbed.

"No, it's German torpedoes," answers the officer, racing for the bridge.

Before he can reach the ladder, the two warheads explode against the iron hull.

Not even the alarm sirens can drown out the tumult. Men in hurriedly donned life preservers run to the lifeboats. From the bridge, Saturnino Furtado de Mendonça shouts orders that are no longer heard, while the first pilot struggles to keep the ship afloat. His efforts are futile. One of the torpedoes had hit the freighter's boilers. The massive 111-meter-long vessel begins to list with the fragility of a canoe. Some of the twenty-six crewmen panic and leap into the water. The others lower the lifeboats and pick up those who jumped. In keeping with the tradition of the sea, Saturnino de Mendonça is last to enter the lifeboats, along with the steward Arlindo. Saturnino takes with him the log and all the papers from the ship. A heavy fog begins to cover the surface, mingling with the smoke from the burning boilers.

The captain remembers his lone passenger and tries in vain to locate him in the boats pulling away from the wreckage. Nowhere does he see him; the fog blocks his vision. The *Macau* takes sixteen minutes to disappear into the depths of the Atlantic. Suddenly, a few meters from the boats, breaking through the mist, U-boat 932 rises from the waters like a steel whale. Captain Wilhelm is the first to emerge from the hatch. Immediately afterward, a sailor appears on the narrow deck of the submarine, quickly stations himself at the machine gun on the stern, and points the weapon at the lifeboats.

"Kommandant, schnell hier gekommen! Schnell!" barks Wilhelm, gesturing for Captain Saturnino to come aboard.

The lifeboat with the Brazilian captain pulls up to the submarine. Saturnino tries to hand the log and the documents to the lead oarsman.

"Nein! Mit den Papieren! Sie müssen die Papieren bringen!" the German gestures again, ordering him to bring the papers.

Saturnino is about to climb aboard when the steward Arlindo grabs his arm: "You're not going by yourself. Wherever you go, I go."

Ignoring the Germans' protests, they make their way to the deck of the submarine. Captain Wilhelm tells one of the armed men to take them below.

With the same quickness with which it emerged, U-boat 932 disappears from the surface, carrying the two Brazilians in its belly. This is the last recorded sighting of Merchant Marine Captain Saturnino Furtado de Mendonça and his faithful, courageous steward Arlindo Dias dos Santos.

Hours later, a Spanish destroyer plucks the twenty-four survivors from the waters of the Atlantic. No one remembers to look for

Owing to his remarkable disorientation, Dimitri had jumped off the other side of the ship. While all the others leapt off the larboard side, Dimo executed a perfect dive into the starboard waters, thus remaining out of sight of both Brazilians and Germans. Fearing he would be taken onto the submarine, he waits for the U-boat to submerge, protected by the fog as he clings to a large piece of flotsam from the deck.

When he decides to call for help, his appeals are lost in the welter of cries of encouragement from other survivors to their shipmates manning the oars. From his improvised raft, Dimo watches helplessly as the lifeboats leave the scene. Exhausted and numb from his time in the frigid waters, he falls asleep as he drifts, hidden in the mist.

Two hours after the torpedoing of the *Macau*, Dimitri Borja Korozec is awakened by strident voices speaking Portuguese with a

pronunciation he has never heard before. They are sardine fishermen from the city of Oporto, who have already furled their nets. He sees the trawler coming quickly toward him.

"Hallo! Hallo!" one of the fishermen calls out, a man named Joaquim, better known as Quim.

"Do you be daft, Quim? Don't you see the feller's dead?" says another.

"None of your footle, Nicolau. I saw him move," Quim assures him.

With a superhuman effort, Dimitri raises one of his arms, signaling that he is still alive. The Portuguese throw hooks into what remains of the floating rubble and haul in the unconscious survivor.

The youth's state of health worries the fishermen. They remove his drenched clothing, paying no attention to the wide leather belt and the cord with the key that Dimo, even semiconscious, clutches tightly. They put warm clothes on him, each of them contributing a piece of his wardrobe. Quim provides loose-fitting denim pants, Nicolau a thick sweater with turtleneck collar, and a third man, named Raul, a pea jacket. They wrap him in a thick wool blanket and the slicker typically worn by fishermen. The garb is completed by a cap that they push down over his ears. Someone pours a vegetable broth down his throat that almost scalds Dimitri's gullet. Even so, the new Moses saved from the waters continues to shiver. Nicolau sees that he's burning with fever. He makes Dimitri drink a mug of brandy. Finally, he asks, "Feeling better?"

Dimitri nods his head, but the bluish color of his skin belies the assertion.

"What's your name?"

"Jacques Dupont," replies Dimitri, fearful of revealing his true identity.

"What kind of name is that? Then you not be Portuguese, eh? You speak with a funny accent."

Dimitri continues inventing: "No, I'm French. I learned to speak Portuguese with a Brazilian friend."

The fishermen accept Dimo's explanation unquestioningly. Nicolau wants to know what occurred. "Can you tell us what happened?"

Dimitri takes another swallow of brandy and begins relating the story of the sinking. After listening to him, Nicolau, who seems to be the leader of the group, says, "You haven't explained why you weren't in the lifeboats."

Dimitri confesses shamefacedly, "I jumped off the wrong side of the ship."

The crew bursts into laughter and Dimitri faints again.

It's clear to the fishermen that Dimo urgently needs rest and more effective treatment. They decide to take him to Viana do Castelo, the nearest port. One of the Portuguese asks, "And where do we put him? He can't stay here exposed, and our bunks are very narrow. The boat's motion could throw him to the floor."

Nicolau solves the problem. He makes a bundle of Dimitri's wet clothes so nothing will get lost and places it between the youth's arms. Then he orders, "Quim and Raul. Put the feller in the hold on top of the sardines."

Raul pauses for a moment and inquires, "But, Nico, what about the smell?"

"Don't be a booby, Raul. Dead sardines can't smell anything."

It is night. Dimitri is awakened amid the fish by the siren of the trawler as it pulls up to the dock. Through the porthole he glimpses the harbormaster. He has no wish to be deported or arrested. He takes his soggy documents from his wet clothes, dries them as best he can, and tears off a piece of the slicker and wraps the papers in it, sticking it inside his cap. He uses his remaining strength to crawl through the narrow opening and slide silently into the sea, swimming to the far side of the boat.

When the fishermen come to look for him, they find only his waterlogged suit. In one of the pockets, overlooked in his haste, is Olga Krupa's letter, in English, which they hand over to the police. While they wonder, intrigued, whether the mysterious individual could really be a spy in the pay of the Germans or merely an ill-fated seafarer, Dimo makes his way to land by a more distant docking area and disappears in the winding streets of the port, leaving in his wake the musky scent of sardines.

FIVE

F rom October 1917 until September of the following year, there is no clue as to Dimitri's whereabouts. It is known that in March 1918, in Coimbra, using the alias Amadeu Ferreira, he won first prize in a typing contest sponsored by Remington. This feat came to light through notes in the firm's publications pointing out that the organizers later disqualified him "because the individual in question had twelve fingers, which gave him an unfair advantage over other contestants."

Other Records of Dubious Authenticity about
Dimitri Borja Korozec during This Period

- A photograph of his hands appear in Robert Ripley's "Believe It or Not" column in the *New York Globe,* with the caption "The incredible dodecadigital man."

- An English anarchist states that Dimitri had a personal involvement with the activist Sylvia Pankhurst in London in the spring of 1918, having participated in demonstrations supporting suffrage for women over thirty while disguised as a suffragette.

- A Spanish informer swears that on June 10, 1918, when Dimitri was twenty-one, one Korozec was rejected by a Barcelona clinic as a volunteer for testing of a new experimental drug, Ergonvine, which when used in small doses causes miscarriage.

- There are some who affirm having seen him in Coimbra during this same period, taking part in a meeting of the Mad Catalans, an independent Portuguese anarcho-terrorist group planning the assassination of President Sidônio Pais.

- In August of that same year, the militant Bolshevik Gregori Propof believes he has identified Dimitri as the man who tripped into Fanya Kaplan as she fired her weapon twice in the assassination attempt that nearly killed Vladimir Ilyich Lenin after a rally in Moscow.

- It is documented that an Italian edition of the *Kama Sutra,* immediately withdrawn from circulation, dedicates a chapter to the pleasure that is attained by a man with two extra forefingers, known by the nickname Il Manusturbatore.

- A German doctor named Kurt Schlezinger claims to have treated a twelve-fingered man suffering from ergotism, an infection that killed thousands in the Rhine valley and is transmitted by the *Claviceps purpurea* fungus, which turns common bread into a hallucinogen.

His presence is finally established with certainty in the early days of September 1918 in Lisbon, in an esoteric session in the home of the poet Fernando Pessoa, on Rua Santo Antônio dos Capuchos. Present at the meeting was the famous English occultist Aleister Crowley, whose poem "Hymn to Pan" Pessoa would later translate. At the gathering, Crowley declares that Dimitri is the reincarnation of the Egyptian high priest Ankh-f-n-khonsu, of the twenty-fifth dynasty. Ankh-f-n-khonsu fell into disfavor when Pharaoh Psamtik II realized that the priest's constant lack of balance was caused by the fact that he had twelve toes.

Aleister Crowley preparing a ritual of Egyptian magic.

In September 1918, the English steamship SS *Demerara* makes a call at Lisbon on its way from Liverpool with four hundred passengers on aboard. Built at the Harland and Wolff shipyards in Belfast, Northern Ireland, the ship is on its way to Rio de Janeiro but must first stop at Tenerife, in the Spanish territory of the Canary Islands, to replenish its water and coal and swap some of the sailors for a Spanish crew. It is on this vessel that Dimitri Borja Korozec embarks for Brazil as a ship's steward.

He had been introduced to the captain by Monoela Craveiro, an obscure fado singer in a cabaret in the port with whom both men maintained sporadic romantic ties. Only at Manoela's insistence did the captain agree to hire Dimitri, for the young man is suffering from a cold that causes a chronic fever. His fragility is attested to by this delirious fragment from his notebook:

[. . .] I cannot understand the constant concern of the ignoble seaman who commands this ship. He avoids me as if the cough that plagues my bronchial tubes were a harbinger of hemoptysis. Shitty seaman. I piss in the pestilent sea. On the waves the boat wavers and wanders. I'm thirsty, very thirsty, but they try to give me sea water. See slaughter. A mass moves over the mast. It's the pelican. I must suck its wet beak to quench this fire that blurs my sight. Away with you, Grim Reaper, my time is not yet come! Mommy called me Malidimo. Little Dimo. Malidimo. Mal and Dimo. Somewhere on the ship someone is murmuring my name. The conspiracy thickens like the fog; first, though, I shall cut the oppressor's claws. Is it night? It must surely be night. Or else it's day dressed in darkness. In my stomach I feel the suffocating heat of the boilers. The gangway! Why don't they lower the gangway? I never had a bilboquet. If I were a girl, they'd certainly have given me a doll. Never had a bilboquet. Beside me, a dying old man keeps muttering a prayer all the time. What time is it? [. . .]

Days later, as they leave Tenerife, all the less fortunate passengers on the *Demerara*, heading for the New World in search of a better life, are infected with the strange illness that afflicts Dimo.

The *Demerara*'s transatlantic voyage turns into a Dantesque adventure. The captain feels like the ferryman Charon cruising the river Styx toward Hell. The only thing missing from the mythology is the coin in the mouth of the sick to pay for the crossing. The constant coughing of the emigrants in steerage is superimposed on the cavernous din of the engines. The germ was caught by Dimitri from a battalion of American soldiers from Kansas City with whom he had fraternized in Bologna. However, because of the period of incubation, everyone erroneously attributed the influenza to the arrival of recently embarked Spanish sailors. From their cots, the less affected yell in voices made hoarse by fever: "It was the Spanish! We caught this damned grippe from the Spanish!"

And thus it was Dimitri Borja Korozec who brought the Spanish Flu to Rio de Janeiro.

The precarious conditions of hygiene and sanitation in Rio de Janeiro in the days of 1918 facilitate the spread of the pandemic. Schools are closed in an effort to contain the plague. Then it is business that locks its doors. Familiar remedies have little or no effect. A few unscrupulous vendors offer exotic elixirs as the miraculous cure. People refuse to leave their homes for fear of infection, but nothing seems to stay the contagion that invades first the city, then the entire country.

There are so many dead that there is no time to place them in coffins. Their bodies are thrown into common graves and hastily covered with earth and lime. Early every morning, hearses patrol the streets gathering up the deceased. São João Batista cemetery witnesses over one hundred forty burials in a single day. The shortage of burial plots is so great, owing to lack of space, that often those in charge merely trade their funereal cargo for fresher corpses.

The plague spreads everywhere, brought by infected immigrants, and in a short time over three hundred thousand die. Panic rules the population and there is talk of an imminent danger of cholera morbus.

Unbeknownst to Dimitri, he claims his first political victim by perpetrating an unwitting biological assassination: President Rodrigues Alves dies in January, killed by the germ Dimitri had introduced to Brazil.

Dimitri emerges unscathed from all this. His long association with the virus generates an antibody that transforms him into a carrier without affecting his health.

Nor is this to be the time when Dimitri succeeds in visiting his mother's homeland. When he tries to disembark in Rio, doctors at Customs discover a late outbreak of measles. Placed in quarantine, he is forced to continue the voyage to San Francisco, California, the next stop.

SIX

HOLLYWOOD—CULVER CITY—MGM STUDIES—
OCTOBER 3, 1925

"**M**ore extras! I need more extras!" shouts Irving Thalberg, the all-powerful Metro producer.

At twenty-six, Thalberg is considered the boy wonder of the industry, a trusted figure in the studio founded by Louis B. Mayer.

His assistant J. J. Cohn approaches, obviously up to his neck in work.

"It's not going to be easy to get extras at eight in the morning."

"How many people do you have now?"

"About four thousand."

"I want twice that number," Thalberg insists.

"Twice as many? What am I supposed to do?"

"Round up people off the street."

That Saturday, under the hot California sun, the great chariot race in *Ben-Hur* will be filmed. The project has already cost four million dollars, and virtually none of the footage shot in Italy was usable. Thalberg has now taken over the reins of the production. He brought the team back to Hollywood, changing the script, the director, and the star, and making the new actor Ramon Novarro the lead. Other more difficult scenes, like the valley of the lepers and the naval battle between Romans and pirates, had been executed without major setbacks. Now, there remains only the grand finale.

In the place of honor in the immense replica of the Circus Maximus are guests who have come especially for the event. Seated there as mere spectators, wearing Roman tunics, are, among other celebrities, Douglas Fairbanks, Mary Pickford, Lillian Gish, and Marion Davies. The final cameras are concealed strategically around the arena, behind enormous statues, in excavations spread throughout the racetrack, on rails, and in the middle of the crowd. On command, all of them must respond simultaneously. Chariots drawn by teams of two and four horses take their place at the starting line.

The collision between the two rivals has been meticulously prepared by the special effects department. Various chariots and horses are to be involved in the crash, which will end with the wheel of Ben-Hur's chariot wrenching away the wheel of Messala's vehicle. There is a certain tension in the air. In the previous attempt, filmed on location in Rome, several horses had died in the simulated accident and Ramon Novarro had escaped by a miracle.

The experienced director, Fred Niblo, gives final orders to his assistants through a megaphone. The costs are exorbitant. The scene has to be filmed in one take.

Beside an extra clad as a gladiator, behind the first turn of the racetrack, is Dimitri Borja Korozec, dressed as a centurion.

After his arrival in the United States, he managed to make contact with various anarchist groups, and the absurd rumor has even circulated that he was the real gunman in the Sacco-Vanzetti case. Knowing the tenacity with which he is dedicated to his cause, it is unlikely that he would have denied being the one responsible.

It is known that he took part in various labor movements, having almost aborted the famous mineworkers' strike of '22 by confusing the dust-covered coal miners with blacks of the ultraradical Back to Africa organization.

In 1924, his travels took him to New York, where he frequented the infamous dance halls of Hell's Kitchen. Soon he was earning a living as a professional dancer. It was in these dance halls that Dimitri met a certain George Raft, also a dancer, with ties to dangerous underworld elements. Raft, who had been a boxer and has just won the dubious title of "fastest Charleston dancer in the world," is the prototype of the Latin lover, with his dark complexion and straight hair always impeccably held in place with Vaseline. He has the habit of tossing a coin into the air and catching it without looking. Dimitri began imitating him, even in his manner of dressing and slicking down his hair. A solid friendship was immediately forged between the two men. Dimitri made him his confidant, revealing his true identity and his still unfulfilled political plans. He even told of his hapless participation in the attack on the archduke in Sarajevo, at which Raft laughed uproariously. Dimitri was taken aback, unable to see the comic side of his misadventure.

Both had success with the ladies, and once Dimo had perfected his imitation of the dancer, George began introducing him as his younger brother.

After a year, and seeing few major opportunities in New York, George Raft persuaded Dimitri that they should move to Hollywood, where they would try to break into the movies. Dimo accepted the invitation, certain that his political objectives would not be compromised. He was convinced that the film industry was the creator of dangerous myths in the service of the bourgeoisie and that the best way to destroy it was from within.

Now it is precisely George Raft who stands beside him, dressed as a gladiator. Dimo still has the appearance of a naive romantic poet, and Raft's thirty years make him appear a lot older than Dimitri's twenty-eight.

George Raft nervously adjusts his helmet. Unlike his friend, he plans to have a career and doesn't want any mistake to hurt his chances: "Are you sure you understand what the assistant director wants?"

"Of course," Dimitri assures him confidently, holding a thick rope half buried in the sand.

"Then let me hear it."

Dimitri rolls his eyes impatiently. He's there more for the free food than because of his minuscule part.

"I wait for the two main chariots to pass and then I yank on this rope hidden in the ground. The horses pulling the pursuing chariots trip over the rope. Simple."

His carefree manner fails to calm Raft completely. Anyone who has lived around Dimitri knows his natural bent for catastrophe.

"Better let me do it. Give me the rope."

Dimo is irritated: "George, I'm not a child."

"Give me the rope."

To Dimitri, the issue has become a point of honor: "I was chosen to pull the rope and I'm going to pull it."

Furious, George Raft throws himself upon him. The pair roll on the ground fighting for the doubtful privilege of causing the disaster. Dimitri throws a handful of sand in George's face and draws his centurion's sword. George gets up, holding his trident and attempting to trap Dimitri in the net that is part of his costume. They are no longer extras. They have become gladiators fighting fiercely with wooden weapons.

From atop a crane, Fred Niblo, unaware of the incident, shouts into the megaphone, "Action!"

They do not hear the crazed screams of the assistant director begging them to pull the rope. The horses of the lighter chariots, which were supposed to stumble, crash in a mad scramble into the two lead chariots, just beyond the turn. The collision causes the inside wall of the track to collapse, toppling a colossal statue of Neptune. Suddenly, the entire set comes cascading down.

Silence falls on the ruined stadium. Standing in the middle of the rubble, George Raft and Dimitri Borja Korozec continue fighting as if their lives depended on it. Aware of the delicate state of Irving Thalberg's health, Mary Pickford and Douglas Fairbanks fear that his heart won't stand it. The melee has just added a million dollars to the production costs of *Ben-Hur*.

Luckily for George Raft, the helmet covering his face keeps him from being identified, and the ex-dancer can go on playing small parts until his breakthrough role in *Scarface* in 1932, as the gangster Guido Rinaldo at the side of Paul Muni.

His trick, acquired in Hell's Kitchen, of tossing a coin and catching it without looking would become his trademark.

Long before this rise to fame, however, the friendship between him and Dimitri had been gravely shaken. Raft feared that someone in the capital of cinema would see them together and associate his name with the hecatomb.

Three years go by and it becomes

Photo of George Raft and Dimitri made by a beginner for an extras agency.

ever clearer that the old ties that united them in New York are coming undone. Besides the small room that they share in a second-
class boardinghouse, they have little in common. While Raft snares
ever better roles, Dimo day by day becomes disenchanted with the
Mecca of cinema. With the exception of a few adventures with star-
lets who later became major stars and whose names are of no interest here, he sees nothing of value in his stay in California. Raft finds
the anarchist's political aspirations ridiculous.

In December 1928, as winter begins, George Raft can take
no more of Dimitri Borja Korozec. Wishing to rid himself once and
for all of his annoying companion, he strikes up a conversation
with him in which he takes notes for a possible book about Hollywood. These notes were discovered by agents of Fidel Castro in
1959 when they closed down the casino of the Hotel Capri, which
George Raft, then at the end of his career, ran as a figurehead for
organized crime.

As an added attraction, the Capri had in its penthouse a pool
with a transparent bottom, and anyone in the bar below could
delight in watching the girls swimming nude.

The following execrable translation, overly literal and sometimes incomprehensible, was made by a Brazilian writer, anonymous and alcoholic, who specialized in cheap detective stories:

[. . .] I really didn't know what else to do with that guy.
After the *Ben-Hur* episode, to be seen together with him was
fatal. His only subject was the "revolution," and how the
true goal of the anarchist was to eliminate all tyrants. As we
were very joined, he confided in me and counted advan-
tages. He wanted to make me believe he was a terrorist
trained in Europe and a lot of other high tales. I couldn't

take his presence any longer in the small rented room we shared in a hostelry near La Cienaga. I then had a brilliant idea of what to do to see him from the back.

We were eating at the Insane Horse, an articulation frequented by extras and production assistants. As always, he was repeating the same steer fertilizer about politics when I interrupted: "Dimo, that's steer fertilizer. I'm going to tell you something, old friend. The real revolutionaries are the personnel of the underworld. Look at how they assault banks. Do you want a greater symbol of capitalism than a bank?"

"You can say that anew," he replied.

I felt that the dunce was crocheted by my rapid parlance and continued: "But in material of anarchy, there isn't who surpasses the Cosa Nostra."

"Cosa Nostra?" he asked, opening his eyes widely.

"The wise men."

"Wise men?" he repeated.

"That's what we call the party of the Mafia."

"May monkeys bite me if I'm understanding," said Dimitri.

Of course the sucker hadn't heard of them. I passed on to explain: "Men who live from crime. They destroy institutions much more than any anarchist with a bomb. They're the real threat to the system. They don't respect order, don't pay taxes, and make their own laws with a .45 or a submachine gun in their hands. Look how they used the Dry Law to their favor. In Chicago, they took advantage of Prohibition to mount a millionaire business. They facture more than sixty millions of dollars per year and eliminate with bullets any foolish who gets in their road. They have the cops and the judges in their pockets upholstered with money."

"Do you know those people?" he asked me.

I took a long drag on my Lucky Strike to create a climate of mystery: "Maybe . . ."

"Stop thrashing around the shrub, George. Do you know or don't you?" he impatiented.

"I think I can say that 'yes.' Now that Johnny Torrio retired, the one who's taking count of things is a youngster I lived with in Hell's Kitchen in New York. If you have interest in knowing real anarchism, persons who act instead of speak, who dominate the contraband of whiskey, the night-clubs where illegal beverages sell themselves, the gambling and the prostitution, I can write a letter of introduction to him. If you are really all that which you say, I have certainty of that he will appreciate your gifts more than anyone in Holly-wood."

I saw his eyes gleam of excitation. I perceived that my proposal had arrived at him like a blow with the fist in the waist. He supplicated me, agitated, that I write the letter at once. I asked paper and a pen of the waiter and began to write the thing right there, in the Insane Horse. Know-ing that Dimitri spoke several languages and could easily pass for Italian, I wrote more or less this following: "Dear Alphonse, the carrier of this one is a man whose talents cer-tainly to you will be of great utility . . ."

I don't remember well of the rest, but it was this way that finally I freed myself of that one who was for me a true ache in the hindquarters.

I presented Dimitri to my old acquaintance Al Capone.

The night train to Chicago would be departing in a few hours. Before leaving California, Dimitri Borja Korozec decides to say good-bye to the city. He wanders about the streets in late afternoon, buffeted by the cold wind of winter that sweeps the sidewalks like an unexpected garbage collector.

He crosses a nearly deserted street and turns onto Hollywood Boulevard, stopping at the corner to observe an oil slick left by some star's limousine. The last rays of sun blanketing the avenue impart a multitude of colors to the stain. "A dead rainbow," he thinks, bordering on the poetic. He feels himself overcome by a certain nostalgia. He remembers distant Banja Luka, where he was born, his parents, Dragutin, and Bouchedefeu. What has become of his dear friend from Paris? In the last letter he received from him, over two years ago, the old anarchist related that he had married the building's fat concierge and that they were very happy, living in Normandy. At his wife's behest, he had given up taxidermy and was now the prosperous owner of L'Excrément Agile, a small business specializing in cleaning septic tanks.

With his usual enthusiasm, he had gone on at great length about his new activity. There were entire pages full of details about the drains of ancient Greece, the gold chamber pots found in the tomb of Ramses I, who died thirteen centuries before Christ, and how the fort of Marcoussy in the Middle Ages had latrines constructed at an inclined angle that permitted the waste to slide directly down into cesspools located outside the walls. Soldiers could withstand months of an enemy's siege without contaminating the castle's quarters with piles of feces. That was Bouchedefeu. Whatever his profession, he loved what he did.

Dimitri also recalls, with affection, Mira Kosanovic, his first and only love, the woman who had initiated him into the pleasures of sex at the Skola Atentatora. He had had various women, short-lived affairs, but his wanderings had left no room for a more serious relationship. He didn't complain; he knew how lonely the life of an anarchist assassin is. "An assassin without victims," he thinks melancholically.

Suddenly, he realizes he's in front of the foremost symbol of Hollywood: the Chinese Theatre. The gigantic movie house had been built a year earlier, and before it stretches the Sidewalk where great stars press their palms into wet cement. He finds the idea ridiculous; nevertheless, as he has never been there, he approaches, curious.

Hours earlier, a star had left her prints there, probably during some grotesque ceremony.

He notices that the cement is still wet. He looks down the street in both directions, then stoops as if to tie his shoe. Before anyone can stop him, he presses his own hands down onto the freshly made marks in the cement.

Only the most attentive observer will realize that now Pola Negri has twelve fingers.

Dimo walks away, satisfied, his spirit renewed by what he considers a courageous act of terrorism. He doesn't notice the small figure dressed as Santa Claus who watches him closely, two blocks away, hidden in the shadows of twilight. When Dimitri crosses the avenue, the figure silently follows him.

CHICAGO—JANUARY 1929

With the same match he had used to light his expensive Cuban cigar, the thick-lipped man with a scar on his cheek sets fire to the letter he has just read.

"George thinks a lot of you. How's he doing?"

"Fine. He's getting bigger and bigger parts in films," replies Dimitri.

"The letter was written in December. Why didn't you look me up before?"

"I tried. I came to see you several times in the Lexington Hotel, but your men wouldn't let me get near you."

The conversation between Dimitri Borja Korozec and Al Capone takes place at the Four Deuces, on Wabash Avenue, simultaneously a cabaret, a brothel, and a clandestine casino. It's said that in the cellar of this one-time office of Johnny Torrio various members of rival gangs spent their final hours of life. Capone's appearance is impressive. He wears expensive tailor-made clothes and an 11½-carat diamond ring sparkling on his pinky. At a table in the back, Frank Nitti, John Scalise, Albert Anselmi, and "Machine Gun" Jack McGurn are playing cards, always keeping an eye on their boss.

There was a good reason Dimitri hadn't looked for Scarface, Al's nickname since the time a juvenile delinquent in New York had cut his left cheek with a razor in a bar fight.

Before the meeting, he had spent a month holed up in a crummy hotel near Union Station, going to the library and devouring everything about gangsters he could find in the archives of the *Chicago Tribune*.

He made friends with an old Sicilian shoeshine man who worked at the door of the hotel and, thanks to his innate gift for languages, had perfected the dialect learned years before from a fireeater in the circus of his childhood. From that same individual he had also assimilated the customs of that distant land.

From articles by the crime reporter James O'Donnell Berinett he learns of the dispute between gangs that is transforming Chicago into a war zone. He reads about the armored Cadillac parked in front of the Four Deuces. The car, made to order at a cost of $20,000, an astronomical sum at the time, has a steel body and bulletproof windows. The doors and hood have combination locks like a safe so that no one can plant bombs in the automobile.

The violence had begun with the assassination of Dion O'Banion, a gangster of Irish origin who was looking to expand his territory. O'Banion's heir, another Irishman, known as George "Bugs" Moran, had vowed revenge, and the war had grown more relentless with the attempt on the life of Johnny Torrio, the former Chicago gang boss. As Torrio had handed over all his businesses to Capone, he thought that his retirement had won him full immunity and went about unarmed and without bodyguards.

One day, returning from shopping, Torrio was caught unawares in broad daylight by Bugs Moran and some of his henchmen. He was hit by two bullets. As he lay on the ground, Moran approached him and, intending to destroy his masculinity as well, shot him in the groin. Then he put his automatic against Torrio's head and pulled the trigger for the coup de grâce. He heard only a metallic click: the gun was empty. Seeing that people were being attracted by the gunshots, Moran and his men ran away, leaving Torrio, a gangster who believed in nonviolence, near death on the sidewalk. In a few minutes an ambulance took him to Jackson Park Hospital, where he miraculously recovered.

Only after he feels duly prepared does Dimo go looking for Al "Scarface" Capone to give him George Raft's letter.

Capone relights his cigar, which insists on going out. He runs his gaze along Dimitri from head to foot and asks, "What did you say your name was?"

"Dim. Dim Corozimo," Dimitri improvises.

"Sicilian?"

"Yes, but I came here when I was very young. I'm from a small village in the province of Palermo."

"What village?"

"Corleone."

The gangster analyzes Dimitri's face and curly hair. He looks more Sicilian than Capone himself. He reminds him of Little Albert, his younger brother.

"How'd you end up here?"

"They sent me to America when my father was shot to death."

To test him, Capone begins speaking in Sicilian dialect. "Tuu patri?"

Dimitri responds in kind: "Sì. I miu patrí é mortu ammazzatu cu'n sparo di lupara."

"Cussi sei veramente sicilianu?"

"Sangu du nostru sangu."

"E comm 'è Corleone?"

"Eru picciriddu, non mi ricordu cchiú." Explaining that he was small and doesn't remember the village where he was born, Dimitri changes the subject: "Sonu un uomo di rispettu, un uomo d'onuri. Fammi truvari un travagghio nella sua famigghia."

Capone decides to welcome him: "Bene. Stai attentu, peró, ch'i testi di mafiusi non ci rrumpunu mai."

"Grazie, don Alfonso, baciu le mannni," says Dimitri gratefully, kissing Al Capone's fat hand.

Before he can have total confidence in Dimo, Scarface must test his abilities: "Are you really any good?"

"I'm trained in any kind of killing, with any type of weapon," Dimitri boasts.

Capone is amused at his braggadocio: "They say the word *Mafia* comes from the Arabic, from when the Moors occupied Sicily. In Arabic it's *mouaffa,* which means 'closed mouth.' Let's see if you're not just talking." He calls Nitti, Scalise, Anselmi, and Machine Gun. "This kid here wants to work for me. Says he's a good shot and knows everything there is to know about weapons."

Albert Anselmi, considered along with Scalise one of the most dangerous gunmen in the group, suggests, "Why don't we go down to the cellar and see how he is with a Tommy gun?"

This was the name given to the submachine gun invented by Brigadier General John Taliaferro Thompson.

The Thompson was capable of firing eight hundred .45-caliber bullets per minute at a distance of almost five hundred yards. The clip was round, giving it a unique appearance. The only problem was that it was impossible to use with accuracy. The bullets came out in bursts, sweeping the area before it. The kick was so strong that it invariably bruised the shooter's armpits.

An advertisement published in the *New York Herald* when the weapon was first released promised "a sure defense against orga-

Thompson submachine gun.

nized criminals and bandits," who ironically were exactly the ones who made greatest use of it.

In a soundproof room constructed in the cellar where the gang practices target shooting, they hand Dimitri a Thompson. He looks at the weapon, fascinated: "I've never seen one of these before. I like to shoot with a pistol."

Capone's men exchange glances, smiling. They think Dimo is afraid. Frank Nitti suggests, "If you like, I can borrow my kid's water gun."

They guffaw, adding similar gibes. Scarface interrupts the fun and directs an icy look at Dimitri. "It's time to find out if you're lying or not. Nobody who tries to put one over on me leaves here alive."

Dimo doesn't hesitate. He turns quickly and, not even taking aim, unblinkingly rips apart the targets glued to the rear wall with four short bursts of gunfire. A respectful silence follows the thunderous machine-gun shots. Dimitri lowers the still smoking weapon. Machine Gun Jack McGurn, a specialist, approaches him and says reverently, "Kid, I never seen anybody handle a Tommy gun like that. How'd you manage to grip it so tight?"

Dimitri, the only one who hadn't protected his ears against the Tommy gun's deafening rat-tat-tat, doesn't hear him well.

"What did you say?"

Machine Gun laughs and repeats the question, shouting: "How do you stand the kick?"

"I don't know. Maybe because of my twelve fingers," he says, showing his hands.

Astonished, Scarface examines the anomaly: "What's that?"

Dimitri replies promptly, even with a buzzing in his ears. "I was born with them. It's a mark of destiny. Ì fatu, don Alfonso."

Impressed, Al Capone immediately accepts Dimo into the organization.

From that cold winter night in the cellar of the Four Deuces, he becomes part of Scarface's gang. Legends says that there was never anyone better at handling a Tommy gun than an unknown gangster dubbed by Al Capone as "Fingers" Corozimo.

At the beginning of February, Capone decides to put an end to the constant attacks by Bugs Moran. In a meeting in a suite at the Lexington Hotel, where he occupies several floors, he puts McGurn, an accomplished organizer, in charge of an operation to eliminate Moran and his entire gang once and for all. McGurn decides to hire out-of-town gunmen so they won't be recognized and also plans to use Dimitri, a new face in the area. He continues to be impressed by the deadly aim of the group's newest member.

Machine Gun's plan is at once simple and a stroke of genius. Four gunmen—the Keywell brothers from Detroit, Fred "Killer" Burke from St. Louis, and Joseph Lolordo from New York—accompanied by Dimitri, will show up disguised as policemen at the garage where Moran carries out his business. Two of them will be in uniforms and Dimo and the others will be in plainclothes.

After the shooting, the fake detectives in civvies will leave with their hands in the air, as if being arrested by the men in police uniforms. To complete the maneuver, he puts Claude Maddox, one of Capone's men, in charge of stealing a police car. To guarantee everyone's presence at the spot, he has a bootlegger unknown in the area set up a meeting with Moran to sell, at an irresistible price, a shipment of whiskey from Canada.

An incurable romantic, McGurn chooses February 14, Valentine's Day, to effect the extermination. They agree to meet at 10:30 that morning.

The only problem is that because the killers are from out of town, they have seen Bugs Moran only in photographs. Dimitri, who also knows him only from the research he's done in newspapers, ventures a small lie to gain stature in Capone's eyes: "I know quite well who he is. I've run into Bugs in several bars on North Clark, where he has his garage."

"Great," says Scarface, giving him a friendly pat on the shoulder.

"Still, I want the Keywell brothers to take pictures of him with them in case anything goes wrong," insists the always meticulous McGurn.

"You can trust me, Jack. Everything's going to work out fine," declares Dimitri in a show of conviction hardly consonant with his past.

Respect for the truth forces one to recognize that sometimes fate conspires against Dimitri Borja Korozec.

Gerardo Machado y Morales, the victorious general in the Cuban revolution of 1898, had been reelected president of Cuba shortly before. In that same month of February, he is braving the cold Chicago winter in search of foreign investments to promote the economic reforms promised during the campaign. His visit is unofficial. The meetings with the magnates have to be confidential in order not to upset Cuban nationalists. For this reason, the general-president takes lodging anonymously with his advisers in a modest hotel in the city. The same establishment houses another illustrious guest: George "Bugs" Moran.

As Dimitri has never seen Moran in person and doesn't know where the garage is located, he has no wish to place his reconnaissance mission in jeopardy. He stations himself at the entrance to the hotel beginning at nine in the morning. He has read in his research that Moran customarily walks the short distance from the hotel to the garage. Dimo's only means of identifying him is a newspaper clipping with his photograph. As soon as Bugs comes out, he plans to follow him to where the killers disguised as policemen are waiting, hidden inside the stolen police car. The automobile should already be parked near the locale. As soon as they pass the car, Dimitri will point out the gangster, get into the car with the others, and leave with them for the garage.

At exactly 10:15, Machado y Morales, president of Cuba, comes out of the hotel. He has an appointment with the magnate Samuel Insull, former private secretary to Thomas Edison and now president of the vast investment firm Middle West Utilities. Some months later, Insull would lose everything in the stock market crash of 1929, but at the moment he is one of the richest men in the country. When Morales makes his way to the sidewalk accompanied by two of his advisers, he is recognized by a honeymooning Cuban couple on their way into the hotel. They greet the Cuban general in a loud voice, repeating his name: "Morales! Morales!"

The president waves and continues in the direction opposite that taken daily by Bugs Moran.

As Dimitri's hearing is still slightly affected by the machine gun shots in the cellar of the Four Deuces, instead of "Morales! Morales!" he understands "Moran! Moran!" He checks the photo of Bugs that he carries with him. There is almost no resemblance between the general and the gangster. But, because both are wearing hats, Dimo attributes the difference to the terrible quality of the faded photograph and begins tailing Morales from the other side of the street. The anarchist's heart starts beating faster. Adrenaline courses through his body and he feels that this time he won't ruin everything.

Two blocks down is a police vehicle on patrol in the area, parked in front of a diner. The police have stopped to get coffee and doughnuts. Dimo takes this for the stolen car and thinks that the real police are the hired killers. He opens the rear door suddenly, jumping into the automobile beside an enormous Irish cop. Slapping the driver on the shoulder and pointing to the Cuban general, he says quickly, "Let's go, boys! That's him!"

As he precipitously clambered into the car, Dimitri spilled the coffee the gigantic Irishman was drinking, soaking him. The cop at the wheel, from the clap on the back, choked on his doughnut.

"Him who?" asks the third policeman, sitting in the front.

"Him! Him!"

The Irish cop, enraged by the bath of hot coffee, pushes him down and slaps handcuffs on him.

Only then does Dimitri realize he got into the wrong car. He still tries to cover up, pointing to the president of Cuba: "Isn't that the singer Bing Crosby? I'm crazy about him. You think you could get me an autograph?"

The enormous Irishman replies by placing his boots on Dimitri's back. "No. You're going to give us yours at the precinct." He turns to the cop at the wheel and says, "Let's take this fruitcake to the station."

After spending the night in a cell with five drunks, Dimo reads in the morning papers about the Saint Valentine's Day Massacre, in which seven members of Bugs Moran's gang were murdered.

The Saint Valentine's Day Massacre.

Without Dimitri's help, the Keywell brothers had mistaken Al Weinshank, another member of the gang who went into the garage at 10:30, for Bugs. The two men were actually quite similar in appearance and this was not the first time such confusion had occurred. Moran, who had overslept and arrived late at the appointment, escaped untouched.

As for President Machado y Morales, he returned safe and sound to Cuba—without, however, having gotten his coveted loan.

Al "Scarface" Capone forgives Dimitri's lapses for only two reasons. First, with his gang routed and fearing he would die in another attempt, Bugs Moran ceases to be a threat. When a reporter asks who could have eliminated his men, he replies instantly, "Only Capone kills like that."

Capone and his son at a baseball game. To the right, the
arrow indicates Dimitri, partially covered by a scorecard.

Afterward, knowing of Scarface's passion for opera, Dimo
invents an uncommon interest in bel canto, memorizing arias and
learning everything about the life of Caruso, the Chicago gangster's
greatest idol. The pair spend nights drinking and singing passages
from *Rigoletto,* Al's favorite work. Little by little, they become inseparable. It is Dimo who drives the car, fortunately armored, which
keeps the light jolts occasioned by the driver's clumsiness from
denting the body. In short, the anarchist has been transformed into
the discreet shadow of the most feared man in America.

Except for a photograph in which Dimo is seen escorting
Capone and his son to a baseball game, there are almost no records
of the time they spent together. Scarface preferred to keep him as a
secret weapon. The friendship between the two comes to give rise to
jealousy among the older members of the gang, like Frank Nitti and
Frankie Rio, but no one dares make any disparaging comment in the
presence of the *capo.*

After the bloody Valentine's Day, Capone's situation begins to deteriorate. Public opinion, which till then considered him, as he himself said, "just a nice guy who sells forbidden drinks," is revolted at the violence of the slaughter.

The condition of the victims, shredded by machine guns and blasts from sawed-off shotguns, was so horrifying that when the coroner arrived at the garage he was unable to examine the bodies on the spot to find out, from their caliber, if the bullets had come from firearms used by the police. A young reporter from the sensationalist *City News,* eager for a scoop, had used the doctor's saw to personally open the skulls of the cadavers and try to remove the projectiles.

The government senses that it's time for immediate action. A special subsection is created in the Justice Department, the Prohibition Division. Men in the division prepare a dossier to indict and arrest Al Capone for income tax evasion. Among them is an obscure agent named Eliot Ness, himself an alcoholic.

The new method of combating gangsterism through the income tax is seen as a veritable revolution. It happens at the beginning of November 1930, in Chicago.

At the same time, almost six thousand miles away, in Brazil, another type of revolution has just brought to power Getúlio Dornelles Vargas, the unknown uncle of Dimitri Borja Korozec.

CHICAGO—OCTOBER 17, 1931

Al Capone's Fate to Be Decided Today

At a table on Adams Street, next to the Federal Building, Dimitri reads once again the *Chicago Tribune* headline. A long black overcoat conceals the heavy canvas bag that he carries over his shoulder. He crumples the ill-starred news item and asks the red-haired waitress to bring him a glass of milk. An excess of spicy Sicilian food and the latest developments have given him an ulcer that reemerges angrily in moments of great tension.

After ten days, the jury is about to begin deliberations on the fate of Scarface. The majority of the public has no doubts about his being found guilty; speculation focuses on the sentence. A few theatrical moves stir up the trial. On the first day, Judge Wilkerson, upon entering the courtroom, orders the bailiff, "Judge Edwards also has a trial that begins today. Ask him to switch jury panels with me."

By that singular measure, Wilkerson avoids any possibility that the twelve jurors have been bought by Capone's henchmen.

Another dramatic episode occurs when the judge notices that Philip D'Andrea, one of Al's bodyguards, is armed and is casting menacing glances at the jury, allowing glimpses of the .38 automatic under his jacket. Even though he has a gun permit issued by the city, D'Andrea is taken into custody. "It's contempt of court to come in here with a pistol," the judge declares.

On Saturday, the prosecution rests its case after calling dozens of witnesses and presenting numerous documents proving that Al Capone, a man who had accumulated an illicit fortune of more than a hundred million dollars, had paid no income taxes since 1925.

Impeccably dressed, Scarface appears bored by the testimony. He displays a calm that surprises the spectators and journalists watching the proceedings.

As soon as the jury withdraws to decide his fate, Al makes an almost imperceptible signal to Frankie Rio, another bodyguard, waiting for him at the door. Frankie nods and leaves the room. Capone and his lawyers return to the Lexington Hotel to await the verdict. He exhibits an enigmatic smile that the reporters take for conceit. They don't know that the king of the underworld is still planning to play his last card.

The idea to pull off a daring operation to rescue Scarface comes from Dimitri. Remembering the ease with which he used to climb ropes in the circus, he suggests to Capone that Frankie Rio go to the top floor of the Federal Building and drop a long rope to the ground. Dimo will climb up it to the floor where the men are deliberating the verdict behind locked doors. He'll force the window, gain access to the room, and bribe the jury.

In the heavy bag beneath the overcoat he carries an offer they can't refuse: six million dollars. Five hundred thousand for each juror. After acquittal, Al promises to pay them another five hundred thousand each, and in Chicago his word is law. In case of betrayal, it's well known what will happen, but the risk is nonexistent; no one betrays Al Capone.

At 2:30, Frankie Rio, from the top of the building, spots Dimo in the alley between Dearborn Street and Adams. He tosses him the rope placed there the night before by a courthouse policeman on Capone's payroll. Dimitri begins his climb along the south face of the building and quickly reaches the floor where Scarface's future is being debated.

Dimo leans against the wall, holding on to the parapet, and through the closed window sees the twelve citizens seated around the table. It's not possible to hear what they're saying, but the discussion appears heated. Gathering momentum, he uses the rope for counterbalance and hurtles through the window, breaking the latch with his feet. The men rise, startled by the sudden invasion.

Before they can say anything, Dimitri makes a gesture asking for silence. He starts talking in a low voice, almost a whisper.

"If you know what's good for you, sit down and listen." He opens the thick canvas bag and dumps the packages of carefully wrapped money on the table. "This is for you. There's $500,000 for each of you. Tomorrow, after the trial is over, you'll receive another $500,000 at your homes. All you have to do is go back in there and return a verdict of not guilty."

As he speaks, Dimo separates the sum into twelve equal parts and pushes the piles toward the stupefied men. They have never seen so much money in one place. Their eyes bulging, they begin stuffing the small fortune into their jackets, their pants, and beneath their shirts. Some stick into their socks the wads that don't fit in their pockets. Two or three hesitate but are persuaded by an Adventist preacher. Another man, older, puts his ear against the door to make certain the guards posted outside aren't overhearing the negotiation. The juror closest to Dimo, an insurance adjuster, starts to say something: "After all—"

"There's no time to lose," Dimitri interrupts. "Do exactly what I'm telling you. It's not every day you get a million dollars for an acquittal. If you ask me, we're being too generous."

Putting away the empty sack, he departs the same way he came, hanging from the balustrade. Before closing the window, he repeats, "Remember: the verdict has to be unanimous."

Everyone agrees, gleeful at that fortune fallen from heaven, and gets ready to return to the courtroom.

With the elegance of a trapeze artist, Dimitri slips down the rope to the sidewalk and quickly disappears in the streets, satisfied at having executed perfectly the task entrusted to him.

Only one small detail gets in the way of the plan to buy the mafioso's innocence.

Owing to his congenital disorientation, Dimitri had climbed one floor too far and ended up invading the room where they were deliberating the case of a nearsighted lady who, driving without her glasses, had run over the Pekinese dog of a retired army colonel. It was these jurors to whom he'd given Scarface's money.

While the aged canicide goes home free and happy, the other jury condemns Al Capone to eleven years in prison.

SEVEN

It is easy to see that after the unfortunate error that occurred in Al Capone's trial the climate in Chicago is no longer the healthiest for Dimitri Borja Korozec. He stops frequenting his usual hangouts, changes addresses, and dares go out only at night, slipping through the streets. He spends the days in his room, reading magazines and newspapers.

An item on the third page of the *Daily News* catches his attention. In Brazil, President Vargas, who had taken office a year earlier, following the revolution, has ordered the burning of millions of sacks of coffee. Through the destruction of the stock, he hopes to bolster the price of the commodity on the world market. Vargas was also his grandfather's name. "Could I maybe be related to that man?" he reflects, intrigued. He once again thinks about visiting the country and keeping the promise made to his mother.

On Friday, October 22, taking advantage of a heavy fog in the city, he packs his bags and heads for Union Station. He plans to go to faraway Miami, a location closer to South America in case he decides to go to Brazil.

He buys the ticket and sits down on a bench very near the departures gate, hiding his face behind a newspaper. He knows that in Chicago his life is in danger. Frank Nitti, Capone's right-hand man, has put a price on his head.

Besides which, Dimitri has the impression that he's being followed by a short figure who pops up wherever he goes. As soon as Dimo catches sight of him, he disappears mysteriously into the darkest corners of the street. He supposes it's some gunman hired to eliminate him.

He's wrong.

The strange figure watching him from the shadows is the same man who, three years earlier in Los Angeles, dressed as Santa Claus, followed him along Hollywood Boulevard. He is a menacing specter from the past. The singular individual stealthily observing him is Motilah Bakash, the dwarf assassin.

The Indian homunculus had escaped with his life upon vanishing, years before, through the window of the Orient Express. He had fainted after tumbling along the rocks at the side of the track, but his size had miraculously cushioned the force of the impact.

He had still been unconscious the next morning, when a Gypsy caravan came to his assistance. Motilah would regain consciousness only three days later, thanks to infusions prepared by Zulima, an elderly sorceress and the matriarch of the nomads. He had, however, lost any recollection of the past, remembering only that his name was Motilah and that he was a dwarf.

The gypsy troupe had adopted Motilah as if he were a talisman. They lavished care on him, gave him typical clothes, borrowed from the tribe's children, taught him the Romany dialect, palmistry, and the Tarot.

As India is also the ancient origin of that people, in a short time Motilah Bakash felt every bit as Gypsy as they.

For three years, during the conflict that swept the Old World, they wandered through countries at war, avoiding battlegrounds.

In mid-October 1917, the caravan had passed through Paris.

There, Motilah saw Mata Hari's photo in a newspaper and learned of her execution. The brutal shock instantly restored his memory. He tore out the page and carefully folded the photo, putting it in his pocket. The hated image of Dimitri Borja Korozec surged clearly into his mind once more. He vowed revenge. If Dimo ever again crossed his path, he would find death at the tiny hands of the last of the Thugs.

At the beginning of the 1920s, the Gypsies had emigrated to the New World, leaving behind a devastated Europe. They disembarked in Canada in the dead of winter and headed south over frozen roads. They passed the border in their wagons, crossing the United States in search of the golden sun of California.

Obsession has radically transformed Motilah Bakash. No longer does he enjoy strolling through the streets with the children looking for customers for the fortune-teller. He seeks Dimitri's face in every man he meets.

In 1928, they arrived in Los Angeles, where the caravan planned to remain for a time. The Gypsies are aware of actors' interest in the occult sciences.

Walking through the streets of Hollywood, Motilah was approached by an assistant director looking for exotic types to take part in *The Circus,* Charlie Chaplin's next film. He was enchanted with Motilah. He had never seen such a perfect dwarf, and a Gypsy to boot! He asked the little man to meet him the next day at United Artists.

When Motilah Bakash was approaching the studio at the appointed time, he feared for an instant that his *idée fixe* of revenge had unsettled his senses. At the corner, walking beside a man he would later learn was George Raft, was Dimitri Borja Korozec.

Motilah immediately forgot the appointment and began following him like a bird dog. At the opportune moment, Kali, the goddess who devours men, would become drunk on Dimitri's blood.

The much-anticipated opportunity does not arise in California. Bakesh is in no hurry. He has prepared another silk *roomal,* the sacred scarf of stranglers, and carries it in his pocket always, along with the paltry money he acquires in the company of the Gypsies. He wants to have funds ready for any emergency, in case his pursuit forces him to depart on short notice.

In December, Dimo deserts Hollywood for Chicago. Motilah, who had been following him hidden behind the Santa Claus costume, quickly leaves after him, without even saying good-bye to his Gypsy family.

In Chicago, Dimo's closeness to Capone and his men prevents Bakash from speedily carrying out the act of extermination. He doesn't care; paradoxically, the dwarf possesses gigantic patience. Killing the enemy becomes the sacred project of his life.

At night, he dreams of Mata Hari, his unconfessed passion. He is tormented by a nightmare in which he sees the dancer being executed. All the soldiers in the firing squad have Dimitri's face.

After the trial of Al Capone, Motilah Bakash feels that the time for revenge has come. He notices that Dimitri is hiding from the men in the gang and begins observing him from a closer distance. When Dimo heads for Union Station, Motilah is a few yards behind.

As he nervously awaits the time of departure, Dimitri watches the entrance to the station. He has no desire for some killer in Frank Nitti's pay to catch him by surprise.

The loudspeaker announces the departure of the express to Miami. Relieved, Dimitri goes to the platform and quickly boards the train. He does notice when a child, wearing a sailor suit and carrying a school backpack, his face partially obscured by an enormous lollipop, gets on the same car. The child in the sailor suit is Motilah Bakash.

Unaware of the danger he is in, Dimitri settles into one of the train's comfortable compartments. The trip is a long one and he hopes to make up for the sleep lost during the last week. He has spent nights on end practically without closing his eyes, for fear that Capone's men would find him. Now, the further the train gets from the city, the safer he feels. He locks the door merely as a precaution and so he won't be disturbed.

He still has some money, as Scarface was generous with his followers. In his luggage is a recently published biography of the anarchist Emma Goldman. He takes out the book and starts reading. Before finishing the first chapter, he is sound asleep.

Motilah Bakash locks himself in the bathroom next to Dimitri's compartment at the end of the car. He rids himself of the lollipop and the sailor suit. From his backpack he removes a strip of black cloth and a gilded Indian tunic acquired at the Marché aux Puces in Paris. On him, the short tunic becomes priestly garb. With the skill of years of practice, he rolls the black cloth around his head to form a turban. He puts in the tunic pocket his wallet and the yellowed photo of Mata Hari cut years earlier from the newspaper. From the bottom of the bag he takes the *roomal,* the sacred silk lasso of Thug stranglers. He stores the child disguise and the lollipop in the backpack. Opening the window, he throws everything into the fields bordering the tracks. Finally, he winds the scarf around his neck as he intones the brief assassin's prayer to the goddess Kali.

Before undertaking his mission of vengeance, he experiences a transitory sensation of frivolity. He wishes to be sure he is correctly attired. He climbs onto the toilet and leans over the sink to inspect himself in the mirror.

At that exact moment a fat traveling salesman from Texas who has drunk over three pints of beer pushes against the bathroom door, breaking the latch. With the momentum of his huge body, the door catapults Motilah out the window.

Definitely, the cosmic forces of the railroads have disastrous influence on the karma of the Indian dwarf. The fat man doesn't even realize what has just happened. He opens his fly and, sighing, relieves his distended bladder.

Motilah Bakash's shrill cry is lost in the sound of the locomotive's whistle.

Little is known of Dimitri Borja Korozec's activities in his first years in Miami. Nevertheless, one can deduce his emotional instability from the diverse professions he practiced in this short period. First, he worked as a clerk in a pharmacy, from which he was dismissed for mistakenly recommending castor oil to a woman suffering from gas.

Later, for a few months, he sold, unsuccessfully, vacuum clean-

door-to-door. To demonstrate the machine, he cleaned at no charge the residences of dozens of grateful housewives.

In mid-1932, Adrian Marley, a Jamaican drummer, convinced Dimitri to manufacture with him a pomade to straighten hair. The enterprise ended when their lives were threatened by two blacks who'd become totally bald.

Later he worked as a truck driver. He took part in meetings of the Teamsters Union until he was beaten for unwittingly helping to break a strike he himself had organized.

He finally found work as a night watchman in a shoe factory. It was at this time that he joined a secret sect made up of anarchist masons, the Black Brick League. At one of the League sessions, in January 1933, Dimo met an unemployed Italian by the name of Giuseppe Zangara.

Zangara immediately caught Dimitri's attention. He identified with his appearance of a lost little boy, with his curly hair, vacant gaze, and awkward gestures. Both of them also suffered from ulcers, and Giuseppe's were constantly bothering him.

On the night of February 13, 1933, a Monday, a meeting of the Black Brick was held, at which was discussed the Depression that had beset the country since the stock market crash of '29. Afterward, the two went to have soup at a small restaurant on Biscayne Boulevard. From his way of speaking, Dimo noticed that Zangara was rambling more than was his wont: "The Oppressor . . . day after tomorrow . . ." murmured Giuseppe between his teeth.

"What did you say?"

"Him . . . he's going to be here . . . day after tomorrow . . ."

"Who?"

"The Oppressor . . . he's coming from the Bahamas . . . on a yacht . . ."

Dimitri understood at once to whom Zangara was referring. He had read in the papers that on Wednesday, following a vacation in the Bahamas, President-elect Franklin D. Roosevelt was coming to Miami.

"Are you talking about Roosevelt?" he asks.

Zangara nods his head.

"President Roosevelt is the Oppressor?"

"All presidents are oppressors . . . I hate all presidents, all governments, all rulers, and all the rich . . ." He takes from his pocket a cheap .32-caliber pistol, bought at a pawnshop. "Wednesday there'll be one less Oppressor . . ."

Dimitri makes him put away the gun.

"Giuseppe, get that thing out of sight. It's still Monday."

Deep down, Dimitri thinks more or less the same way. He had been trained to rid the world of tyrants, he had just never imagined Roosevelt to be one of them. Little by little, the disjointed logic of the Italian anarchist takes over Dimitri's confused thinking. What did it matter that Roosevelt had been chosen by the people? The same thing had happened with Mussolini in Italy and Hitler in Germany. Hitler, Mussolini, Roosevelt—all tyrants, all oppressors.

Fate had led him to discover that Zangara was planning to kill Roosevelt. He too could eliminate the president-elect. He had brought his .45 from Chicago; it was hidden in his room, in the top of the closet. As they silently finished their soup, the idea began to germinate in his head to claim for himself the assassination of Franklin D. Roosevelt.

MIAMI—WEDNESDAY, FEBRUARY 15, 1933—9:30 P.M.

The convertible slows and parks at a downtown square. Seated in the rear of the automobile is the new president. Smiling and tanned from his boat trip, he addresses a short speech to the twenty thousand people gathered to greet him. He speaks of the New Deal, his extraordinary plan to end the Depression.

Oblivious of the event, a hungry beggar named Tobias O'Leary turns his attention to stealing a banana from a fruit cart.

Less than ten feet away, Giuseppe Zangara, his weapon cocked, prepares to climb onto a bench in the park to get a better view of his target.

Between Zangara and the beggar appears a woman wearing a print dress, her hair in disarray. She walks uncertainly on her high heels. She opens the purse distended by a large, heavy object and checks its contents. In it is a .45 automatic like those used by gangsters in Chicago. The woman who can barely keep her feet is Dimitri in a wig.

Having filched the fruit, the beggar Tobias O'Leary moves away from the cart and hides behind a tree to keep out of the vendor's sight. The tree he chooses is between Dimitri, who is approaching it, and the bench onto which Zangara has just climbed, revolver in hand.

Everything that happens next occurs all at the same time, in a synchrony dictated by chance.

The beggar quickly eats the banana and throws the peel on the ground. Zangara, from the bench, shouts "The people are starving!" Dimo, a pace away from him, struggling to keep his balance because of the high heels, steps on the banana peel, slips, and bumps into Zangara, who is raising his arm to shoot. His heavy purse collides with Giuseppe's hand just as five shots leave the revolver. The impact causes the bullets to miss the President though several people are hit and the mayor of Miami, Anton Cermak, who was standing beside the car, is fatally wounded.

Thanks to Dimo's slip, Franklin Delano Roosevelt escapes the assassination attempt unharmed.

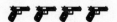

On Thursday, all the newspapers carry the same story on their front page:

Facsimile of newspaper report of the incident in Florida.

Without fear of contradiction, it can be said that Dimitri Borja Korozec was indirectly responsible for the success of the New Deal.

Passage from the incomplete manuscript *Memories and Lapses: Notes for an Autobiography*, by Dimitri Borja Korozec.

MIAMI, FRIDAY, JUNE 7, 1935

Now that I've turned thirty-eight, I see no cause for celebration. To date, fate has willed that I show up late for every
rendezvous with destiny. Nothing has worked out. Only my
ineffable determination forces me to remain faithful to the
ideals of my youth.

Roosevelt's smile, the cigarette holder between his teeth,
still haunts my dreams. The gods of assassins must hate me,
since I saved my own victim.

Sometimes I think it would have been better to stay in
Europe. Last year, in Marseilles, a group of Croatian terrorists assassinated King Alexander of Yugoslavia. Two of them
were classmates of mine at the Skola Atentatora.

I feel so alone. True, I've had several love affairs. I've
given up trying to understand the strange attraction I have
over women, but I try not to get emotionally involved. The
wandering life I lead doesn't permit me deeper ties.

Six months ago, I thought I had found the ideal companion in the person of Helen Murray, a horse trainer and dissi-
dent of the American Communist Party. I was attracted to
her blonde hair, her full breasts, her firm thighs, and above
all, her interest in anarchist ideals.

Helen had come from New York to forget a tumultuous
affair with Victor Allen Barron, a militant in the Red Labor
International. Through her I learned that he had left for Rio
de Janeiro, where the communists were preparing a revolution led by one Luís Carlos Prestes. Barron had studied elec-

tronics and radiotelegraphy in Moscow and would be the communications man, in charge of setting up a clandestine station.

Unfortunately, there was something about Helen that bothered me a great deal and finally brought about the end of the relationship. Every time she had an orgasm, she would scream at the top of her lungs, "Proletarians of the world, unite!"

Knowing about the ongoing conspiracy, I am once again pulled by the longstanding decision to visit Brazil. Maybe the chance to exercise my deadly skills will come about in my mother's native land.

This time, Dimitri Borja Korozec prepares carefully for the journey with which he yearns to change his life. He has obstinately preserved the gold coins given him by Dragutin, keeping them as a last resort, as he has no idea of what future awaits him.

A new means of transportation is beginning to shorten distances: the airplane. Commercial enterprises are spreading around the world, reducing the size of the planet. Among them is Pan American World Airways, one of whose lines, with eight stops, links Miami to Rio de Janeiro. Dimitri signs on as a loader in the shipping department. For five months he studies the baggage-handlers' routine and the Pan Am route.

He also learns all he can about Brazil in the city library. Félix Ortega, a Mexican comrade in the Black Brick, provides him with a letter to a pair of Basque anarchists, the Samariego brothers, who work as candymakers at the Colombo confectionery in Rio de Janeiro.

Dimo packs only his essentials, a .45 automatic, and his remaining money, into a suitcase, which he hides along with a thick blanket in the company hangar. All that's left to do is prepare provisions with canned food and bottles of water for the day of the trip.

The crossing is made in a Sikorsky S-42, a thirty-two-seat hydroplane dubbed the *Brazilian Clipper,* which takes off from its mooring at Dinner Key and lands, days later, at Ponta do Calabouço in Rio, almost opposite Fiscal Island.

As one of the loaders, Dimitri plans to trick the security men with his Pan American overalls and hide in the baggage compartment at the rear of the powerful four-engine plane. He anxiously waits for the first flight whose tiny hold isn't stuffed with trunks, thus leaving room for him.

The long-awaited opportunity arises on November 24, 1935. The Sikorsky S-42 lifts off from the waters, carrying twenty-three passengers and one stowaway, Dimitri Borja Korozec, to Brazil.

EIGHT

Wonderful city,
Filled with a thousand enchantments . . .
Wonderful city,
The heart of my Brazil!

Aboard the plane, the returning Brazilians joyously sing André Filho's march, which has become the official anthem of Rio de Janeiro. The *Brazilian Clipper* circles the statue of Christ the Redeemer and alights like some gigantic albatross on the warm waters of the Bay of Guanabara. The airship docks at the moveable bridge at Ponta do Calabouço and the passengers begin to disembark after their exhausting journey.

In the baggage hold, Dimitri pushes aside the blanket that protected him from the cold, stretches his numbed arms and legs, and gets ready to leave his hiding place. He shrinks into the rear of the compartment, piling bags in front of him. As soon as the land personnel leave with the first load of luggage, he grabs several suitcases, including his own, and joins the other workers.

From the first moment he sets foot on Brazilian soil, Dimo falls in love with the city. He is enchanted by Sugar Loaf, which reminds him of a naturally formed sphinx lying in a splendid cradle. From the top of Corcovado mountain, the outstretched arms of Christ seem to bless his arrival.

He observes his surroundings as if hypnotized by nature itself; dazzled by the landscape, he makes his way to Marechal Âncora Square. The men and women with whom his path intersects walk as if responding to some sensual rhythm. Unconsciously, Dimo begins to imitate the sway of their hips. The afternoon sun is still enough to burn his face and warm sweat slowly floods his body. He finds this humid tropical sensation agreeable. Dimitri feels the pulse of the mulatto blood in his veins accelerate. Concealed behind a bush, he removes the Pan American overalls covering his clothes and throws them beneath a bench in the park. He stops a young man, grabbing him by the arm, and asks the location of the famous Colombo Confectionery. The youth is startled, looking anxiously to both sides. "It's on Gonçalves Dias, between Sete de Setembro and Ouvidor," he says in a melodious accent unfamiliar to Dimo, then quickly withdraws.

His manner of replying intrigues Dimitri. How could such an everyday question cause that reaction? He is unaware that the Communist uprising that brought him to Brazil had failed the night before, in less than twelve hours.

Nor does he know that the nervous young man whom he asked for the address of the Colombo is a young Bahian writer on his way into hiding, known as Jorge Amado.

As he crosses Primeiro de Março, Dimitri Borja Korozec notices that an atmosphere of war is in the air. Armed troops are circulating in the streets in military vehicles and civilian buses. Asking along his route, he finally spots the confectionery.

Founded in 1894, the Colombo had quickly become the meeting place for the city's high-society, political, and intellectual sectors. Its decoration recalled the best French establishments, and its sweets, pies, and pastries rivaled European delicacies. Dimitri approaches one of the waiters in the salon and asks for the Samariego brothers.

Julio and Carlos Samariego had emigrated to Brazil in 1928, fleeing Mexico after having participated in the assassination of President Obregón.

Arrows indicate the Samariego brothers at the obelisk, still in Mexican sombreros.

They established themselves in Pôrto Alegre, capital of Rio Grande do Sul, the southernmost state, where they worked in a cookie factory. They enthusiastically adapted to the country's habits and took an active part in political movements.

In 1930, they left for Rio de Janeiro, the core of the revolution. They were two of the men from Rio Grande do Sul, known as *gaúchos* despite being Basque, who tied their horses to the obelisk on Avenida Rio Branco to celebrate the victory.

Disillusioned by the messianism of the revolutionary leaders, they distanced themselves from their comrades and went back to their pastry-making activities, and their culinary gifts won them the coveted job of candymakers at the Colombo.

The Samariego twins are as alike as two drops of water. Stocky and dark, they wear the same wide mustache from the time they lived in Mexico. While still young men, in Galdácano, they used to drive barbers in the city crazy. Julio would sit down to get his hair cut and say, "Since I'm a Muslim, you have to turn the chair toward Mecca. Otherwise, my hair will grow back in ten minutes."

The barber would ignore him. When the job was done, Julio would warn, "If it grows back, you'll have to cut it again for free."

He would leave the barbershop and, ten minutes later, Carlos would come in with long hair: "Didn't I tell you?"

Astonished, the poor barber would redo his work without charge.

The brothers receive Dimitri in the two-story house where the workers' quarters are located. They are dressed in the traditional white uniform of pastry-makers.

Julio and Carlos have the disagreeable habit of constantly arguing. Julio reads the letter of introduction from the Black Brick and comments, "I remember Ortega very well. He's a short, fat man."

Carlos replies, "You're crazy. Ortega is tall and thin."

They begin a violent altercation in a gibberish that Dimitri presumes is Basque. Finally, they turn to Dimo and ask, "Is Ortega short and fat?"

"Or is he tall and thin?"

"Both," answers Dimitri, not wishing to contradict either of them.

Considering the matter closed, Julio returns to the letter: "It doesn't matter. The fact is that you got here too late. The coup failed. It began last night at three in the morning and ended at one-thirty in the afternoon. They arrested Captain Agildo Barata, the leader of the uprising, at the Praia Vermelha barracks, and they're looking for Prestes and the other revolutionaries. A state of siege has been decreed and the country's on a war footing."

"The worst part is that Getúlio's given Filinto Müller, the chief of police, carte blanche to use methods the Gestapo would envy. This isn't the ideal time for someone like you to get to know the Wonderful City."

An intense depression descends upon Dimitri. Fate insists on putting him in the right place at the wrong time. The twins try to cheer him up: "Take it easy, man. The important thing is not to lose hope."

"Of course. As Bakunin said, despair is typical of those who don't understand the causes of an evil, see no way out of it, and are incapable of fighting it," states Julio.

"Except that it was Kropotkin who said it," retorts Carlos.

"Bakunin," insists Julio.

"Kropotkin."

"Bakunin."

"Kropotkin!"

"Bakunin!"

In front of the downcast Dimitri, the two engage in another violent debate in Basque.

"Lenin. Actually, it was Lenin," states Dimitri, interrupting the argument.

Placated, they begin to analyze the situation. They conclude that there is nothing to be done but wait.

They put Dimitri up at a boardinghouse on Catete and a week later, taking advantage of their criminal connections, get him a job as ambulance driver for the city. For this, they obtain false documents for him. In addition to the forged French passport in the name of Jacques Dupont, he now has other papers. He is no longer Dimitri Borja Korozec but Demétrio Borja, Brazilian, unmarried, born in Vassouras.

RIO DE JANEIRO—*JORNAL DO COMMERCIO*—
DECEMBER 14, 1935

Hail! O São Borja's gallant son
For your proud and heroic decision
To take communists by the throat
In your rigid, ready, inexorable grasp.

You, with feelings forged in civic pride,
Who firmly held the tiller in your hand
Could have no fear of that rabble
Or submit to wretches such as they. No!

Bought with Russian coin
They would reduce us to a colony
Of the Slavs, savage and glacial.

They wantonly killed,
But by the president's hand was saved
The inviolable honor of the nation.

This sonnet by Geraldo Rocha in honor of Getúlio Vargas offers some idea of the climate that reigns in the city immediately after the putsch. A state of war is declared, reinforcing the repression even further. Dimitri tries to be as discreet as possible. He rarely leaves his room at the boardinghouse on Rua do Catete, whose owner, Dona Pequetita, a young widow, quickly takes a liking to him. He shows up for work every day at the hospital and is considered a model employee.

Afraid of being arrested and searched, he hides his belt with the gold coins in a hole made in the underside of the heavy autopsy table at the morgue, a hole that he covers with plaster from the emergency room. He has been working for less than a month in the first-aid station in República Square, where he has made friends easily. His air of vulnerability appeals to both the nurses and the doctors. The other drivers quickly welcome him, mainly because, having no family, he volunteers to cover the most thankless shifts, such as happened the day before, on Christmas. "You can always count on Borja," they comment in the halls, using the name by which he is now known.

On Thursday, December 26, after his shift, having nowhere to go, Dimitri remains around the hospital. Eager for information, he asks everyone for the latest news. There are countless rumors: Prestes had fled the country; from north to south various army battalions were involved; Moscow had financed the uprising with millions of dollars and had infiltrated hundreds of agents into Brazil. The more lucid among them comment that if the support of international communism were as great as people say, the revolution wouldn't have failed.

Around two in the afternoon, Dimitri is approached by the head driver. "You still here, Borja? Then take an ambulance and go pick up Dr. Otelo Neves in Ipanema."

At 3:30, Dimitri is on his way back with a young doctor beside him, a physician from Minas Gerais who has been in Rio only a short time. When they pass Rua Prudente de Morais, Neves points to a young blonde woman walking along the sidewalk: "What a pretty woman. She looks like a foreigner."

Dimitri slows down so both can take a look at her. They notice something strange about the young woman's behavior.

"How odd. She got to the corner, stopped, turned around, then ran in the opposite direction."

His curiosity piqued, Dimo parks the ambulance. "If you don't mind, doctor, I'm going to find out what's going on."

Before Neves can stop him, Dimitri jumps out of the vehicle and turns the corner at Paul Redfern to find out what startled the woman so badly. He is horrified at what he sees. Three limousines are stopped in front of number 33. From inside the house, men are tossing books and packages out the windows. Meanwhile, other armed men are shoving a couple into one of their automobiles, hitting and kicking them as they do so. The man is stout, very blond, and is bleeding. The woman is thin, with a light complexion and brown hair. Dimitri quickly evaluates the situation: "Robbery followed by kidnapping," he imagines. Without thinking twice, he runs and launches himself onto the attackers, catching one of them with a violent punch in the face. He is easily overcome by the others and begins yelling for help: "Police! Police!"

One of the men finds this amusing: "Of course it's the police. What'd you think it was, you communist son of a bitch?"

Two other policemen push Dimo into the car and all three vehicles pull away at top speed, their tires squealing.

Sitting in the ambulance, Neves witnesses the scene, powerless in the face of such brutality. Unwittingly, Dimitri had tried to prevent the arrest of Arthur Ewert and his wife Elise Saborovsky, two important Comintern members sent by Moscow to aid the revolution. The fascist police of Filinto Müller had, however, allowed a bigger prey to escape. The beautiful blonde woman who had run away toward Leblon was Olga Benario, wife of the revolutionary leader Luís Carlos Prestes.

Why do you drink so much, man?
That's enough for now!
If it's over a woman, it's best to stop
Because not one of them knows how to love.

Late on the night of February 26, Ash Wednesday, the prisoners at the House of Detention on Frei Caneca hear in the distance a straggling group of drunk revelers pass by singing Rubens Soares's hit of the 1936 Carnival. King Momo's reign was ending in the same melancholy fashion in which it began: surveillance at dances, masks forbidden, and rehearsals of carnival blocs and revelers only at specified hours. The street festivities alone retained something of the contagious gaiety characteristic of those days. However great the tyranny, the soul of the people is free.

Since November, hundreds of civilians and communist militants, anarchists, innocent people, or simply enemies of Getúlio have had dossiers created on them or had been taken to the First Offenders wing.

Originally intended for criminals with no previous record, the wing was emptied out to house political prisoners. Among them, Dimitri Borja Korozec, known as Borja, incarcerated along with

more illustrious individuals such as Aparício Torelli—Aporelly—
the famous humorist who wrote under the pen name Baron of
Itararé. His criticisms of the government in the newspaper *A Manhã*
are considered highly subversive by the chief of police, whose sense
of humor is second only to Himmler's. The baron, after Müller's
men invaded the newspaper and cowardly beat his fellow workers,
hung on the door to the editorial offices a sign that read THE BEATEN
PATH.

The detainees comment on the terrible tortures that go on in the
cellars. It is learned that the torturers stuck a wire up Arthur Ewert's
urethra, then heated the exposed portion with a blowtorch. His
wife, Elise, had her nipples burned off with cigars and was raped by
dozens of soldiers in front of her husband.

Dimo is spared these torments because, having rid himself of his
driver's license, he presented himself as Jacques Dupont, a French
citizen. His story that he had gotten into the fight thinking it was a
robbery and kidnapping, as the police were in plainclothes and
driving unmarked cars, failed to convince his interrogators, but as
there was no record of his previous activities and fearing a diplo-
matic incident, they left the case for later evaluation. There were
more important prisoners to torture.

At the First Offenders wing Dimitri learns about Vargas's life
through other prisoners.

He discovers to his astonishment the blood ties that unite them.
Getúlio is the son of the old *gaúcho* general Manuel Vargas, of whom
his mother so often spoke, and therefore his natural uncle. He keeps
this revelation to himself. He is afraid his companions will think
prison has driven him mad, as had happened with Ewert.

From that moment on, he comes to nurture a mortal hatred for
the dictator. He no longer has any doubts about his mission: Dimitri

Borja Korozec had been born in faraway Bosnia to kill Getúlio Vargas.

In the first days of March, a piece of news spreads like wildfire around the House of Detention: Prestes and Olga Benario had been captured in the Méier district. Dimitri will never encounter them during his time at Frei Caneca.

It's also known that some of the male prisoners will be transferred to the prison ship *Pedro I.* Most are heartened by the thought of trading the dark, squalid cells where they are piled for sunlight and the open sky. Others fear the separation from their wives, held on the wing's second floor.

The *Pedro I,* which earlier could be seen opposite the beach at Flamengo, was now anchored half a mile off Governador Island. The prisoners find this out thanks to an ingenious system of communication invented by Dimitri. He had realized that by keeping the level of water in the toilets low, sound could be propagated through them from one cell to another. The secret was in the handling of the flushing chain, which had to be executed with a jeweler's precision.

On the night of the eleventh, a conversation is heard through the coprological network: "The first levy leaves tomorrow for the *Pedro I.* Over."

"Do they know who's going? Over."

"I bribed a guard for the list. Over."

"Then go ahead. Over."

"Borja, Fe——"

At that instant, some uninformed person flushes the toilet in one of the cells and the rest of the names are drowned in the bubbling waters. Dimitri is the only one to know that this will be his last night in the prison on Rua Frei Caneca.

Compared to the fetid dungeons of the First Offenders wing, the prison ship *Pedro I* is almost a pleasure cruise. The prisoners, civil and military, can talk, circulate on deck, and breathe the sea air. What makes the two prisons similar is the food, as awful in one as in the other. The prisoners take their meals in the immense mess hall, where the filthy napkins provoke a facetious comment from the Baron of Itararé, Aporelly: "These napkins are dirtier than Getúlio's conscience."

The same baron also makes his thoughts known in what would come to be called "the oxtail incident."

One day oxtail was served that was already in a state of decomposition and smelling rotten. A committee of prisoners went to complain to the captain, who ordered a lieutenant to take care of the matter. The lieutenant entered the mess hall and saw the meat floating in its own juices in the steaming cauldron: "I don't see anything wrong with this oxtail."

Aporelly replied instantly, "We don't want you to see it, we want you to eat it."

The lieutenant withdrew indignantly, while the others tossed their plates into the air.

With his deep-seated idea of killing Vargas, Dimitri can think of nothing but flight. At first he finds it difficult to join any of the several factions among the prisoners of the *Pedro I*. No one knows him, for he has not taken part in any revolutionary movement in Brazil.

The Bolsheviks think he's a Trotskyite, the Trotskyites think he's a Bolshevik, and the anarchists think he's crazy.

His natural likability, however, coupled with the information provided by his House of Detention companions that he was the inventor of the latrinophone, finally overcomes all resistance.

In the first days of April, along with a naval officer, Captain Roberto Sisson, he begins to organize a plan to flee the ship. Many prisoners join the undertaking with alacrity. Sisson draws a map of Governador Island and in the dead of night they gather secretly to analyze the best way to make it to the island.

"The thing to do would be to lower the lifeboats," Roberto Sisson suggests.

"Are you crazy? The noise would bring the guards down on us," states Tourinho, a young lieutenant, in total disrespect of rank.

"What if we overpowered the guards first?" Sisson asks.

"Impossible," insists Tourinho. "All it would take is for one of them to sound the alarm and we'd be discovered immediately."

Dimitri offers the most obvious solution: "Swimming. We have to swim out of here."

"Swim? But it's almost a mile through open sea!" says Sisson, worried.

Another participant agrees: "Borja's right. It's got to be swimming."

Sisson again insists: "I think that swimming—"

"It's going to be by swimming. End of discussion," Tourinho interrupts.

Dimo finishes his idea: "We drop ropes to the water and go down them so as not to make any noise. At night, because the watch isn't as strict."

"When do we leave?" an officer asks.

"The earlier the better. Tomorrow we'll steal the ropes and we can leave the next day."

"What beach are we going to?" inquires another prisoner.

"Leave that to me. I'll study the map and all you have to do is follow me," Dimo says.

The group disperses, leaving Dimitri alone with his thoughts of assassination. He carefully examines the island's beaches. Fleeing is just the first step. To him, the dictator's days are numbered.

On the appointed night, they slide silently down the side of the *Pedro I* and disappear into the dark waters of the ocean. After swimming for three hours, floating countless times to rest, the several men led by Dimitri finally come to the island. Exhausted but elated at their feat, they embrace each other expansively and roll in the sand. They raise enthusiastic cheers to the author of the idea: "Viva Borja! Borja's the greatest!"

Suddenly, the cries of joy are interrupted by a siren and spotlights sweeping the beach. One of the lights stops on Dimo's face. They all stand motionless, rigid as statues. By a cruel coincidence, Dimitri and his followers have arrived precisely at the spot on the island where a marine base is located. The elaborate plan has failed completely. Only two of the fugitives are not found: Lieutenant Tourinho, an expert swimmer, who decided to head for the Maria Angu beach a mile and a half away, and Captain Roberto Sisson. The latter, as soon as he touched the water, opted to return to the ship by the boarding ladder. He did so because, despite being a naval officer, Sisson didn't know how to swim.

NINE

In the boardinghouse on Rua do Catete, number 25, the widow Maria Eugênia Pequeno, better known as Pequetita, has just stepped from her shower. Intelligent and ingenious, Maria Eugênia had had an immense 500-gallon tank built on the roof of the building, thus solving the water-shortage problem that constantly plagues the city.

Pequetita looks younger than her thirty years. Bathing in the sea at Botafogo beach and the Danish exercises developed by Professor Müller, which she does every day, make her body firm and tanned. Her almond eyes, high cheekbones, and dark hair tied in a bun betray the Arabic blood of her Portuguese ancestors, born in the Algarve. In her rosy face, with skin soft as a peach, it is her fleshy, well-formed lips that stand out. The young widow radiates a sensuality that she tries to conceal, without great success.

Pequetita slowly dries herself in front of the large mirror in the bathroom. She lightly touches her large, firm breasts, their pink nipples, her ample thighs, and her rounded buttocks with the linen towel. Everyone wonders why such a pretty woman is still single.

The truth is that Maria Eugênia, a widow for four years, remains faithful to the memory of her dead husband. Tulio Pequeno had died of tuberculosis in 1932. He was an insurance salesman and had two passions in life: Pequetita and opera. He sang in the chorus of the Municipal Theater, and during a performance of *Aïda* had suffered a hemoptysis on stage, dying a few days later. Because insurance was his profession, Tulio had left a policy that allowed Pequetita to buy a two-story dwelling on Rua Catete that she transformed into a boardinghouse. Maria Eugênia ran the establishment with the utmost competence, always efficiently and objectively. With neither children nor close relatives, she had taken refuge in reading the novels of Rafael Sabatini and Alexandre Dumas. She conjured up images of love affairs with the books' heroes while rejecting the idea of falling in love with another person. She remembered a phrase she'd heard as a young girl from Father Rodrigues, in Grajaú, about a neighbor who had recently married for the second time: "The worst adultery is by the widow who remarries. Betraying the dead finds no pardon, whether in heaven or on earth!" The anathema had been burned into her childhood memory.

However, since Dimitri had come to live at the boardinghouse, occupying the room next to hers, Pequetita had begun to feel a strong affection for him. She had immediately noticed the new guest's extra index fingers. The perfect anomaly, far from repelling her, had evoked an even stronger attraction. She had erotic dreams in which the handsome man with green eyes and curly hair was sucking the tumescent nipples of her breasts, exploring with his twelve fingers the most intimate recesses of her body, kissing her pubis, and penetrating her with the ardor of Sabatini's Captain Blood. She moaned languidly in her widow's bed. She would awake in the middle of the night drenched in sweat and exhausted from her solitary climax. During the day, using her master key, she would go into Dimo's room, roll in the unmade bed, sniff the pillowcase and placing the pillow between her damp thighs, rub against it until achieving the paroxysm of pleasure.

This is why, the more time that passes, the more worried she becomes about Dimitri's mysterious absence. Normally, a guest who disappeared for a week would have his luggage confiscated as payment and the room would be let to another lodger. For six months Maria Eugênia has had no word from her tenant; still, she keeps the room as it was. Her woman's intuition tells her that there is something strange about Dimo's disappearance.

On that rainy autumn evening, as she dresses, Pequetita decides to do something that runs contrary to all the standards she has observed as owner of the boardinghouse: she will search Dimitri's belongings looking for clues to his whereabouts.

This time, she enters with lynx-like eyes the room that has witnessed so many secret acts of pollution. She searches the dresser drawers, lies on the floor to look under the bed, and finally comes upon the valise hidden in the closet. Taking out the few items of clothing stored there, she realizes it has an improvised false bottom fashioned from a thick sheet of cardboard. Removing it, she makes a discovery worthy of the adventure novels she admires so much. Along with several forged documents bearing the photo of the man she secretly loves is a large-caliber pistol wrapped in oilcloth, a small bundle of dollars in a rubber band, and Dimitri's worn notebook. She impatiently turns the pages with an excitement she has never felt when reading her favorite authors.

She quickly becomes aware that the object of her passion is no ordinary man and that he is in danger. The censored newspapers publish nothing, but everyone knows of the large number of arrests made since the communist putsch. It's likely that Dimo has fallen into the hands of the police or the army. Resolved to find him at any cost, Pequetita remembers a distant cousin of her husband's who is in the marines. Although not of high rank, he's the only military man she knows. Maybe he has connections that can help her discover Dimitri's fate.

She returns to her room and looks through her husband's old address book. There, in Tulio Pequeno's cramped handwriting, which she rereads without the least remorse, is the young man's name: Sergeant Olegário Ferreira. Marine Barracks, Governador Island.

"It's been so long! How are you, aunt?" Sergeant Olegário greets her, citing a nonexistent kinship that she always detested.

"Very well, thank you," replies Maria Eugênia Pequeno as they stroll around the sunny courtyard at ten in the morning.

She wants this visit to be over as quickly as possible. She dislikes the somber atmosphere of the barracks, which reminds her of the school run by nuns that she had been sent to in Teresópolis. Besides which, she never liked the sergeant. Extremely thin, with small, lifeless eyes set too far apart, and a reddish, hooked nose, Olegário Ferreira looks like a Christmas turkey about to be sacrificed.

On the rare occasions she'd seen him, when her husband was still alive, Olegário had always cast lascivious, almost obscene glances in her direction. Even when he called her "aunt," the form of address was laden with hidden intentions. Nevertheless, he is her only hope to find Dimitri. The sergeant is no paragon of intelligence; he abuses platitudes and his ignorance is recognized as invincible.

"What can I do for you? That's what family is for, isn't it?" Olegário says, perpetrating a phrase that he considers the greatest wisdom. "Did I mention that you're looking lovelier than ever? Good enough to eat."

Pequetita ignores the pathetic flattery. "I don't want to take up your time. I'm looking for a guest at the boardinghouse who disappeared without a word."

"Don't worry, aunt. Where there's life there's hope. Am I right or am I right?" says Olegário sententiously, using one more inopportune cliché and sending chills through Pequetita as she imagines Dimitri dead.

"My fear is that he's been taken prisoner by mistake."

"I don't think that's likely, aunt. Chief of Police Filinto is competitive."

"You mean 'competent,' " Maria Eugênia corrects.

"Right, competent. They're only arresting communists because the Reds want to destroy the three pillars of society: God, Country, and Family. Communists are a plague. Worse than fire ants. Either Brazil puts an end to fire ants or they'll put an end to Brazil. Am I right or am I right?"

"I don't know, Olegário."

"I've heard that communists eat babies."

"I'm not acquainted with their gastronomical preferences," Pequetita answers.

"They attack at night. That's why I sleep with two revolvers under my pillow. Having just one's like not having any. Am I right or am I right?"

"In any case, the person I'm looking for isn't a communist," the widow interrupts.

"What's his name?"

"I don't remember," Pequetita lies. If he's been arrested, she doesn't know what name Dimitri might have given. "But it's easy to identify him. The man I'm looking for has twelve fingers."

This information surpasses Olegário's capacity to assimilate it. "Huh? The guy's in charge of a dozen police informers?"

"Not at all. He has an extra forefinger on each hand."

"He has what?"

Pequetita begins to lose her patience. "The forefinger, Olegário. The pointer! The man has four pointers! One extra on each hand! A pinky, a ring finger, a middle finger, a thumb, and two pointers!"

"Take it easy, aunt. Don't get excited. How come you didn't say so right away? Talking is what leads to understanding. Am I right or am I right?"

"I'm sorry, Olegário," she apologizes, "it's just that I'm a little nervous."

"Well, aunt, at least I'm going to be able to help you. I don't even need to ask anybody. Around six months ago a bunch of prisoners swum away from the *Pedro I* and landed here on the beach, right in front of the barracks. Ha ha! And they say that communists are smart. I noticed one of them had that thing you're talking about. From the name I think he was French. It's a small world. Am I right or am I right?"

Pequetita thanks heaven for the coincidence and asks excitedly, "What was his name?"

"Oh, I don't remember, aunt. Am I supposed to remember some gringo's name six months later?"

"And is he being held here?"

"No, aunt, they sent him to the prison on Grande Island."

Pequetita quickly takes her leave: "I'm very grateful, Olegário. I don't know how to thank you. It was a pleasure seeing you again. Now, if I may, there are a lot of things I have to do back at the boardinghouse."

"Come back anytime, aunt. I miss you," replies the sergeant, undressing her with his eyes.

As she is about to go through the barracks gate, the sergeant shouts from the middle of the courtyard: "But he *is* a commie, or he wouldn't be in prison. We reap what we sow. Am I right or am I right? Be careful, aunt. I don't know if besides babies the communists eat widows too."

Maria Eugênia never managed to discover whether or not Olegário's words had a double meaning.

Grande Island, slightly over 100 square miles in area and located in Angra dos Reis, less than 90 nautical miles from Rio, is covered with the luxuriant vegetation of tropical forests. A structure was built there in 1884, initially as a health outpost for quarantine of passengers and slaves from abroad who might be carrying contagious diseases. The hospital, known as the Leprosarium, would later be transformed into a prison, having housed among others the rebellious lieutenants who participated in the famous Revolt of Copacabana Fort in 1922.

From the docking point, through seven and a half miles of mountain range, is another prison: the Dois Rios Correctional Colony, located on the old Dois Rios plantation.

This notorious penitentiary is situated on the escarpment of the island, and next to it are crude, filthy sheds surrounded by an immense barbed-wire fence where some nine hundred prisoners are massed. In the colony, political prisoners and common prisoners are lumped together. Conditions of hygiene and nutrition are extremely precarious, and inmates waste away before one's eyes.

It is in this virtual concentration camp that Dimitri Borja Korozec has been imprisoned for the months since his ill-fated flight, suffering in a hell built by the hand of man in the midst of the paradise created by nature.

One of Dimitri's companions in misfortune is Professor Euclides de Alencar, a renowned entomologist with no connection to any political party. The professor had been arrested merely for criticizing the regime to his colleagues at the Instituto Vital Brasil, in Niterói. At fifty, squat and with taxi-door ears, his face hidden behind a long white beard, he seems more like a gnome from the Grimm Brothers' fairy tales. In a few months of incarceration the scientist has lost over forty pounds, but not his enthusiasm for insects. He harbors a true passion for the tiny invertebrates. His eyes light up when he speaks of mosquitoes, fleas, and bedbugs.

To fill the time, Dimitri joins Alencar in the study of cockroaches. He spends hours on end listening to the professor discourse about the small, dark bugs that infest the cells.

"My dear friend, the cockroach, whose name comes from the Spanish *cucaracha,* is the most misunderstood creature on earth. I can't fathom the aversion that humans feel for this marvelous animal."

"What's so marvelous about it?"

Alencar launches into a veritable lecture about the disgusting insect.

"To begin with, its capacity for survival. We have found roach fossils over three hundred million years old. There are thirty-five hundred species spread all over the globe. In Costa Rica there's a winged cockroach, the *Blaberus giganteus,* so large that it feeds on fishes and frogs. It buries its stinger in its prey and sucks out their vital fluids. Isn't that fantastic?"

"What about the ones here—what type are they?" asks Dimo, pointing to three specimens creeping along the front wall.

"*Periplaneta americana.* My favorite. It's the most common cockroach, easy to raise in the laboratory and highly intelligent."

"Intelligent?"

"Of course. All roaches are intelligent. They can be said to have two brains."

"*What?*"

Alencar is amused at his disciple's astonishment. "There are two pairs of ganglia in the head, linked to a ganglion at the end of the tail. This permits it to receive sensory impulses in a fraction of a second."

"What impresses me more is the ability they have to eat anything," says Dimitri, pointing to a fourth roach gnawing on a piece of paper.

"That's because they possess minuscule teeth in their stomachs, with which they chew any food ingested."

As the days go monotonously by, Dimitri begins to look upon those animals with different eyes. He no longer finds them so repulsive. He brings crumbs from the pestilential dining hall to feed them.

In a short time, his cell is the roaches' preferred spot. He patiently trains the insects to push empty matchboxes and to take small messages stuck to their wings to the prisoners in more distant cells.

Overcoming his natural repugnance, he manages to have them cover his body on command, as apiculturists do with bees. Even Professor Alencar is surprised at the feat. Guards and prisoners alike begin calling him, in an admixture of respect and disgust, the Roach Man of Grande Island.

This sudden fame brings prisoners from the other barracks to approach Dimitri. Among them is the writer Graciliano Ramos. Arrested in the state of Alagoas in March and transported first to the House of Detention in Rio and later to the Correctional Colony,

Graciliano had not had a formal trial. Of the meeting between the two we have only this brief mention, recorded later by Dimo on one of the pages of his notebook:

[. . .] I was very impressed by this sensitive, thin man with the sunken cheeks. He was only a few years my senior, but he looked like my father. I saw that incarceration had made him a ghost of his former self. He told me that his wife, Dona Heloísa, had managed to contact a certain general and that he was expecting to be transferred at any moment back to the First Offenders wing. He took an interest in my ability to train insects. I explained that it was just a pastime, to stay sane until I found a way to get out of that hell. He told me that if he didn't succumb to the hardships of prison, when he was freed he would write an account relating its horrors. He wanted to dedicate a chapter to me, telling about my experiments with the roaches, but I begged him not to. They might think I'd gone crazy [. . .]

A common criminal named Henri Mathurin, a Frenchman, had also become close to Dimitri. Slender, dark-haired, with smooth skin and soft-spoken, Mathurin had approached Dimo under the impression that he was French, as Dimitri continued to claim that nationality.

Henri was a homosexual and a safecracker. Those who tried to mock his sexual preferences were taken aback by the violence and speed with which he operated the stiletto made from a spoon handle, his inseparable companion.

Whether legend or reality, it was said that Mathurin had escaped years before from Devil's Island, in French Guiana, where he was serving a life sentence for killing his lover. He had come to Brazil by crossing Venezuela through the Amazon jungle. It is with him that Dimitri plans to get away from the Correctional Colony. The Frenchman has the experience necessary for the dangerous undertaking—to anyone who escaped from Devil's Island, fleeing Grande Island is a picnic; all they lack is the money essential to the flight. This fundamental item will be provided during the visit that the widow Maria Eugênia, after moving heaven and earth, is to pay the new great love of her life.

The trip from Mangaratiba to Grande Island takes place without incident, despite the choppy sea that rocks the launch. Maria Eugênia has obtained special authorization. General Góis Monteiro himself, brother of the poker partner of a brother-in-law of the son of the nephew of the grandfather of one of Pequetita's neighbors, had granted her the pass. He had been enchanted by the young widow's beauty and perseverance.

At the Correctional Colony, the duty sergeant examines the credentials and orders a private: "Go get the Roach."

"Captain La Roche?" asks the private, referring to Antônio La Roche, who was also confined on the island.

"No, idiot. The Roach Man. He's got a visitor."

In a small room next to the prison infirmary, under the watch of a sleepy guard, Pequetita finds herself at last in the presence of Dimitri. They speak softly, almost whispering.

"How did you find me, ma'am?"

"That doesn't matter, and please don't call me ma'am."

The visit makes Dimo painfully shy. "Do you take the same interest in the fate of all your guests?"

"I'm not afraid to admit that to me you're more than a guest," she says, amazed at her own brazenness.

A shiver runs through Dimitri at this revelation. He had felt attracted to Pequetita from the first moment he saw her, but had hidden his feelings, for nothing in the widow's behavior indicated that the attraction might be reciprocal.

"In any case, you've taken a risk coming here. Who told you I was being held prisoner?"

"No one. I found out on my own. I have to confess that I went into your room and saw what you had hidden there."

Pequetita recounts in detail the agony she had gone through after Dimo's disappearance. In an outburst of daring, she tells how her heart would beat faster every time she heard the doorbell, in the hope of seeing him returning to the boardinghouse. She speaks of the sleepless nights during the endless months without news of him. Finally, she confesses to having read, with mounting anxiety, every page of his notebook.

"I know everything."

"And even so, you came to find me?" Dimitri says, astonished.

"Of course. I was sure you needed help. I took the liberty of exchanging some of the dollars I found in your valise. The money will be a lot more useful here than stuck away in your suitcase."

She takes the bundle of folded banknotes hidden in her waistband and discreetly passes it to Dimo. When the two touch, a wave of heat runs through their bodies. Dimitri doesn't want to release the hands that have brought him love and salvation. "Thank you. I don't know what to say."

"Then don't say anything," concludes Maria Eugênia, a smile lighting her face.

They stay there, their eyes glued to each other, fingers interlaced, mingling the tepid sweat that appears in their clasped palms.

Finally, united in a minute that has the flavor of eternity, together they achieve an intense and silent orgasm.

"Time to go, lady."

The guard's hoarse voice breaks the enchantment of the magic moment. Her face flushed, Pequetita reluctantly pulls free of the hands of the man she loves. From the door, she casts him a last look replete with promises: "The room is still waiting for you. Goodbye."

"See you soon," replies Dimo.

He knows that now no force known to man will be powerful enough to keep him in the fetters of captivity.

The following day, as they leave the dining hall, Dimitri approaches Mathurin. "I got the money for the escape. I'm just afraid they'll decide to search me."

"Don't worry about it. On Devil's Island I learned a way to hide things that will get by any search," Mathurin assures him.

"How?"

"I'll show you. Come with me."

Henri takes Dimitri to the bathroom and asks him to watch the entrance. Lowering his pants and squatting next to the wall, he begins contorting himself as if he were about to evacuate. Suddenly, a polished bamboo tube approximately six inches long and two inches in diameter emerges from his anus. It is divided into two parts that screw into each other. Twisting both ends, Mathurin opens the unusual cache. From inside the tube he takes out a delicate gold chain and four rolled-up photos of his mother.

"It's my little safe."

Dimitri contemplates the menacing cylinder. Henri explains, "I've made one just like it for you. You have to stick it in really far, up to the colon in the large intestine. All you do is take a deep breath and it goes right in. Even if they strip you and spread your legs, there's no way to discover it."

After a long pause, Dimitri says to his companion, "On second thought, I think I'll stay here. The Colony isn't really so bad. The food's tolerable at best, but the place has a lovely view, the air's clean, and I need to look after my roaches."

Henri is amused at the terror the bamboo inspires in Dimitri. "Don't be silly. If you're that scared of the tube, I'll carry yours too."

"Is there room?" Dimo asks, amazed.

"Of course!" Mathurin answers, slapping his buttocks good-humoredly. "Where there's room for one, there's room for two."

GRANDE ISLAND—CORRECTIONAL COLONY—JULY 14, 1936

Symbolically, the two choose the date of the French Revolution for their flight. At eleven at night, the sentinel of the west wing, seduced by the charms of Mathurin and the 100 milréis offered by Dimitri, allows them to dig a passage under the barbed-wire fence. To cover himself, he asks Mathurin to give him a sharp blow on the head with the shovel, an act that the Frenchman carries out with great pleasure. Avoiding the path leading to the mooring spot, they cross the forest between the Pedra d'Água and Papagaio peaks toward Saco do Céu.

At every turn, Dimitri, unaccustomed as he is to life in the forest, hears strange nocturnal sounds. It is almost morning when they arrive at a village hidden among the trees at the foot of a hill.

"What place is this?" asks Dimo.

"Don't be frightened. It's the lepers' colony. Few people know of its existence."

"Lepers?"

"Yes, lepers and merchants. They're the ones who're going to sell us the boat to take us out of here. That is, if they take a liking to us. Otherwise . . ."

"Otherwise what?"

"They'll kill us and keep the money."

Before Dimitri can say anything, they are surrounded by a band of men carrying shotguns. Even in the darkness, it is possible to see that they are all disfigured by leprosy. Both the fugitives try to disguise the panic invoked by the circle of horrors.

One of the lepers, unarmed and probably the group's leader, a hat pulled down over his eyes, addresses them with an ironic smile on what remains of his lips. "Where you going in such a rush? You in a hurry to catch the disease?"

Once again, Dimitri misses his roaches. Mathurin steps forward and faces the man. "We're running away from the colony."

"They ran away from one colony to stumble on another," the boss says, laughing.

Dimo and Henri find themselves surrounded by lipless laughter. The Frenchman attempts to begin negotiations: "We want to buy a boat."

"What do you have by way of money?"

"We have money."

"*Had* money. You won't need it after you're dead," says the man suffering from Hansen's disease. "It's better to die quickly from a bullet than stay here rotting with leprosy."

The lepers around them cock their weapons and take their positions for the execution, awaiting their leader's command. Mathurin closes his eyes, resigned, but Dimitri says confidently, "I'll never die of leprosy, because I've already had it, and there's a cure right here on the island."

The lepers' leader interrupts the shooting. "What's that?"

"I contracted the disease on a trip to India. My body was covered with lepromas and my face was deformed by leontiasis. They had given up any hope of my living, when a Pakistani guru gave me the sacred recipe for an infusion made from three types of herbs. Those herbs grow in abundance in these forests. Right here, around that tree, there's a thicket covered with them," says Dimitri, pointing to a nearby area.

The man scrutinizes Dimo suspiciously. "And what proof do I have that you're not lying to save your skin?"

"I'm the living proof. I was disfigured, and within a few weeks the potion rebuilt my nose and extremities. There was only one aftereffect. In my anxiety to be cured, I took too much of the medicine and grew an extra finger on each hand," asserts Dimitri, holding up the twelve fingers with which he was born.

The lepers are amazed at that unimpeachable demonstration.

"What are the herbs and how do you prepare the tea?" the leader asks, anxiously.

"Easy. First I want to know if we're getting the boat."

"Of course, friend! You don't even have to pay!"

"I insist. Business is business."

"How soon does the treatment start to take effect?"

"It varies. Sometimes it takes days, sometimes weeks. The first signs show up in less than a month."

At Dimitri's command, Mathurin and the lepers spend the next hours gathering innocuous plants in the woods around the hidden village.

As they climb into the boat, Dimo makes his final recommendations about the recipe. "It's simple. Boil the herbs for five hours over a slow flame of green wood. Then allow the cauldron to cool overnight."

As Dimo and Henri lean into the oars to begin their journey of freedom, the leader of the lepers shouts from the shore, "Thank you again. The only reason I don't shake your hand is because I don't have one."

TEN

RIO DE JANEIRO—NOVEMBER
1937

> *[. . .] President Getúlio*
> *Dissolved in a wink*
> *The Chamber and the Senate*
> *Faster than you can blink . . .*
>
> *[. . .] Brazil from north to*
> * south*
> *Has only admiration*
> *For this great statesman*
> *Who now directs the nation . . .*
>
> *[. . .] Implanting his*
> * dictatorship,*
> *The leader of the New State*
> *Soon brought the rich to heel*
> *And won the people's heart*
> *In every corner of Brazil . . .*
>
> *—Popular street poem*

The minister of war,
General Eurico Dutra,
beside Getúlio Vargas
on the day of the
promulgation of
the New State.

Since his escape, over a year earlier, Dimitri has withdrawn from his revolutionary dreams into Maria Eugênia Pequeno's soft bed. Immediately upon reaching shore, he had separated from his companion. Mathurin had continued to the Mangue area, where he found work as bouncer in the brothel of Madame Rosaly, a fat procuress who was a friend of his and ran a trysting spot on Júlio do Carmo, while Dimitri wrapped himself in the widow's sensual arms.

Dimo and Pequetita spend weeks practically without leaving the bedroom, and she has to admit to herself, with a twinge of remorse, that she never experienced such intense sensations when making love with her deceased husband. Dimitri's hands expunge the memory of past caresses from her flesh. The sex never becomes routine. Daily, they invent and reinvent new, inexhaustible sources of pleasure, their bodies shuddering in unsuspected voluptuousness.

The management of the boardinghouse is left to Francisca, a Portuguese governess who has been with Pequetita since childhood. Far from being annoyed by her new tasks, Francisca rejoices at seeing her mistress happy once again.

Dimitri doesn't even bother to read the newspapers anymore, except for the sports pages. He has developed an almost fanatical interest in a game that he knew little or nothing about, soccer. He roots for the Flamengo team, attracted by the red-and-black colors that symbolize the club, and is thrilled at the "bicycle" goals of Leônidas, the Black Diamond.

Mustache grown by Dimitri.

As a precaution, he decides to alter his looks by growing a thick mustache, which accentuates his appearance of a romantic anarchist. Whenever the idea of eliminating Getúlio Vargas comes to mind, he puts it aside and postpones any action, convincing himself that the moment has not yet arrived.

At eight o'clock on the evening of the tenth, Dimitri is lying beside Pequetita in the rumpled bed, whose sheets still exude the scent of another amorous encounter, when the announcer's voice interrupts the usual program on the radio on the night table: "Ladies and gentlemen, His Excellency the President of the Republic."

Vargas's voice assails his ears: "Workers of Brazil . . ."

In his long speech, Getúlio announces the new order. Under the pretext that there is a communist plan to overthrow the government by armed struggle, he states that he has shut down Congress, dissolved the political parties, and suspended the elections scheduled for next year. With the support of the armed forces, he is now concentrating all power in the presidency. The New State is created. All this, he says, is being done in the name of national security.

When the pronunciamento is over, Dimitri realizes, not without a degree of guilt, that he has been mistaken in his aims. He turns the radio off, lights a cigarette, and sits on the bed, downhearted. Maria Eugênia notices his despondency.

"What happened?"

"Everything we just heard could have been avoided."

"What do you mean?" asks the widow, intrigued.

"You know very well what I mean. If I hadn't been remiss in my duty, the dictator would already be dead."

Pequetita wraps him in an embrace. "My love, forget that craziness."

"Craziness?" Dimitri replies, freeing himself from her arms. "So you think the greatest goal in my life is crazy?"

Pequetita tries to apologize. "One man by himself can't do anything."

"That's not what history teaches us. Sometimes, one man is enough. One man and a bullet," says Dimitri sententiously, his gaze vague, remembering Sarajevo.

Maria Eugênia becomes desperate, foreseeing the possibility of losing a loved one for the second time. She must dissuade him from any act of insanity. She takes off her nightgown and displays her perfect breasts, trying to drag him back to the comfort of the sheets: "Come. I want you," she says, opening her generous thighs.

Dimo moves away in order not to succumb to that act of seduction. Getting up, he quickly puts on his pants and shirt.

"Where are you going?" asks Pequetita anxiously.

"To my room. I need to think."

Dimitri leaves the cozy bedroom and closes the door behind him. Sadness comes over the widow and she covers her proffered nakedness with the wrinkled bedspread. Two tears form a trail of pain on Maria Eugênia Pequeno's face.

[. . .] I went to the bullfights in Madrid,
Paratiboom, boom, boom.
Paratiboom, boom, boom.
And almost didn't return.

[. . .] I met a señorita from Catalonia.
She wanted me to play castanets and grab a toro barehanded.
Caramba, caracoles,
I'm a samba man, don't put me through the mill!
I'm running away to Brazil.
That's just a lot of bull.

Paratiboom, boom, boom . . .
Paratiboom, boom, boom . . .

Passage from the incomplete manuscript *Memories and Lapses: Notes for an Autobiography,* by Dimitri Borja Korozec.

RIO, APRIL 19, 1938

Carnival has been over for two months now, but the happy refrain from the march "Bullfights in Madrid" won't leave my thoughts. Paratiboom, boom, boom . . . To me, that repeated sound, far from recalling the jovial atmosphere of celebrations, has a demonic meaning. It reminds me of the Spanish civil war that the Republicans are losing to Franco's Fascist army, supported by German airplanes of the Condor Legion. The onomatopoeia of the chorus is associated with the sound of the shrapnel and the bombs dropped on defenseless cities. Paratiboom, boom, boom . . . García Lorca shot to death: Paratiboom, boom, boom . . . Guernica pulverized by bombs: Paratiboom, boom, boom . . . Catalonia and the Basque country decimated: Paratiboom, boom, boom . . . The blood of my anarchist comrades drenching the sunny soil of Spain: Paratiboom, boom, boom . . .

In the early part of the year I looked up the Samariego

brothers at the Colombo to organize the assassination of Vargas with them; the dictator must be overjoyed at the victories of his Spanish counterpart. But they had gone back to their native land to join the Republican forces. Naturally there was no way they would stay out of that bloody struggle.

Today is Getúlio's birthday. Last night the radio program *Hour of Brazil,* also known as "Talking to Yourself," promised a program in his honor. The transmission, normally tiresome, will be even more unbearable. Hitler's birthday is tomorrow. The two dictators could celebrate on the same day.

My raptures with Maria Eugênia have become less frequent, though losing nothing in intensity. Whenever I'm away, she says good-bye to me as if it were the last time we'd ever see each other. I can tell from her expression that she fears for my life. Her fear is, at least for now, unfounded, since the occasion has not arisen for me to carry out the task I have given myself. It must be the widow's curse.

Last December, knowing that Vargas is an assiduous golfer, I got a job as caddy at the club where he plays. But before I could cross his path I had to give up the position because of lumbago brought on by the weight of the bags.

In February of this year, wearing the typical regional costume of the *gaúchos,* I applied for work as a barbecue assistant in the kitchen at the presidential palace, but my inability to carve out a rump roast betrayed my lack of practice.

A month ago, after long reflection and with no alternative, I made a pragmatic decision that cost me dearly. Despite the loathing that I feel for the Integralists, I managed to infiltrate the group through César Albanelli, an idiot of a millionaire that I met one day, half drunk and bragging, in a bar in Copacabana. To win him over, I told him I was Italian, that I knew Mussolini, and that he should call me Corozimo, the same name I used to gain the confidence of Al Capone.

I have nothing but contempt for Integralism, the Brazilian political faction that apes Nazism and Fascism and their racist theories, but I know they've been planning an assassination attempt against Vargas ever since the party was outlawed. To me, the end justifies the means.

At last, I can glimpse the possibility of killing the tyrant.

RIO DE JANEIRO—MAY 2, 1938

"Anauê!"

"Anauê!" shouts Dimitri in response, answering the Integralist greeting, which means "hail!" in some Indian language or other.

He feels rather ridiculous at the secret meeting in Botafogo, wearing the proscribed uniform of black pants, green shirt, cap, and the armband with the Greek letter sigma imi-

Meeting at Albanelli's mansion. Dimitri's hand is to the left.

tating the swastika. The more excited among them are holding banners sporting the same symbol. The mansion where they are meeting was lent by César Albanelli, a friend of the Integralist leader Plínio Salgado and a founding member of the party. With the banning of the party, the Integralists disguised themselves as a civil-recreational club, but the high command of the Green Shirts, the Chamber of Forty, has decided to seize power by force.

The plan, formulated by the Integralist doctor Belmiro Valverde along with a few military men, is to invade the Guanabara Palace, the presidential residence, and arrest Getúlio Vargas. If he resists, the dictator will be eliminated.

Dimitri listens in silence while Valverde lays out his scheme. He is little concerned with the homegrown Fascists' childish ideals. He is there only for the opportunity to penetrate the palace and assassinate Getúlio.

At his side, César Albanelli is irritated at Valverde's leadership. After all, the meeting is in his house and he feels offended in his Pharaonic vanity. Fat and truculent, bald as an egg, Albanelli prides himself on his resemblance to Mussolini. The obligatory use of the uniform that night had been his idea, a sine qua non for his allowing the use of the mansion. As it was impossible to go through the streets in those outfits, the guests were obliged to change clothes in the kitchen. Interrupting Valverde, he suggests, "Before anything else, so we can get used to it, it would be good for us to address one another by our code names. Mine is Maringá. What's yours, Corozimo?"

"Queiroga," improvises Dimitri, somewhat embarrassed at the ridiculousness of the situation.

"Excellent!" says Albanelli encouragingly, clapping him violently on the back. "How about the rest of you?"

After an awkward pause, each man introduces himself.

"Tibiriçá."

"Macedo."

"Carvalhaes."

"Bulhões."

"Albanelli," shouts a short, dark, fat man who resembles Goebbels, from the back of the room.

César interrupts the roll call. "Hold on there. That can't be. Albanelli is my name."

"Exactly."

"What do you mean, 'exactly'?"

"To spread confusion among the enemy."

Everyone bursts into laughter at the fat man's inopportune jest. Albanelli turns purple with rage and frustration. Valverde again takes up the reins of the meeting: "This doesn't strike me as the time for jokes."

Leaning on a table where a map is laid out, he turns to Lieutenant Severo Fournier, a tall, handsome young naval officer, and begins to review the plans.

"Fournier, the assault on the palace is under your command. The bedrooms are located in the right wing, facing the chapel. While you and your men are attacking, other teams will be encircling the ministries of the army and the navy, as well as the residences of other government authorities. The operation is set for the night of the eleventh."

"Should we encounter much resistance?" inquires the lieutenant, smoothing his brown hair.

"I doubt it," replies Valverde. "Lieutenant Júlio Nascimento, commandant of the marines that protect the palace, is part of the conspiracy. He's volunteered to give us access to the locale. He's going to open the gate to the sentry post so the two trucks with our men can enter the gardens."

Fournier studies the map, seeking to memorize every detail. "We have just one problem," he says. "We need a technician to cut off communications from the palace. If they get help from outside, we're finished."

Remembering the training and the intensive courses he had at the Skola Atentatora, Dimitri offers to take on the assignment: "As far as that's concerned, you can rest easy. I'll see to isolating the area. I'm an expert in the subject; I know everything there is to know about telegraphy and telephony."

Valverde, who barely knows the new member of the group, asks apprehensively, "Are you sure?"

His chest swelling with pride, César Albanelli vouches for his most recent protégé's statement. "If he says he knows, it's because he knows. My friend Corozimo isn't given to boasting."

Shortly before midnight, Alzira Vargas, the dictator's daughter, is awakened in her bedroom by the sound of an isolated gunshot. She attributes it to some drowsy sentinel inadvertently pulling the trigger. Similar incidents had occurred on other occasions. She covers her head with the pillow, attempting to go back to sleep. A second shot convinces her that something is wrong. She takes from a drawer the .38 revolver she had received as a gift some days earlier, for target practice. Without even changing clothes, she dashes to her father's bedroom. Getúlio is strapping on his weapon, over his pajamas.

"What's going on?" she asks, worried.

"The palace is under attack, Bunny," Vargas advises her, using one of his several nicknames for his daughter.

"Who?"

"It must be the Integralists. They've been disgruntled ever since I dissolved the party."

The two head for the private office next to the library. By now, enemy machine gun fire is sweeping the walls of the building. There are not many in the palace who can offer any resistance: only a few police, two or three assistants, the duty officer, and the president's family. Vargas looks out the windows at the garden, trying to assess the situation, oblivious of the bullets that threaten his life. Displaying uncommon bravery, Alzira leaves the office and rushes down the stairs, weapon in hand, in search of information. On the lower floor, the defenders answer machine gun fire with shots from their handguns. The only machine gun in the palace wasn't working.

Alzira returns to the upper floor and informs Getúlio that the palace is surrounded by rebels. Father and daughter cock their revolvers, an indication that they intend to extract a high price for their defeat.

"We can't hold out for long. We have to call for help," he suggests, his *gaúcho* accent heightened by tension.

"I've already tried. The phone lines are dead."

"Did you cut all the lines?"

"Yes."

"Including the direct line?"

"What direct line?"

"The direct line between the palace and Police Headquarters."

The sound of troops under the command of Colonel Cordeiro de Farias coming to Vargas's rescue answers Dimitri's question.

As a result of Dimitri's disastrous oversight, the Integralist putsch failed. It is nevertheless worthy of mention that the combined forces of the army and a contingent of the notorious Special Police in their red berets took almost five hours to penetrate the Guanabara Palace.

They went in by way of the Fluminense Football Club field, next to the gardens. The reason for the hesitation: they were awaiting specific orders. In addition, the door linking the field to the palace was shut and no one had the key. Instead of breaking down the door, they contacted Filinto Müller at Police Headquarters, who got in touch with Alzira Vargas, who, furious at the delay, ordered one of the besieged palace guards to slip through the shadows with the key and open the gate.

Upon hearing this news days later in the Café Lamas, Max Cabaretier, one of the bohemians who frequented the place, commented, "It's because of things like this that there'll always be a Brazil."

Three months after that ridiculous misadventure, when things have calmed down, Dimitri tries to recover the money belt with the pounds sterling which is still hidden under the autopsy table in the morgue at the Public Hospital. He's afraid that renovations at the hospital will reveal the hiding place of the coins.

For weeks, he watches the building on Republic Square, observing the comings and goings of its employees and studying the best course of action. He has no desire to be recognized by some former coworker. He chooses the night of August 28, a Sunday, the day with the least traffic, to carry out his plan.

At eleven o'clock, he breaks one of the rear windows on the ground floor and silently enters the building. He heads for the morgue, being careful to hide whenever anyone comes down any of the hallways. As a precaution, when he enters the autopsy room he doesn't turn on the lights. In the near-darkness Dimitri sees a body on a table, covered with a sheet. He curses his bad luck. The table is already heavy enough without that added dead weight. He crawls toward it and begins to drag the table, expending every effort not to make any noise.

Suddenly, the corpse rises in terror and runs screaming toward the door, throwing aside the sheet and shouting: "God help me! There's a ghost in here! The table's moving by itself!"

In reality, the corpse was an orderly who had taken advantage of a quiet moment to catch some sleep in the morgue. Dimo, who also had a scare, quickly opens the plaster-covered hole with a knife and retrieves his treasure.

Before the bogus dead man can return with the guards, Dimitri slips out of the hospital to the safety of Republic Square.

The incident leaves him so excited that when he returns home he makes love to Pequetita until daybreak.

ELEVEN

RIO DE JANEIRO—DECEMBER 1939

> *Brazil, where hearts were entertaining June,*
> *We stood beneath an amber moon*
> *And softly murmured "Someday soon."*
> *We kissed and clung together,*
> *Then, tomorrow was another day,*
> *The morning found me miles away*
> *With still a million things to say;*
> *Now, when twilight dims the sky above*
> *Recalling thrills of our love,*
> *There's one thing I'm certain of,*
> *Return I will to old Brazil.*

A ri Barroso's samba of exaltation sung by Francisco Alves, known as the King of Voice, broadcast constantly by Rádio Nacional, enchants the first refugees arriving in Brazil. Europe is once again at war. After annexing Austria and subjugating Czechoslovakia, Hitler invaded Poland, provoking reaction on the part of France and England.

The country that welcomes them to the sound of the samba "Brazil" resembles a tropical paradise, an "island of tranquillity" far from the bombings of the German Luftwaffe.

This is not what Dimitri Borja Korozec thinks. A palpable melancholy has permeated his being since the ill-fated attempt to assassinate Getúlio. He had escaped the encirclement by the soldiers, and when he returned home had burned the hated Integralist uniform he had been obliged to wear against his will.

After rescuing the gold coins, he spends hours on end contemplating the belt given him by Dragutin, wondering how to use that legacy to achieve his objectives. Discouragement prevents him from thinking clearly.

At the start of the year, Maria Eugênia makes him go with her to Cambuquira, but neither its springs rich in radioactive particles nor Pequetita's vibrant body relieves his feelings of failure. The vacation, which the widow extends until after Carnival, serves only to make him lose ten pounds thanks to the dysentery caused by the powerful effect of the waters.

In June, the widow seeks to motivate him by holding an intimate gathering to mark his birthday. The celebration only sharpens his awareness that, at forty-two, all of his assassination projects have been frustrated.

At the beginning of September, he thinks about putting together a homemade bomb to hurl at the dictator during the Independence Day festivities. On September 7 of every year, Getúlio appears at the Hour of the Fatherland, a ceremony held at the Vasco da Gama stadium. Maria Eugênia succeeds in dissuading him by pointing out that hundreds of innocents would die as well. When he gets rid of the materials for the bomb by throwing them in the trash, Dimitri almost causes a fire in the boardinghouse.

One Saturday afternoon in December, a news item in the *Jornal do Brasil* leaves him especially depressed. Professor Euclides de Alencar, his fellow prisoner on Grande Island who had taught him about roaches, had died the day before. He had been freed a year earlier and reinstated in his position, but the long months of incarceration had left indelible marks on his health. The wake is at the Instituto Vital Brasil in Niterói. Dimitri decides to attend and pay his last respects to the wronged entomologist.

When she hears of his intention, Pequetita, hoping to raise his spirits, convinces him that first they should go see a parade to be held downtown in the Cinelândia area.

"Don't you know I hate military parades?" Dimitri grumbles.

"It's not that kind of parade, silly. It's to promote a film from Metro that's about to open."

"What film?"

"*The Wizard of Oz.* They say it's wonderful. It's a musical in Technicolor, with Judy Garland. Brazil is the first country to see the film after the United States," Pequetita proudly informs him.

Dimitri hasn't the faintest idea who Judy Garland is. His time in Hollywood had left him with a true loathing for the seventh art. The last time he'd been in a movie theater was in 1932 to see *Scarface,* and even then just to find out whether Paul Muni had faithfully portrayed Al Capone and to see his old friend George Raft, who was considered a discovery. He left disappointed with both. Still, it does no harm to please Maria Eugênia. As soon as the parade ends in Cinelândia, he'll leave for the wake in Niterói.

"Who's going to be in the parade?"

"MGM is bringing some of the less important players and

they've hired Brazilian actors to wear the costumes of the Tin Man, the Scarecrow, and the Cowardly Lion." Pequetita is an assiduous reader of movie magazines.

"Well then, let's go now," Dimitri decides, smiling at the child-like happiness on the widow's face.

Starting in 1920, the daring impresario Francisco Serrador had constructed various buildings in the area occupied for a century and a half by a monastery, the Convento da Ajuda.

The Império, the Capitólio, the Glória, and the Odeon, facing Floriano Square, had modern cinema halls on their ground floors. The area quickly became known as Cinelândia. At night and on weekends it was one of the liveliest spots in the city. Those who didn't attend the shows would stroll around the square, delighting in the bustle.

In that square are Dimo and Maria Eugênia, having a *jaboticaba* ice cream cone. As if they were new lovers, they lick it together, which allows their tongues to touch without calling the attention of passersby. The sunny afternoon and the festive atmosphere seem to have temporarily dispelled Dimitri's mournful thoughts.

The couple remain near the edge of the sidewalk in order to have a better view of the parade, which is about to begin. The brass band is already in sight, coming around the corner in their colorful uniforms, launching into the opening chords of "Over the Rainbow," the film's theme song. The crowd shouts and applauds happily. Just behind the brass band come the Tin Man, the Scarecrow, and the Cowardly Lion, suffering the heat of summer in their heavy costumes. With them, an actress in pigtails and clothes identical to those of the character Dorothy, created by Judy Garland, dances and throws kisses to the crowd. Another, dressed as the Wicked Witch of the West, runs along the street mounted on a broom and cackling evilly.

For the children, however, the great attraction is the Munchkins who comprise some of the population of Oz. MGM has brought from the United States ten midgets who were in the original cast. In the same elf costumes worn in the film, they throw imported candy to the boys and girls, who shriek with joy.

Dimitri must admit that all that gaiety improves his mood. He doesn't notice that one of the dwarfs, darker than the others, has stopped tossing the coveted American caramels and is staring at him intensely. His eyes pour onto him a long-distilled hatred; the Munchkin, who now begins to draw away from his fellows, is the Thug Motilah Bakash.

Adepts of the occult will believe that it was due to the protection of the goddess Kali that Motilah had escaped death when he twice fell from a rapidly moving train, as he himself had stated in a letter to his adopted Gypsy family from his time in the Big Sur, in California.

Actually, the second time he was hurled from a train window, on the Chicago–Miami route, while pursuing Dimitri, the killer dwarf had gotten caught on the hook of the pole at trackside where the mailbag was picked up as the train rushed by.

He had remained there for several days, until rescued by an employee of the postal service. His hatred of Dimitri kept him alive as he swung like a watch fob at the mercy of the elements. Weakened by his terrible ordeal, Motilah Bakash had returned to Los Angeles, where he was welcomed back into the Gypsy caravan.

Mayara, a fat, pampered Gypsy princess with a luxuriant growth of hair on her upper lip that gave her a certain masculine appearance, took pity on the little Indian. Compassion quickly turned to love. It was touching to see the couple walking hand in hand among the carriages, with fat Mayara dragging the diminutive Motilah as if he were the whimsical princess's doll.

At night, she would place him on her vast, rotund body, exhausting the little man who had metamorphosed into an erotic toy. In Bakash's sexual fantasies, the voluminous anatomy of the Gypsy woman would take on the svelte contours of Mata Hari. After orgasm, he would seek refuge in the warm folds of Mayara's flesh, in search of restorative sleep.

Little by little he resumed his normal activities, traveling the streets with the children in the group. Besides snatching ladies' purses, he becomes a highly skilled pickpocket. After months of training on a dummy covered with sleigh bells, Bakash can fish out the contents of anyone's pocket, even someone moving quickly. To make up for his short stride, he learns to skate and circulates on wheels with extreme agility.

By pure chance, after some years of relative happiness, Motilah Bakash picks the pocket of a man on Rodeo Drive. Upon examining the documents, he discovers that their owner is Victor Fleming, the director who is preparing to film *The Wizard of Oz*.

Fleming is beginning screen tests to select the more than forty midgets who will be in the picture. Mayara, an inveterate cinephile, suggests to Motilah that he return the director's wallet and claim to have found it on the sidewalk. She wants to see her loved one made a giant by the camera's lens. Bakash, who can deny her nothing, carries out his beloved's wish, taking care first, however, to remove the $311 from the billfold's contents. He leaves only the documents, useless to him but of great value to the director. Victor Fleming immediately falls in love with Motilah. His perfect proportions and his Lilliputian bearing win him a spot in the front row of the people of the forest.

One can only imagine Motilah Bakash's surprise at spotting, in Brazil, the object of the revenge for which he has longed so fervently. The thick mustache is no obstacle to Bakash's recognizing the features he has cursed through all this time. The years have been generous to the anarchist, who still retains the jovial, romantic look of an undernourished poet and the same dark, curly hair. If he could, the little man would pierce Dimitri's green eyes with the power of thought.

As the group passes along Rua Alcindo Guanabara, Motilah hides in a corner and pulls off the long false beard. He throws away the small Tyrolean hat. He no longer looks like an elf but like a little boy in short pants and suspenders. The parade moves into the distance, turning onto Treze de Maio, and the music of the brass band mixes with the normal sounds of city traffic. The spectators in the square begin to disperse. Under Bakash's furtive gaze, Dimitri checks his watch and kisses Maria Eugênia good-bye. He doesn't want to be late for Professor Alencar's wake. Going up Avenida Rio Branco, he heads for the Niterói ferries.

Motilah Bakash, the killer dwarf, follows, taking two steps to Dimitri's one.

As soon as they cross Almirante Barroso, Motilah's diminutive legs can barely keep up with the lengthy strides of his prey. Fortunately, Dimo delays at a kiosk, reading the newspaper headlines.

At the same time, from the other side of the street, Bakash spots a sporting goods store. Sensing a solution, he quickly crosses the street and buys a pair of skates. The salesman watches in amazement as the tiny figure leaves his establishment weaving expertly among the pedestrians. Passersby wonder who the irresponsible parents are that let the child skate downtown.

When Dimitri goes down Rua da Assembléia in the direction of Quinze de Novembro Square, from which he will head toward the ferries, Motilah finds no difficulty in trailing him as he glides elegantly along the opposite sidewalk.

Since 1834, steam-powered boats have traveled between Rio de Janeiro and Niterói. This curious plaque was displayed on all the vessels:

> **PASSENGERS MUST NOT TALK
> WITH THE PILOT OR THE
> HELMSMAN. IN THE REAR
> SEATS IT IS NOT PERMITTED
> TO SMOKE OR SEAT SLAVES.
> THE INSIDE CHAMBER IS FOR
> LADIES, AND NO PASSENGER
> IS ALLOWED THERE.**

Twenty-eight years later, the Englishmen Jones and Rainey created a ferryboat service linking the two sides of the Bay of Guanabara. The ferries, in the style of the barges that navigated the

Mississippi, became known as the Cantareira boats because of the name of the firm, Companhia Cantareira de Viação Fluminense—the Cantareira Transport Company of Rio de Janeiro.

Dimitri arrives at the station in time to catch the 4:00 ferry. Without losing sight of him, Motilah also buys a ticket and dexterously leaps onto the floating passageway. The boat pulls away from its moorings, plowing through the waters of the bay.

All that remains is for Motilah Bakash to wait for the ideal circumstances to finally realize his mission and liquidate his nemesis. He doesn't have his *roomal* with him, but the sacred lasso will not be needed. So intense is his desire for vengeance that he plans to hurl himself on Dimo and rip out his jugular with his teeth. Kali thirsts for Dimitri's blood.

Unaware of the danger, the anarchist leans against the railing at the stern of the boat and watches the ocean, his nostalgic thoughts on the wake being held for his friend. When the vessel is halfway across, a summer gale seeds the blue sky with dark clouds and a strong wind churns the waves into whitecaps. "Now," thinks Motilah. It has not yet begun to rain, but he doesn't want Dimitri to take shelter inside the boat. He approaches silently, ready to pounce. This time the hated enemy will not escape.

At the instant he starts to launch himself onto his victim's back, a wave whipped up by the gale lifts the boat's prow. Losing their traction, the wheels of Motilah's skates slip backward on the waxed boards of the deck.

Without a sound, Motilah Bakash is tossed into the ocean. The weight of the skates drags him to the bottom and the cry rising from his throat is stifled by the waters.

The same adepts of the occult might say that the first drops of rain were the tears of Kali, devourer of men, weeping over the loss of her most faithful follower.

The next day, on the island of Paquetá, upon slicing open the belly of a shark they have just caught, two fishermen stand paralyzed in bafflement at the contents of its stomach. Motilah had been swallowed in a single bite by the enormous fish. His mortal remains are intact. Crossing himself, one of them asks, "You think it's the prophet Jonah?"

"Saints preserve us, Raimundo! That's not a whale, and Jonah wasn't a midget on roller skates."

TWELVE

RIO DE JANEIRO—SEPTEMBER 1940

[. . .]
But why pour such venom on me?
How can I be Americanized?
I was born with the samba in my blood
And live to hear the old rhythms all night long

And here I say "te amo" and never "I love you."

The orchestra of Carlos Machado attacks the final bars of the song and the audience at the Urca Casino gives Carmen Miranda a frenetic standing ovation. The opening night, a benefit performance for the City of Children, sponsored by the First Lady, Senhora Darcy Vargas, and marking the return of Carmen Miranda after her smashing success on Broadway, had been disappointing. Songs written in the United States, such as "I Like You Very Very Much" and "Chica Chica Boom Chic" had left the public cold and indifferent.

With her characteristic resilience and professionalism, Carmen had suspended the show and, in a few weeks of rehearsal, radically changed the repertoire. She had added "Ela Disse que Tem" and "Voltei pro Morro" to her old Brazilian numbers, as well as the vibrant samba by Vicente Paiva and Luís Peixoto, a reply to the detractors who claimed Carmen Miranda had lost her Brazilianness.

From his table, Bejo, the nickname of Colonel Benjamim Vargas, the president's brother and a frequent visitor to the casino, shouts "Bravo," accompanied by his coterie.

The luxurious Urca Casino was the realization of a dream by a visionary from Minas Gerais named Joaquim Rolla. A man of humble origin who had begun life as a muleteer herding beasts of burden along the trails in the interior of the country, Rolla had risen to become a builder of highways. After gambling away several fortunes, he had decided to switch sides of the roulette table and within a few years had become the emperor of gambling in Brazil. He had establishments scattered throughout the nation, but the jewel in his crown was the Urca Casino. The shows in the grill room were headed by world-class stars. Brazilian and international attractions, from Grande Otelo to Virginia Lane, from Mistinguett to Bing Crosby, left their talented mark on the casino's stage.

Tall and elegant, Joaquim Rolla was rarely seen in the salons. He ruled his empire from his private table in the grill room, where even the notables of the New State would go to pay homage to him. Endowed with quick and brilliant intelligence, he was nevertheless semi-illiterate and could barely write his name. His vocabulary was inversely proportional to the riches he had accumulated. The story is told that while downtown one afternoon he had run into a well-known politician who'd been in the casino the night before. The politician had greeted him:

"Rolla! What a pleasant coincidence!"

Maintaining his affectation, Rolla had replied, "The coincidence is all mine, Excellency."

It is precisely at the Urca Casino that Dimitri Borja Korozec is employed as a croupier. He obtained the job thanks to Mário the Cigar, a casino worker who, like him, lives at the boardinghouse on Rua do Catete.

Mário the Cigar, whose nickname comes from the perennial Corona clamped between his teeth, had been impressed by Dimo's dexterity in handling a deck of cards at a no-stakes poker game one lazy Sunday afternoon in the backyard of the boardinghouse. Dimitri's twelve fingers impart an almost magical speed to the dealing. Dimitri, in turn, is interested in the job when he hears that Bejo Vargas is an inveterate gambler and an ardent habitué of the casino. Bejo has an outgoing personality. Whenever he wins at roulette or baccarat he laughs loudly and tosses heavy mother-of-pearl thousand-réis chips to the waiters and the musicians. A sinister idea takes shape in Dimitri's mind: he can get to Getúlio by kidnapping the dictator's kid brother.

Casinos of the period.

"Place your bets, ladies and gentlemen!"

"Rien ne va plus!"

"The point is six!"

"The house wins!"

"Banco! Banco!"

"A card to the player!"

"No further bets!"

The croupiers enliven the game by spinning the roulette wheels. The newly installed air-conditioning system can barely keep up with the increasing heat. The smoke from cigars and cigarettes, pierced by the lights in the salon, forms an almost palpable fog. Elegant women in long dresses and men in tuxedos crowd around the tables. The more fanatical gamblers stick to the green cloth like flies in honey. In the distance, the sound of Carlos Machado's orchestra, playing in the grill room, completes the festive casino atmosphere.

At one roulette wheel the retired notary Luciano Solfieri, a consistent loser, yanks from the croupier's hand his last chip, which he has just lost: "You're not getting this one. This is for the children's milk."

Everyone laughs at the rejoinder and the employee kindly lets it pass. Solfieri is an old "customer" and a friend of Rolla's. The fat notary takes it all good-naturedly. Ever since Getúlio expropriated his notary office, Solfieri has been signing his name Solfieri—Pigeon.

But the irresistible attraction of the game room is the new croupier at the baccarat table. Even nonplayers gather around to watch Dimitri's acrobatics as he shuffles six decks before placing them in the sabot. He handles the paddle that distributes the cards and rakes in the chips as if he'd been doing it all his life.

"Three thousand in the bank," he announces as he shuffles the cards, forming a colorful cascade.

"Go, Borjinha!" the onlookers say encouragingly.

Dimitri marvels at how his twelve fingers, which greatly hindered him when he was trying to learn the tricks of the circus, adapt so perfectly to baccarat.

One of the biggest admirers of his skills is Colonel Benjamim Vargas. Even shorter than Getúlio, Benjamim looks like a miniature version of his brother. Bejo forgets to play as he stands there watching Dimitri's nimbleness with the deck. As Dimo had foreseen, the good nature of the president's brother allows them to establish contact almost at once. Bejo takes an immediate liking to the accomplished croupier. Besides which, there's something in Dimitri's mannerisms that reminds him of his father, old General Vargas.

Often, when the gambling salons close at three in the morning, the colonel invites him to have a whiskey at the bar, where they talk until dawn. Dimitri makes up stories, based on his past adventures, that fascinate Bejo. Little by little, he achieves familiarity with the other man, followed by his complete trust. It is during one of these late nights that the plan comes to him of how to kidnap Benjamim Vargas.

He will first get him drunk to the point of unconsciousness and then, under the pretext of personally taking him back to the palace, whisk him away to a hiding place. All that's missing now is a safe spot to keep the prisoner, but he knows someone who can help him in the undertaking.

"You're completely mad," states Mathurin, having another glass of beer.

"Not mad, determined. What must be done, must be done," replies Dimitri resolutely.

The conversation between the two escapees takes place in a bar on Júlio do Carmo, in the Mangue district, near Madame Rosaly's sporting house where Mathurin now works as manager. They speak French to avoid being overheard by curious neighbors. The ex-safecracker has put on weight from the peaceful life at the brothel. He no longer has the lean and muscular body he boasted on Grande Island despite the hardships of the Correctional Colony. Nor does he chase the deadbeats, young bohemians who make use of the prostitutes' service and run off without paying. He contents himself with administering Madame Rosaly's affairs like a prosperous businessman. But he is still feared in the area. Not even the toughest pimps from the red-light district, hardened men accustomed to razor fights, dare mock his homosexuality. His respected sobriquet is spoken only in whispers: Madame's Behind.

Dimitri quickly tells him of his wanderings and misadventures of recent years, and about his relationship with Maria Eugênia, leaving for last his employment at Urca Casino and the idea of the kidnapping. He hopes his friend will provide him with a place to hide Bejo Vargas.

"Don't you see you're going to ruin everything? Even if you succeed in kidnapping the man, you won't be able to go back to the boardinghouse or the casino. What does your widow think of that?" he asks, concerned.

"In the first place, she isn't *my* widow, as I'm still very much alive," answers Dimitri, rapping his knuckles on the wooden table, a superstition acquired in Brazil. "Second, naturally I haven't told her anything. I don't want her to be involved. I know quite well the risk I'm taking."

"I'm against it," Mathurin insists.

"If money's the problem, I have two hundred pounds sterling in

gold coins given me many years ago in Belgrade by my old commander in terrorism, Colonel Dragutin. They're yours."

A dark shadow passes over Mathurin's eyes: "Don't insult me."

Dimitri realizes he has offended his old comrade. "I'm sorry.
That's desperation speaking, not me."

Mathurin sighs resignedly, faced with his friend's determination. "Well, if you've made up your mind to go ahead with this
insanity, I'll help you. I have a house in the woods, in Barra do Piraí,
where I take my boys. You can hold him there. I'll draw a map for
you, but I won't give you the keys. I want you to break down the
door, because if there's any problem I can say I didn't know anything."

"Thanks, Mathurin. This is another thing I owe you," states the
anarchist, moved.

"Forget it," says Mathurin, disguising his own emotion. "What
do you plan to do if everything works out?"

Dimitri's eyes gleam with excitement at his anticipated triumph.
"Force the tyrant to confess his crimes in a speech on the radio and
resign. Otherwise, I kill his brother."

Mathurin is unsure whether to attribute the absurdity to an
attack of madness or to the heat wave that is besieging Rio de
Janeiro.

Dimitri chooses a Friday night for carrying out his plan to get
Benjamim Vargas drunk. He imagines the anguished weekend that
Getúlio will spend in the Rio Negro Palace, in Petrópolis, the president's summer residence. He has prepared the place, in the garage
of Mathurin's cottage in the woods, where he will hide the colonel.

After the tables close down at three in the morning, he accompanies Bejo to the bar where, as usual, they begin drinking. Unnoticed

by the colonel, for each shot of whiskey he downs, Dimo pours two for Bejo. Everything seems to be going well. All he has to do is shake the two plainclothes bodyguards accompanying Benjamim. Appealing to the vanity of Getúlio's brother, he says scornfully, "You're always with those lugs. What're you afraid of?"

"Nothing," says the colonel boastfully, showing a .38 revolver in his waistband.

In an act of bravado not uncommon to him, he dismisses the bodyguards.

Dimo congratulates himself on his cunning. He continues recounting incredible tales about his past and keeps on refilling Bejo's glass while drinking small amounts from his own. "It won't be long now," Dimo thinks, seeing no more obstacles to realization of the kidnapping.

The audacious plan had everything it needed to work, if not for one detail unknown to Dimitri: despite his short stature, Benjamim Vargas possesses an extraordinary tolerance for drink. He can absorb two full bottles of Scotch without the alcohol affecting his senses.

The same cannot be said of Dimitri Borja Korozec. Notwithstanding the frugality with which he serves himself, by four in the morning Dimo is completely drunk. The binge awakens a personality opposite to his own, characterized by maudlin and repetitive sentimentality. The dictator's brother becomes transformed into the target of the most cloying affection.

Dimitri embraces Benjamim, his face almost brushing the other man's, and declares in a slurred voice, "Bejo, you know I love you, Bejo. I don't want anything bad to happen to you!"

"I know, Borjinha," replies the sober Benjamim with the patience of one accustomed to the long-winded yakety-yak and high-octane breath of hundreds of drunks.

"To me, you're family. A mother's a mother, a father's a father, and family is family. Isn't that right?"

"Of course it is, Borjinha."

"Bejo! Give me a kiss, Bejo! I love you, Bejo! Give me a kiss!"

These vows of esteem are interspersed with exclamations of unimaginable religious fervor: "May God our Lord bless you and protect you, Bejo!"

"Amen, Borjinha."

Unexpectedly, remorse takes hold of Dimitri. "You know what I am? I'm a son of a bitch! And you know why? Because a father's a father, a mother's a mother, but a grandfather is a grandfather! That's why you're a great friend and I'm a big son of a biiiitch!"

Dimo sobs copiously and falls asleep in Benjamim Vargas's arms.

The bartender, who has been watching everything impassively, offers his help. "Not to worry, colonel. We'll put Borja in a taxi."

"No need. I'm going to call it a night and I'll drop him off on the way. Do you know where he lives?"

The bartender provides the address and the two of them carry the unconscious Dimo to Bejo's automobile. In the lobby, the anarchist's muffled snoring provokes repressed laughter from the custodial staff, just beginning the cleanup of the gambling rooms.

Contrary to what Dimitri had planned, the intended kidnap victim deposits the would-be kidnapper at the door of the boarding-house on Catete.

THIRTEEN

> *Carrying Chico, Ferreira, and Bento went the raft*
> *And the raft returned alone.*
> *Without a doubt, a gale out there capsized the craft*
> *And the raft returned alone.*

The melancholy lament of Caymmi's song seemed to presage the tragedy that befell a fisherman known as Jacaré. He and three companions traveled seventy-one days on a balsa raft from Fortaleza, on Brazil's northern coast, to Rio to petition Vargas to extend workers' rights to their occupation. The journey, a true odyssey, moved the country. When they disembarked at the dock at Mauá Square, the raft was placed on a truck with the four heroes, who continued to the Guanabara Palace accompanied by a veritable multitude. Vargas granted their request.

Some time later, Orson Welles, who was in Brazil directing *It's All True,* decided to include the adventure in his documentary. The voyage was re-created for the cameras and the fishermen set out to sea. In the midst of the filming, a tall wave swamped the crude vessel, hurling its occupants into the water. One of them didn't return to the surface: the leader of the expedition, the fisherman Jacaré.

On November 15, six months before the fatal accident, the raft is still a symbol of courage and hope. In late afternoon, Getúlio will receive the four men from Ceará in the palace.

Dimitri Borja Korozec has an especial interest in that same date for reasons unrelated to the feat of the brave navigators from the northeast. For on that same day the president will be at the Jockey Club for the Getúlio Vargas Grand Prix.

The gargantuan drinking bout that had prevented his absurd kidnapping plan forced Dimitri to leave the Urca Casino. Not that he'd been fired; instead of harming him, the episode had won him greater popularity, for Bejo had found the situation amusing. Dimo gave up the employment out of pure embarrassment, despite Rolla's insistent pleas for him to stay on as croupier.

The binge also provoked the ire of Maria Eugênia, distressed to see him arrive home intoxicated almost at daybreak. The incident led to their first quarrel. Pequetita is beginning to become irritated at the anarchist's childish attitudes.

Ignoring the widow's complaints, Dimitri plunges headlong into a new project. He had read about the Grand Prix in *O Globo,* one of the events marking the anniversary of the Republic. As is his custom, Getúlio will attend the race bearing his name. Vargas enjoys parading around the track in an open car, the suggestion of Lourival Fontes, head of the Department of Press and Propaganda, to improve his image. A week early, Dimitri visits the racetrack to evaluate the possibility of eliminating Getúlio Vargas at the Jockey Club.

As he strolls along the grass, his attention is drawn to the men removing the discarded betting tickets from earlier races. These uniformed employees use a wooden stick with a pointed spike at one end to pick up the slips of paper, which they then deposit in a bag draped over their shoulders. Dimitri stops to observe their routine. He notices that the bettors, absorbed in their calculations, pay no attention to them. When the last race ends, Dimo approaches one of the workers and, claiming to be a collector, offers him good money for his jacket and cap. He also buys the bag and the stick used to spear the tickets on the ground.

Upon returning home, he knows how he will assassinate Getúlio.

In the small workshop he has put together in the boardinghouse garage, Dimitri applies the finishing touches to the object he has prepared for the attack.

Using an aluminum tube, sections of an exhaust pipe, and an old revolver that had belonged to Pequetita's husband, he fashions in

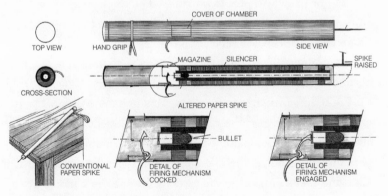

Homemade rifle fashioned from a paper spike.

metal a replica of the wooden stick, transforming it into a single-shot .22-caliber rifle. Its innocuous appearance conceals a silent weapon with great penetrating power.

All that remains is to test the instrument. Knowing that Maria Eugênia has gone shopping, he goes to the backyard, where a fruit-laden mango tree is ideal for his purposes. He still possesses the sharpshooting talent that so impressed his comrades at the Skola Atentatora. He calibrates the aim, correcting the angle and the trajectory, using the mangoes as a target. Within a short time, virtually automatically, he is hitting the fruits dead center.

Saturday, at the Jockey Club, a bullet in the dictator's forehead will put an end to the New State.

The previous evening's rain had left the ground soft and the young women sauntering along the *pelouse* showing off the latest fashions stained their cloth-lined shoes in the damp earth.

It is only moments before the Getúlio Vargas Grand Prix. During the canter, when the horses are shown before the race, the splendid form of Trunfo, one of the favorites, ridden by Agostín Gutiérrez, had been well received.

Tenor and Albatroz had also shone; fine mudders, both had a chance of winning on that heavy turf.

From the gallery of honor, surrounded by authorities and flatterers, the president greets the crowd, smiling and slowly waving his arm in a gesture that has become his trademark. He frequently whispers something to his friend Salgado Filho, president of the Jockey Club and first man to head the recently created Air Force Ministry. Vargas will leave immediately after the Grand Prix to receive the

At the Grand Prix, Minister Salgado Filho and a show-off boy. In the rear, Dimitri disguised as a litter collector.

raftsmen from Ceará at the Guanabara Palace.

On the other side of the track, the horses are lining up at the 2,000-meter mark. Even the litter collectors momentarily interrupt their task so as not to miss the start of the race. Only one of them, his back turned to the event, goes about his work, spearing the torn tickets from the lawn. The motion is mechanical. His eyes are glued on the president.

The indifferent litter collector is Dimitri, who is waiting for the start of the race, when all attention will be focused on the track, to shoot Getúlio. Without neglecting the discarded tickets, he takes his position in front of the gallery of honor. Any noise escaping from the silencer will be covered up by the yells of the crowd. Dimitri is ready to fire. Angrily, he spears the last muddy piece of paper before the starter's shot.

The race begins, and the jockeys spur their mounts, seeking to gain the advantageous pole position. The spectators shout the names of their choices: "Go, Adonis," "Run over him, Tenor!"

As they round the final turn, Trunfo, under the whip of his Chilean rider, pulls away from the pack, opening up a lead of two lengths over Albatroz in second place. Further back, Tenor and

Adonis hold on to the third and fourth positions. Hundreds of pairs of binoculars follow the horses into the homestretch. Dimo raises the stick, points it at Getúlio Vargas's head, and pulls the trigger. There is a muffled explosion and the anarchist falls to the ground, writhing in pain.

There is a scientific explanation for what happened to Dimitri when he put his ingenious device into action. Because the grass was still soaked from the previous night's rain, each time he stuck the instrument in the ground to pick up paper, wet earth accumulated in the weapon's barrel, sealing the projectile's exit path. The gases produced by the explosion, prevented from leaving the barrel by the blockage, expanded in the opposite direction, propelling the cylinder's rear cover into Dimitri's face. The force of the impact had knocked the gunman off his feet. Luckily, the racing fans were so involved in the action on the track that no one had noticed the accident.

Dimitri Borja Korozec escapes from the adventure with a black eye and shattered pride.

FOURTEEN

I never saw so many demands
Or anyone who does the things you do
Don't you know what conscience means
Can't you see I'm just in love with you?
[. . .]
Amélia didn't have a trace of vanity,

Amélia was a woman through and through.

𝄞 𝄞 𝄞 𝄞

From the pages of *Memories and Lapses.*

RIO DE JANEIRO—APRIL 30, 1942

I rewind the Victrola and listen to Ataulfo Alves sing the samba for the fifth time. I'm alone in my room. The music makes me recall Mira Kosanovic, the beautiful Albanian woman who was my first love. "Mira didn't have a trace of vanity, Mira was a woman through and through." I hum the refrain, changing the name. Not that I've lost interest in the widow. It would be unjust to ignore what Maria Eugênia has done for me, risking her own freedom. What bothers me is that, more and more, Pequetita is concerned about my activities. Instead of encouraging me, as an anarchist's companion should do, she discourages any action that places me in danger.

The oddest part is that I'm sure that when she read my notebook she was fascinated by my revolutionary past. Naturally I don't want her as an accomplice and I understand that her religious upbringing condemns violence, but I would still like to make her understand that my life is dedicated to the overthrow of tyranny, whatever the cost.

I still remember her reaction when I came from the Jockey Club after the failed attempt. She berated me as if I were a mischievous child. True, she attentively treated my injury, which even so didn't prevent my losing 50 percent of the vision in my right eye as the result of an infection from the gunpowder, but she threw into the Rodrigo de Freitas lagoon my .45 automatic from the days in Chicago. When I questioned her about it, she said she wanted no more weapons in the house.

She also made me get rid of the workshop that I had put together with such effort and then she had four locks installed on the garage. Now, I have to conceal in the water closet of my toilet, wrapped in plastic bags, the thirty sticks of dynamite that I stole from a quarry in Jacarepaguá. Every time I go to the bathroom I can't forget to disarm the valve. I feel like a boy sneaking smokes behind his mother's back.

I don't know why I sometimes think that Pequetita has doubts about my sanity. I want to share my next project with her and see her quiver with enthusiasm, but I feel I need to keep it secret. Tomorrow, May 1, Getúlio will appear at the big labor rally at Vasco da Gama stadium to commemorate May Day. I know his itinerary and also that the dictator doesn't use a motorcycle escort on such occasions. I plan to crash Maria Eugênia's car, loaded with explosives, into his automobile. My only protection will be jumping from the moving vehicle before the collision. Something tells me Pequetita won't look kindly upon the plan.

On the morning of May 1, Dimitri suffers a disappointment. Upon removing from the water closet the materials with which he plans to build the car bomb, he sees that the protective plastic covering has torn, wetting the dynamite sticks. For a moment, he considers postponing the operation; then, on reflection he decides that the explosives are unnecessary. The Cadillac used by Getúlio isn't armored. If he hits the side of the automobile with enough force, the collision will kill the occupant. The streets are empty because of the holiday, which will make it easy to arrange the accident. Dimitri gets behind the wheel and hot-wires Maria Eugênia's old Ford, then heads for Rua do Russell, where he will wait for Vargas to appear.

The 1941 Cadillac Fleetwood with wide running boards is the president's favorite. Getúlio, short and plump, feels more at ease in the spacious backseat of the limousine. The driver takes the route along Flamengo Beach by way of Rua Silveira Martins.

Vargas, who has come down from Petrópolis for the festivities, uses the time to read the address he will deliver at the stadium. Relaxed, he pushes his rimless glasses down the bridge of his nose and is about to light another cigar when a car comes at high speed from Rua do Russell, crashing into the Cadillac like a meteor. The impact catches him completely unprepared and he's tossed from one side of the car to the other, his unprotected body bouncing around in the vehicle's interior like a rag doll.

O ACIDENTE COM O CARRO DO PRESIDENTE VARGAS

O acidente havido com o auto do presidente Getulio Vargas, quando este se dirigia ao local onde era comemorado com um desfile o "Dia do Trabalho".
        O desastre teve lugar na Praia do Flamengo, e reuniu imediatamente um grande número de populares, que, como se pode ver nas fotos que publicamos, acorreram a prestar ajuda, sendo, então fotografados junto à limousine que conduzia o chefe da Nação.

Photo of the accident in the *Noite Ilustrada*. The arrow points to the streetcar in which Dimitri hid.

Vargas narrowly escapes death, incurring multiple fractures in his left leg, jaw, and one hand.

Nor does the collision spare the perpetrator of the deed. Dimitri was unable to leap from the moving automobile: as he tried to open the door, his coat sleeve caught on the handle.

Perhaps as divine punishment, the anarchist suffers the same injuries that he inflicted upon his victim.

The Fleetwood resists the shock reasonably well, but Maria Eugênia's 1934 Ford is reduced to a pile of metallic rubble.

Dragging himself away from the twisted metal remains of the car, Dimo seeks refuge in a streetcar whose driver has stopped to rubberneck. He hopes to hide from the enraged mob that wants to lynch the individual responsible for the accident.

At the instant that the crowd prepares to execute the would-be assassin of the head of the nation, the characteristic voice of the beloved leader, distorted by his broken jaw, is heard from inside the limousine: "Don't do it! He didn't mean to!"

The people reluctantly obey the order of the injured president. The irony of the situation leaves Dimitri mortified and embarrassed. The pain in his soul is greater than that from his bruises. His life has just been saved by the man he planned to kill.

Getúlio Dornelles Vargas and Dimitri Borja Korozec are rescued at the same time. One of the passersby volunteers to take the president to the Guanabara Palace, where he will be attended to by several doctors, among them Castro Araújo, Juscelino Albuquerque, and Florêncio de Abreu. Soon after that, a taxi transports

Dimo to the Pedro Ernesto Hospital, where he is treated by an anonymous fifth-year medical student.

His injuries oblige Getúlio to spend three months in bed at the palace. Doctors and nurses are amazed at his recuperative powers. With identical fractures, it takes Dimitri twice as long to get back on his feet.

As proof of the generosity that his political opponents call demagoguery, Getúlio insists on paying all of Dimitri's medical expenses.

During the time he is stuck in bed with his leg elevated, his hand in a cast, and with stitches in his chin, Dimitri wonders about Maria Eugênia's absence. The widow calls the nurses' station daily to inquire about him, but she never comes to visit. "She must be angry that her car was destroyed," he thinks, attaching no importance to the fact. The truth is that Pequetita, tired of the adventures that endanger the anarchist's life, after much reflection has decided to put an end to the madness. She still loves Dimitri, but can no longer bear to live with her heart in her mouth.

In November, on the day that Dimitri is released from the hospital, Maria Eugênia is waiting for him at the boardinghouse door. He approaches to kiss her, but she turns her head and says, "We need to talk."

"I know. You're upset because of the car."

"If that's what you think, you don't know me at all."

She begins walking down Rua do Catete and Dimo follows, trying to hug her. "Then what is it?" he asks, puzzled.

Pequetita removes his arm from around her waist. "What's wrong? You have the audacity to ask what's wrong?"

"Of course. It's the first time I've seen you so irritated."

"What's wrong is that I can no longer stand going to sleep at night not knowing if you're going to be alive the next day. I can't bear the thought of being a widow again."

"There's no danger of that."

"Why not?"

"Because we're not married," says Dimitri, smiling, trying to be funny.

That irritates Maria Eugênia even more. She turns on her heel and heads back to the boardinghouse, voicing a threat over her shoulder.

"I've had enough. Either you give up this craziness or I never want to see you again."

The anarchist retorts, raising his voice, "What you call craziness is the reason for my life!"

Pequetita doesn't reply, which infuriates Dimo: "Go! I never needed you for anything!" he shouts, immediately regretting that immense expression of ingratitude.

The residents on Rua do Catete come to their windows to witness the unusual scene. When he realizes he's become the center of attention, Dimo enters the first café he sees and orders coffee and a pack of Petit Londrinos. He regrets the unjust words with which he has just attacked Maria Eugênia. He sees no answer to the dilemma confronting him. He must choose between Pequetita's love and the uncertain path of the political assassin.

He draws in the dark smoke from the strong cigarette, holding it in his lungs until out of breath. Once again he is alone. Alone, literally alone. Maybe it's better that way. Solitude is the hallmark of warriors.

──── FIFTEEN ────

RIO—MARCH 1943

Etelvina, my gal,
I made a big score.
I won five thousand,
I don't have to work no more.

L istening to Moreira da Silva in a cabaret in the Lapa district, Dimitri Borja Korozec, slightly intoxicated, finds inspiration for his next occupation. The sadness brought about by Maria Eugênia's absence must have contributed to blurring his thought processes, as there is no apparent reason for him, at age forty-six, to opt for the profession of banker of the *jogo do bicho,* the illegal lottery based on animal names.

Adapting to the fashion, he had trimmed his mustache and gone back to plastering down his curls with Vaseline, as in the days when he imitated George Raft's hairstyle. He hung around nightclubs, unresigned to the separation from the widow.

One of his recent bohemian companions was Mário Pereira, a

twenty-seven-year-old law student who attends class so infrequently that he's now in his last year of law school for the fourth time.

It is into his ears that Dimitri pours the habitual lamentations of the lovelorn—without, however, any mention of his terrorist activities. "The woman doesn't understand me. She doesn't appreciate my work."

"What do you do?"

"A little of this, a little of that, whatever, you know," replies Dimo, avoiding the subject.

"They like us to have a stable profession, Borjinha. I suffer from the same prejudice merely because I'm a student."

"That's why Moreira's samba's given me an idea. I think I'm going to become a banker for the animal lottery."

Mário is surprised at Dimitri's statement. "Banker for the animal lottery? You need a lot of money for that."

"There's money. . . . There's money. . . ," Dimo assures him, smiling enigmatically.

Mário shrugs and changes the subject, attributing the presumptuous declaration to the effects of alcohol.

Dimitri finishes his drink and takes his leave of the would-be attorney. He is eager to return to his new lodgings. Shaken by the widow's irrevocable decision and not knowing where to live upon leaving the boardinghouse, Dimitri had been taken in by Mathurin at the brothel on Júlio do Carmo.

Thanks to his ability to adapt, developed over the years, he quickly accommodated to life there.

His polyglot talents help him make friends with the foreign prostitutes assembled there in these times of crisis from poor villages in Hungary, Austria, and Poland by the men of the Zwig Migdal, an organization of Jewish procurers who were a disgrace to their people. These pimps dangled the promise of marriage and fortune in Brazil before the poor young women. Unprotected and far from their families, not knowing the language, they were forced into prostitution. Some manage to get rich and become famous madams, others are unable to bear it and kill themselves. The instinct to survive, however, causes most to adjust to the new reality.

Dimitri often observes the girls walking half-naked around the bordello under the watchful eye of Madame Rosaly. He is amused to see them at the window setting the price with customers or refusing those who fail to inspire confidence. When they want to withhold their services, they claim they're sick, shouting in German as they shake their heads, "Nein! Ich habe eine Krankheit. Eine Krankheit!"

"Let's get out of here, the whore's got an *encrenca*," is what the customers hear, creating a neologism that even today means "confusion" or "difficulty" in Brazilian Portuguese.

Mathurin's business acumen had not gone unnoticed by the brothel's owner. Madame Rosaly had made him a partner soon after the ex-safecracker suggested expanding operations by opening a branch in the Laranjeiras district.

When he arrives in Lapa that Saturday, March 6, Dimitri informs his friend of his decision. The pragmatic Mathurin replies, "What does the lottery have to do with political terrorism?"

"Nothing. That's the best part. Don't you see?"

"No."

"I can convince Maria Eugênia that I've given up anarchism for good. Besides which, lottery banker is the perfect disguise for my revolutionary mission."

Mathurin weighs the pros and cons. "You know, the animal lottery isn't viewed very favorably by the police. It's tolerated but illegal. Not to mention that there's a lot of competition."

"Anyone who worked for Al Capone isn't afraid of competition."

The plan isn't to Mathurin's liking. As a last resort, he uses the argument raised earlier by Mário Pereira: "What about money? Where are you going to get the money to bankroll the game?"

Dimo locks his gaze on his old comrade with the expression of one who has an answer for everything.

"I've thought of that. I'm going to sell the pounds sterling that Dragutin gave me."

If he could have heard Dimitri's words, the old Serbian colonel would surely have turned over in his grave.

In 1892, the government subsidy for maintaining the zoo at Vila Isabel having been cut off, Baron Drummond came up with a means of stimulating the sale of admissions. Each ticket was marked with numbers corresponding to the animals' cages. At the end of the afternoon there was a drawing, and the lucky visitors received the equivalent of 20 times the price of the ticket. The animal game was born. It was an immediate success. The tickets, soon available in stores, had generated middlemen, the future bankers of the animal game.

In a short time, the game that had begun so innocuously becomes transformed into runaway gambling. The bankers organize the lottery. The numbers corresponding to the twenty-five animals divided into "groups" further expand into 100 batches of tenths, 1,000 batches of hundredths, and 10,000 thousandths.

To find out the tenth to which the chosen animal belongs, its number is multiplied by 4; that number and the three preceding it constitute its tenth. For example, the tenths for the camel (Group 8) are 32, 31, 30, and 29.

The great attraction of this ingenious lottery is the thousandth. Whoever hits the thousandth receives 5,000 times the value of his bet. "Spots," the term for the places where bets are made, proliferate throughout the city.

At the beginning of the twentieth century, the game was outlawed by the authorities, which only contributed to its propagation. Now it was more spicy, the forbidden fruit. There was no one who didn't make his small "leap of faith" at least once a week.

The hunch is everything; the person who dreams about a river plays the crocodile; about a fat man, the elephant; and dreaming about milk is a sure bet on the cow.

In 1923, when the statesman Rui Barbosa, the beloved Eagle of The Hague, died, there was massive betting on Group 2, and the eagle came up, ruining several lottery bookies.

With the astuteness of international financiers, the bankers began to lay off high wagers among themselves to avoid similar calamities.

It is into this fascinating and risky activity that Dimitri Borja Korozec plunges, body and soul. Part of the small fortune obtained from selling the gold coins he invests in renting a "fort," the term for the bookmaker's headquarters, on Rua Benedito Hipólyto; the rest he uses for working capital. With great satisfaction he struts in front of the house, sporting a tailor-made white linen suit.

Still, he is not completely happy. Contrary to his expectations, Maria Eugênia does not approve of his activities. He phoned her to explain his new pursuit: "It was because of you that I embarked upon this profession."

"Profession? You call that a profession? Gambling is against the law. You tell me you've given up anarchism, which I don't believe, but you're still the same criminal you always were."

"Don't you understand that I'm exercising a social function?"

"The only thing social about the animal lottery is the social diseases a lot of the bookies have!" says Pequetita in exasperation.

"I had no idea you were such a reactionary. Are you going to tell me you've never gambled?"

"Never, but if someday I dream about you, I'll bet on the snake!" screams the widow, slamming down the phone.

Offended, Dimitri opts to downplay the importance of the incident and attempts to forget Maria Eugênia by dedicating himself with tenacity to his business. In time, he plans to expand his territory, but first he wants to establish himself as the biggest lottery banker in the Mangue area.

For the first few weeks everything seemed to go well. Even Mathurin, who had been against the undertaking initially, had become resigned to the sight of Dimitri parading around as a lawbreaker.

The paradisiacal serenity was shattered in the nightmare of Friday, April 23, the day of Saint George, the warrior saint. His inexperience and ignorance of the ins and outs of the trade prevented Dimo from laying off with other bankers the numerous bets placed on Group 11.

To his despair, the horse came up.

In less than twenty-four hours, Dimitri Borja Korozec, the popular Borjinha of the Mangue area, had neither money, a lottery business, nor the widow.

In an inexplicable flight of folly, Dimo holds Getúlio Vargas responsible for his sudden ruin. The bankruptcy awakens in him the sleeping anarchist and the need to execute his mortal enemy. He must avenge those oppressed by the regime.

At one in the morning, after paying the final winning bettor with the little money remaining, he closes the "fort" and hands the keys to Mathurin.

"Where are you going?" his friend asks, concerned.

"I don't know."

Like some ominous black witch, a dark butterfly-shaped cloud covers the moon, casting its light on the sidewalk. Dimitri raises his eyes heavenward and predicts, "Tomorrow the butterfly's going to hit."

Raising the collar of his wrinkled coat, he descends Rua Benedito Hipólyto toward downtown. Avoiding the street lamps, he disappears into the darkness.

SIXTEEN

Do you know where I'm from?
I come from the Engenho hillside,
From the forests, from the coffee fields,
From the rich coconut lands,
From the huts where one is too few,
Two are just right, and three is too many.

I come from beaches with silky sands,
From majestic mountains,
From the pampas and the rubber plantation,
From the rivers' rugged shores,
From the fierce green seas,
From my native land.

I left behind my cleared fields,
My lemon, my lemon trees,
My jacaranda tree and my little house
At the top of the hill
Where the thrush lifts its song.

However many lands I may roam
O God, don't let me die
Until I return home,
Until I can wear the V
That means the victory to come.

T he Brazil of 1944 is marked by two relevant facts. First, having declared war on the Axis almost two years earlier in
reaction to the sinking of several vessels in its fleet, the
country sends the first soldiers of the Brazilian Expeditionary Force
to Sicily. The brave boys are saluted in the verses of Guilherme de
Almeida in "The Song of the Expeditionary Corps." The second is
the mysterious disappearance of Dimitri Borja Korozec.

Regarding the first of these, there is copious documentation of
the courage of the twenty thousand Brazilians armed by the United
States, as in the heroic taking of Monte Castelo in the Apennines.
The pilots of the Brazilian air force, in the cockpits of the famed
Senta a Pua ("Give 'em Hell") squadron, left their trail of glory in
the skies of Italy. The participation by women did not take a backseat to the men. From the first moment, hundreds of young women
formed lines to enlist as nurses in the field hospitals.

The symbol of the troops was a patch depicting a snake smoking
a pipe. It had been said that it would be easier to get a snake to
smoke than to get Brazil to enter the war. Well, the snake smoked.

The conflict motivated every Brazilian citizen. Pyramids of
metal were piled in the streets to contribute to the war effort. Because of gasoline rationing, automobiles ran on gasogene, the chim-
neys stuck onto the rear giving them the appearance of moving
kitchens. Not to mention the blackout, a precaution against possible
air attacks. At night, a darkened Copacabana recalled remote times.

Families already apprehensive about sons shipped off to the battle-fields feared that those not yet recruited would be drafted.

As for the second event, surely the more intriguing, it must be conceded that there is no reliable record of Dimitri's whereabouts during the ensuing decade.

Despite exhaustive research, his fate from 1944 to 1954 constitutes a real enigma; nothing concrete is known about the anarchist's designs. In the notebook entitled *Memories and Lapses,* an indispensable wellspring for this biography, the pages relating to this period either were lost in the course of Dimitri's wanderings or were destroyed by the author himself.

It should be mentioned that there are the usual rumors, highly inauthentic in nature, that no reputable researcher would credit.

It would be frivolous, for example, to affirm, as some perhaps well-meaning individuals swear, that in 1945, when Getúlio Vargas was forced to resign the presidency, Dimitri, armed with a rifle with telescopic sight, was in a tree on Rua Farani, in Botafogo, along which the dictator's car would pass on his way into exile.

They are mistaken who claim to have seen him lurking around the São Borja ranch in the southern state of Rio Grande do Sul, to which Getúlio had withdrawn, waiting for an opportunity to poison his *maté* tea.

Only a hallucinatory mind could believe the fanciful episode that identifies him as the cameraman who put the camera out of commission at the 1950 inauguration of TV Tupi in São Paulo.

Even more absurd is the notion that the terrorist had left for Europe, where he had built for the German generals the bombs used in the frustrated attempt to eliminate Hitler on June 20, 1944, and that his face had been identified in the angry mob that lynched Mussolini.

The least implausible version of what happened to Dimitri during those ten years, even though entirely undocumented, is that after his ill-fated experience as a lottery banker he suffered a violent depression and was taken by monks of charity into a Trappist monastery in Fribourg.

It is at times like these that the conscientious biographer has the obligation to verify his sources thoroughly, separating the wheat from the chaff and historical truth from lies forged around myths.

In reality, the first indisputable news of Dimitri after his disappearance in 1943 comes in his notes for the month of August 1954. In the elections of 1950, Vargas had come to power democratically. Three years later, Dimo returned from an unknown past on the wings of vengeance.

The genuine notes that survive begin on the lower half of a sheet torn from the diary of Dimitri Borja Korozec:

[. . .] with their skirts tucked up around their knees, and despite my insistence, neither of the two could explain why. We continued laughing and drinking till dawn.

On Sunday, August 1, 1954, at the age of fifty-seven, I had almost given up my intention to kill Getúlio. It was becoming harder and harder to get close to the president, now elected by the people. It was totally by chance that our paths crossed once again.

When they closed the casinos in '46, several of the croupiers went to work in amusement parks. They operated the stands where bets were placed, just as earlier they had managed the games on the green felt. To survive, they had been obliged to trade the elegant gaming rooms for the vulgar atmosphere of outdoor fairs.

I had been employed in one of those traveling amusement parks, running the Wheel of Fortune, a kind of vertical roulette that rewarded players with prizes rather than money.

Once when we were set up in Petrópolis, I heard someone yell my name from an automobile passing through the square.

"Borjinha! I don't believe it! Borjinha!"

It was Colonel Benjamin Vargas.

Bejo seemed happy to see me again, and ordering the driver to park, he got out, accompanied by his bodyguards. He couldn't believe I was working at an amusement park: "What are you doing here?"

"I'm responsible for the Wheel of Fortune," I explained with great dignity.

"It's been ten years since I saw you. Let's go have a few drinks."

"I can't right now. My break isn't for another half-hour."

"Are you kidding? I'm the Inspector of Public Amusements. If they don't let you come right this minute, I'll shut down this piece of crap."

At this point, the owner of the park, recognizing the president's brother, approached, oozing obsequiousness.

"Borja, why didn't you tell me you were a friend of Mr. Bejo? Go ahead, I'll take over for you. Take your time! Take all the time you need!"

At the tent where drinks were sold, Bejo ordered a whiskey of doubtful provenance and I a Cuba libre. We strolled around the stands under the eye of the two security men. Bejo wanted to know what I'd been doing in the last few years. I skirted the subject without saying anything concrete. The colonel took my discretion for embarrassment, thinking I was ashamed of what I'd had to do in recent years to survive. He offered to find me a better job: "I don't know in just which office, but I'm sure we can find you a soft spot in some ministry."

Our conversation was interrupted by the sound of a child crying. The little girl, with curly hair tied in a blue velvet ribbon, couldn't be older than ten, and her father was trying to console her. "Sweetie, Daddy missed the target. That's why the man can't give you the teddy bear."

We were in front of a stand where you shot air rifles at a target. If you hit the eight small plaster ducks spinning in the moving track in the rear, you could claim one of the prizes on the shelf. The item that had aroused the little girl's interest was a plush blue bear in a sailor's suit. The child's sobbing moved me. Paying for a load of pellets, I raised the Daisy airgun, a harmless replica of the Winchester 73. I shot from hip-level. Even without aiming, I shattered all the spinning ducks. From behind the counter, my carnival mate gave me an irritated look. I told him to give the girl the bear. The child was beside herself with happiness and her father couldn't thank me enough.

I saw that the colonel had witnessed it all, flabbergasted. "Holy smoke! I didn't know you were so good with a gun, ché! Where'd you learn to shoot?"

"Oh, here and there," I replied vaguely.

"Is it just with an air rifle?"

"No, I shoot well with any type of weapon. I guess it's a gift."

"I know the type of job I'm going to get for you," he said, very happy.

He scribbled a note on a business card bearing the seal of Brazil and stuck it in my pocket. "Tomorrow you'll go back to Rio and on Wednesday look up Gregório in the Catete Palace. Give him this card. You're going to work in Getúlio's personal guard."

Thus it was that Benjamin Vargas unwittingly offered me the great opportunity to kill his own brother.

SEVENTEEN

RIO—CATETE PALACE—THURSDAY, AUGUST 5, 1954

Sea breeze on my face
And the burning, burning sun.
The sidewalk filled with folks
Seeing and being seen.
Rio de Janeiro, how I love you.
And love those who love
This sky, this sea,
This happy people.

Gregório interrupts the song by Antônio Maria and Ismael Neto by turning off the showy Standard Electric radio with its ivory Bakelite case, a gift from a general. Every time he hears the music, he wonders how a man from Pernambuco and another from Pará could compose such a pretty waltz about Rio de Janeiro.

Gregório Fortunato, the Black Angel, was a man of humble origins, tall and beefy, raised on the ranches of São Borja. For almost thirty years he had been Vargas's companion, serving as bodyguard and factotum. His doglike devotion had won him Vargas's affection.

When Bejo relinquished his position as head of the personal guard, Gregório had assumed the post. His proximity to the chief led him to become the object of flattery by those seeking to worm their way into Getúlio's good graces. He had even been awarded the Maria Quitéria Medal by the Minister of War, one of the armed forces' highest honors. Thanks to the favors granted through his intermediation, Gregório was a rich man. The influence he exercised in the shadow of the throne was often greater than that of the cabinet ministers.

Unlettered, unprepared for the power he possessed, he had revealed himself to be an arrogant and dangerous man whose desires were interpreted as direct orders of the president. The personal guard, called the "black guard" by his enemies, carried out his orders without blinking.

The Black Angel scrutinizes from head to foot the man standing before the desk in his office. He reads, with some difficulty, the note written on the card from Benjamim Vargas that Dimitri has given him. Putting away the card, as he does with any document, however minor, signed by a person in authority, he addresses him: "Demétrio Borja. You from Rio Grande do Sul?"

"No, Vassouras."

"You come highly recommended. Bejo says you can be trusted and that you're a good shot. Were you in the military?"

"I served in the army, like everybody."

"You start today. Later I'll introduce you to the men in the guard."

"Thank you, Lieutenant," says Dimitri, addressing Gregório by the rank won in the Constitutionalist Revolution of 1932.

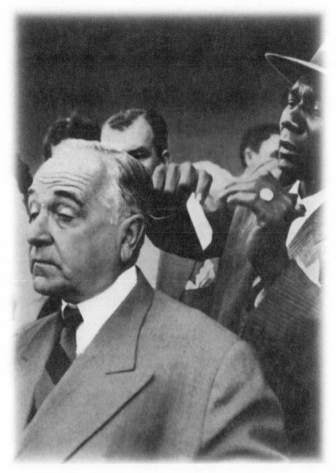

Gregório, the Black Angel, combs President Vargas's
unruly hair.

The Black Angel caresses the omnipresent dagger on his desk
and, his expression vacant, comments as if speaking to himself,
"Too bad I didn't meet you earlier. I had a job right down your
alley."

Facsimile of the *Tribuna da Imprensa* for August 5, 1954.

The next day, upon reading the extra editions of the newspapers, Dimo suspects what Gregório had been hinting at by those words.

The Blood of the Innocent

Today, what more can I say? The sight of Rubens Vaz, lying in the street, with two bullets at point-blank range; the interminable journey I took with him to the hospital, see-

ing him die in my arms, prevent me at this moment from coldly analyzing last night's heinous ambush. But, as God is my witness, I accuse a single man as responsible for this crime. He is the protector of thieves, whose impunity gives them the audacity to commit acts like those of last night. That man is Getúlio Vargas.

Sitting in the duty room of the personal guard, Dimitri reads Carlos Lacerda's article. For months the attacks by the journalist of the *Tribuna da Imprensa* had been becoming more and more violent. He accused Vargas of covering up shady deals, enriching his friends, and plunging the country into unbridled corruption.

In February, the "Colonels' Petition" decrying low salaries and "the negligence into which the army has been cast," linked to discontent in the air force and the navy, both openly opposed to Vargas, had exposed for all to see his lack of support among the military. Inflation is gnawing away at Getúlio's 100-percent raise in the minimum wage.

With the political cunning that characterized him, Vargas had said nothing, waiting for the accusations to blow over, managing the crisis "without rest, without haste." He wasn't counting on his enemies' strength growing with the vehemence of Lacerda's attacks, not only in the *Tribuna da Imprensa* but also through a new and powerful vehicle placed at his disposal by Assis Chateaubriand, the owner of Diários Associados: television. A superlative orator, Lacerda succeeded, through his pronunciamentos on TV Tupi, in mobilizing public opinion as had never been done before.

To protect him from physical indignities, a group of air force officers volunteered to guarantee Lacerda's safety. One of them, Major Rubens Vaz, accompanied him on August 4 to a talk given at the Colégio São José.

Around twelve-thirty that night, Lacerda, his son Sérgio, and the major were returning to Rua Tonelero, where the journalist lived. As they were saying good night in front of the car, they were caught unawares by gunmen waiting in ambush. Lacerda escaped with a bullet in the leg, but Major Rubens Vaz was killed in the attack.

Dimitri has a hunch the disastrous assassination attempt had been organized by Gregório Fortunato. He fears that the personal guard will be disbanded before he has a chance to kill Getúlio.

The next few days are the most agitated in the history of the Catete Palace, which turns into a powder magazine waiting to explode. Civilians and military linked to the government talk in whispers, commenting on the latest news. An anonymous call to the *Tribuna da Imprensa* states that the order for the crime came from the personal guard. The informant claims he can't go into detail because he himself belongs to the guard.

The air force sets up the "Republic of Galeão" at the airbase and, superimposing itself upon the political authority, begins an inquiry of its own. The investigation points suspicion in the killing at the Catete. There is proof that Gregório maintained ties to known criminals.

Denunciations surface of corruption in the president's circle. The clues do not point directly to Getúlio but nevertheless demonstrate the "sea of mud" into which his government has plunged. Some say that Getúlio will be forced to resign. Others swear that Vargas will leave the palace.

Dimitri takes advantage of the reign of confusion to make a minute study of the blueprint of the palace. Using credentials provided him by Gregório, he examines the servants' quarters of the building, studying each floor, memorizing every detail of the structure.

As he had been admitted to its ranks only the day before the attack, he is the only member of the guard not under suspicion. For this reason he has no difficulty making friends with Albino, the Catete's elderly janitor. Thin and laconic, Albino had first entered service during the administration of Nilo Peçanha, who governed from 1906 to 1910.

Alzira Vargas relates an unusual episode in which the janitor played a key role. When Washington Luís was deposed in 1930, he entrusted to Albino the presidential sash with the gold escutcheon and the twenty-eight diamonds representing the states of Brazil, advising him to turn it over only to someone in legitimate authority. Fearful that the sash would disappear, Albino began wearing it under his clothes and would remove it only to bathe. Until he handed it over to Vargas, the janitor of the Catete went to sleep and awoke as president of the Republic without anyone's knowledge.

Dimitri and Albino have long conversations lamenting the unfolding palace drama. Albino admits that he's never seen Getúlio so unhappy, wounded by the betrayal everywhere around him.

On Monday, the personal guard is disbanded. All the agents under Gregório's command return to the offices from which they came. Dimitri, however, who does not belong to any security organ, continues to visit Albino, taking him small presents, fascinating the janitor with his attentions. Little by little, he learns the routine in the palace and the president's habits.

On Thursday, August 12, when political tension is at its height, Vargas leaves for Belo Horizonte, where he will inaugurate the Mannesmann steel mill. That day, Dimitri pays yet another visit to Albino. He finds him depressed by the somber atmosphere in the

Palace of Eagles: "It seems more like the Palace of Vultures," he comments sarcastically.

"Take it easy. It'll all work out, you'll see," Dimitri says in an effort to cheer him up.

Albino has grown fond of him. He finds it comforting to exchange ideas with this likable and attentive man.

At a certain moment, under the pretext of using the bathroom, Dimitri takes his leave from the janitor and heads for the interior of the Catete. The gloomy palace is almost empty because of the president's trip. Dimitri rapidly goes to the third floor and enters Getúlio's bedroom.

The austere appearance of the chamber mystifies him. In contrast to the ceremonial wing of the palace, the room is furnished with heavy, dark, unattractive furniture. There is a plain wooden bed, a chest of drawers, armoires, and a mirror. No luxurious carpet warms the setting. The worn paint on the walls and the cracked ceiling contribute to the air of desolation. The windows are covered by long, unadorned curtains.

Dimitri pushes one of them aside. The space between the window and the curtain is enough to hide a man. He returns the curtain to its place and hurries back downstairs before Albino can notice his prolonged absence.

Satisfied, Dimo now knows where to conceal himself to carry out the long-awaited execution.

Transcribed from *Memories and Lapses.*

RIO, MONDAY, AUGUST 23, 1954

In my room at the rear of the Hotel Novo Mundo, at the corner of Flamengo beach and Rua Silveira Martins, near the Catete Palace, I assess developments. Yesterday, officers from the air force called for Vargas to resign and today were joined by generals in the army. It's said that Vargas would agree to take a leave for the time it takes to complete the inquiries by the police and the military but would never resign definitively. An emergency cabinet meeting is predicted.

Within a matter of days, those in charge of the investigation succeeded in identifying the men who took part in the ambush. Alcino do Nascimento, a professional gunman, Climério de Almeida, a police agent from the personal guard, Nelson de Souza, the cabby who drove the killers, and Gregório Fortunato, who ordered the attack, are under arrest.

Gregório's files were opened by the military, bringing unbelievable findings to light. Compromising letters from generals, deputies, and even the president of the Bank of Brazil, toadying up to the Black Angel, have appalled the nation. Events are moving at dizzying speed.

I feel I must act while there is still time. I have to strike the final blow before my prey escapes once again, taking refuge on the ranch at São Borja.

At this moment of confusion, with the unwitting help of my new friend Albino, it won't be hard for me to get into the Catete and, covered by the curtains, wait in the old caudillo's drab bedroom. Even if I have to stay awake all night, I won't leave until I complete the mission that will justify an entire life dotted with mistakes. For someone who has waited so many years, a few sleepless hours will make no difference.

As I write these lines, perhaps the last of this diary, for if I'm discovered I don't plan to give myself up alive, I think longingly of Dragutin, Mata Hari, Bouchedefeu, Marie Curie, George Raft, Al Capone, Mathurin, and Maria Eugê-nia, the generous widow. I recall my father's dreams as a frus-trated terrorist and, especially, I think about my mother, the Brazilian mulatto woman exiled in a foreign land.

This time, nothing will prevent the bastard grandson of the old general Manuel do Nascimento Vargas from extermi-nating the ex-dictator-despot-tyrant-president Getúlio Var-gas, my uncle.

CATETE PALACE—TUESDAY, AUGUST 24, 1954—8 A.M.

Wearing a striped pajama, President Getúlio Vargas sits on the inhospitable bed in the room furnished with Franciscan parsi-mony. The meeting with the Ministry, which began at three in the morning, had ended in an impasse. The majority of the civilian min-isters tended toward a solution that would avoid a bloodbath—i.e., removal from office. General Zenóbio da Costa was in favor of putting troops into the streets. Osvaldo Aranha had declared himself on the side of resistance, but had stated that the decision must be Vargas's.

For the first time in his life, the skillful seventy-one-year-old politician, the president considered by the oppressed as the Father of the Poor, sees himself vanquished.

There is only one way to transform defeat into victory. He places a white envelope on the night table and takes from his pajama pocket the Colt .32 with mother-of-pearl handle that he has carried for years. He contemplates the weapon, lost in thought.

Dimitri observes everything from his hiding place behind the curtains. He had planned to strangle Getúlio, clutching his throat in a lethal tourniquet between his twelve fingers. He realizes, however, that he cannot allow the president to commit suicide. Dead by his own hand, Vargas will become the martyr of the people. Dimitri understands at a glance that if he is to fulfill his goal as anarchist and destroy the man, not even he must kill him in such circumstances.

The best way to extinguish the myth is to force him to live. True revenge will be to see him execrated and pursued far from power, like a hunted animal. Thus are oppressors annihilated.

He must stop the final act of that tragedy. He pushes aside the curtain and shouts, "No!"

For a moment, Getúlio is astonished at the unexpected intrusion. Recovering from the shock, he asks, "Who are you?"

"Dimitri Borja Korozec."

"What are you doing here?"

"I came to stop you from committing suicide."

"Why?"

"Because the only way you can die is by staying alive."

Vargas stares at him in confusion. There is something familiar in those features. The man's face merges with the memories of his father when he was young, on the cattle ranches of Rio Grande.

"Where are you from?" asks the president, still intrigued.

"From Bosnia. I'm your nephew, the son of a sister you never knew."

Vargas suddenly remembers the woman from Sarajevo who wrote him a letter many years earlier saying the same thing. In his mind, the resemblance between the intruder and the old general is becoming more and more unmistakable. At that decisive instant, he doesn't know whether he's delirious and imagining phantoms from the past.

Getúlio forces himself to remain lucid and resumes the inter-rupted gesture, cocking the small Colt with the mother-of-pearl handle.

With a catlike leap, Dimitri throws himself upon him and grasps the arm gripping the pistol. The president struggles for control of the gun. The two roll silently on top of the Spartan bed. Finally, Dimitri manages to wrap his hands around the weapon.

Just as Dimitri thinks he has won the battle, Getúlio, with a tug, wrenches the Colt to his chest. Inadvertently, Dimo's index finger pulls the trigger.

Horrified, Dimitri Borja Korozec realizes that his finger has just caused the suicide of Getúlio Dornelles Vargas.

Dimo tries to revive the dying legend lying prostrate on the bed. Futile. Vargas remains lifeless in his arms. He curses himself for his clumsiness, the fate that has tormented him since childhood. His awkwardness has led him to kill, with a bullet through the heart, the one man he could not kill.

Dimitri hears nervous footsteps in the corridor, people attracted by the sound of the shot. He must leave that bedroom, which has become a funeral chamber. He opens the windows and prepares to scale the walls to the building's roof, having laid out plans beforehand for such an escape.

First, however, an almost morbid curiosity compels him to return to the night table. He opens the envelope and unfolds the letter. Someone is knocking on the door and shouting. Dimo has time to read only the final sentence of the letter on the stationery of the Republic: "Serenely, I take the first step on the road to eternity and leave life to enter History."

He quickly closes the envelope and leaps toward the window on his way to the roof of the Catete Palace.

Broken by his failure, Dimitri Borja Korozec disappears into the fog of the August morning by climbing to the top of the Palace of Eagles.

EPILOGUE

FRANCE-PRESSE—ASSOCIATED PRESS—REUTERS—TASS

EGYPT—ALEXANDRIA—WEDNESDAY, OCTOBER 27, 1954

President Gamal Abdel Nasser escaped death yesterday when several shots were fired at him by a fanatic during a ceremony in this city. When arrested, the terrorist Mahmoud Abdel Latif declared himself to be a member of the radical Muslim Brotherhood sect. Based on his information, military commandos charged with wiping out the organization quickly arrested several members of the sect who were in hiding near the marketplace in the district of Anfushi. In the assassins' hideout were found copious materials that will lead to final annihilation of the guerrilla group.

Among the documents was a half-destroyed notebook entitled *Memories and Lapses: Notes for an Autobiography,* by Dimitri Borja Korozec. Judging by the name, the author is not of Arab origin.

Only one of the terrorists managed to escape, in a spectacular getaway, by leaping from a terrace on the fourth floor at the rear of the

293

building. Zigzagging through the streets in a headlong flight, he was recognized by a merchant in the area who, disturbed by the uproar, shouted at the top of his lungs, "Etnashar esbaa! Etnashar esbaa!" which in Alexandrian Egyptian dialect means "twelve fingers."

ILLUSTRATION CREDITS

Page 11: Seal of the Black Hand: Jô Soares.

Page 12: Dragutin Dimitrijevic: *Crapouillot,* No. 20. Office de Livres de *Crapouillot,* p. 50.

Page 17: Bergmann-Bayard, 1901: *Pistols and Revolvers,* by Major Frederick Myatt, M.C. London: Salamander Books, 1980, p. 154.

Page 17: Schuler-Reform, 1904: *Pistols and Revolvers,* by Major Frederick Myatt, M.C. London: Salamander Books, 1980, p. 154.

Page 18: Guernica: Museo Nacional Centro de Artes Reina Sofia, Madrid/ Herdeiros de Pablo Picasso. Copyright © Sucession Picasso 2001.

Page 19: Mira Kosanovic letter: Jô Soares.

Page 26: Map of Sarajevo: Sírio Cansado.

Page 30: Archduke Franz Ferdinand entering a car: Undated, uncredited photo.

Page 33: Princip being taken into custody: *Crapouillot,* No. 20. Office de Livres de *Crapouillot,* p. 48.

Page 33: Illustration of the assassination: *Le Petit Journal Illustré,* in *Crapouillot,* No. 20. Office de Livres de *Crapouillot,* p. 51.

Page 33: Archduke Franz Ferdinand's tunic: *História Universal,* Vol. 9, by H. G. Wells. São Paulo: Companhia Editora Nacional, 1970, p. 458.

Page 33: Garvilo Princip: Undated, uncredited photo.

Page 33: Browning model, 1900. *Pistols and Revolvers,* by Major Frederick Myatt, M.C. London: Salamander Books, 1980, p. 199.

Page 39: Pound sterling: Jô Soares.

Page 40: Dimitri with bandaged hand (detail): *Political Murder: From*

Tyrannicide to Terrorism, by Franklin Ford. Cambridge: Harvard University Press, 1985, p. 248.

Page 44: One of the cars on the Orient Express: *The Last Express: A User's Manual.* Broderbund Software, Inc., p. 23.

Page 45: Map of the Orient Express route: Sírio Cansado.

Page 48: Mata Hari: *The Fatal Lover: Mata Hari and the Myth of Women in Espionage,* by Julie Wheelwright. A Julliet Gardiner Book. London: Collins and Brown, 1992, plate 3. Courtesy of Mander and Mitchenson Theatre Collection, London.

Page 57: Photo of Dimitri's and Mata Hari's feet: Jô Soares.

Page 67: Gérard Bouchedefeu: Jô Soares.

Page 85: Door of the Croissant: *Jaurès: La Parole et l'acte,* by Madelaine Rebérioux. Paris: Découvertes Gallimard, 1994, p. 15. Courtesy of Centre National et Musée Jean-Jaurès, Castre bos.

Page 86: Map of Paris (detail): Sírio Cansado.

Page 87: Dimitri's notebook: Undated, uncredited photo.

Page 98: Javert's letter: Undated, uncredited photo.

Page 106: Taxi convoy: *Le Roman Vrai de La IIIe e de la IVe République, 1871–1958,* Vol. 1, by Gilbert Guilleminault. Paris: Robert Laffont, 1991, p. 28. Collection of Sirot-Angel.

Page 110: Photo taken by Madame Bourdon: *Le Taxis de Marne,* by Phillippe Bernett, p. 158.

Page 111: Routes taken by the taxis: Sírio Cansado.

Page 111: Prussian medal: *Le Taxis de Marne,* by Phillippe Bernett, p. 93. Collection of Roger Viollet, Paris.

Page 120: Brasserie Lipp: Undated, uncredited photo.

Page 122: José Patrocínio filho: *O Fabuloso Patrocínio filho,* Vol. 3, by Raimundo Magalhães, Jr. Rio de Janeiro: Civilização Brasileira, 1957, p. 74. Courtesy of Brício de Abreu.

Page 122: José Patrocínio filho: *Gazeta de Noticias,* 1957. *O Fabuloso Patrocínio filho,* Vol. 3, by Raimundo Magalhães, Jr. Rio de Janeiro: Civilização Brasileira, 1957, p. 156.

Page 123: Portrait of Dimitri: Jô Soares.

Page 145: Aleister Crowley: *The Confession of Aleister Crowley: An Autobiography,* edited by John Symonds and Kenneth Grant. New York: Arkana, (Penguin Books), 1989.

Page 153: George Raft: Undated, uncredited photo.

Page 162: Thompson submachine gun: Drawing by Carlos Fuentes, 1998.

Page 168: Saint Valentine's Day Massacre: *Capone: The Man and the Era,* by Laurence Bergreen. New York: Simon & Schuster, 1996. Courtesy of Chicago Historical Society (ICHI 14406).

Page 169: Al Capone: *Capone: The Man and the Era,* by Laurence Bergreen. New York: Simon & Schuster, 1996. Courtesy of Chicago Historical Society (DN 96548).

Page 185: Newspaper facsimile: Undated, uncredited photo.

Page 191: Samariego brothers: Undated, uncredited photo.

Page 220: General Eurico Dutra and Getúlio Vargas: *Getúlio Vargas na Literatura de Cordel,* by Origines Lessa. Rio de Janeiro: Editora Documentário, 1973, p. 91.

Page 226: César Albanelli: Undated, uncredited photo.

Page 245: Casino advertisement: *Nosso Século,* 1945–1950. Editora Abril.

Page 254: Homemade rifle: Drawing by Carlos Fuentes, 1998.

Page 256: Jô Soares and Salgado Filho, August 8, 1943: Private collection.

Page 261: The accident photo: *Noite Illustrada.*

Page 271: Animal drawing: *Aparência do Rio de Janiero,* Vol. 2, by Gastão Cruls. Rio de Janiero: José Olympio, 1965, p. 754.

Page 281: Gregório Fortunato and Getúlio Vargas: *O cruzeiro,* 1950.

Page 286: Newspaper facsimile: *Tribuna da Imprensa,* August 5, 1954. Private collection.

BIBLIOGRAPHY

Amado, Gilberto. *Presença na política*. Rio de Janeiro: José Olympio, 1958.

Avrich, Paul. *Sacco and Vanzetti: The Anarchist Background*. Princeton: Princeton University Press, 1991.

Beaupré, Fanny, and Roger-Henri Guerrand. *Le Confident de ces dames*. Paris: La Découverte, 1997.

Berger, Paulo. *Dicionário Histórico das ruas do Rio de Janeiro*. 4 vols. Rio de Janeiro: Olímpica, 1974.

Bergreen, Laurence. *Capone, The Man and the Era*. New York: Simon & Schuster, 1994.

Bernett, Philippe. *Les Taxis de la Marne*. N.p., n.d., p. 93.

Bornstein, Joseph. *The Politics of Murder*. New York: William Sloane Associates, 1950.

Borsa, S., and C.-R. Michel. *La Vie quotidienne des hôpitaux en France au XIXᵉ siècle*. Paris: Hachette, 1985.

Bragance, Anne. *Mata Hari: la poudre aux yeux*. Paris: Belfond, 1995.

Câmara, José Sette. *Agosto 1954*. São Paulo: Siciliano, 1994.

Carneiro, Glauco. *História das revoluções brasileiras*. 2 vols. Rio de Janeiro: Edições O Cruzeiro, 1965.

Carrillo, E. Gomez. *Le Mystère de la vie et de la mort de Mata Hari*. Paris: Charpentier et Fasquelle, 1926.

Charrière, Henri. *Papillon*. Paris: Robert Laffont, 1969.

Coarcy, Vivaldo. *Memórias da cidade do Rio de Janeiro*. Rio de Janeiro: José Olympio, 1955.

Collier, Richard. *The Plague of the Spanish Lady*. London: A&B, 1974.

Le Crapouillot, no. 20 (n.d.): 50.

Crespelle, Jean-Paul. *La Vie quotidienne à Montmartre au temps de Picasso.* Paris: Hachette, 1986.

Crowley, Aleister. *Aleister Crowley, An Autobiography.* London: Penguin Books, 1979.

Cruls, Gastão. *Aparência do Rio de Janeiro.* 2 vols. Rio de Janeiro: José Olympio, 1965.

Curie, Eve. *Madame Curie.* New York: Da Capo Press, 1937.

Daraul, Arkon. *A History of Secret Societies.* New York: Citadel Press, 1995.

Delporte, Christian. *Histoire du journalisme et des journalistes en France.* Paris: Presses Universitaires, 1995.

Dulles, John W. F. *Anarquistas e comunistas no Brasil.* Rio de Janeiro: Nova Fronteira, 1973.

Edmundo, Luiz. *O Rio de Janeiro do meu tempo.* 2 vols. Rio de Janeiro: Imprensa Nacional, 1938.

Facer, Sian, ed. *On This Day.* New York: Crescent Books, 1992.

Fausto, Boris. *A Revolução de 30.* São Paulo: Companhia das Letras, 1997.

Flamini, Roland. *Thalberg, the Last Tycoon.* New York: Crown Publishers, 1994.

Fonseca, Rubem. *Agosto.* São Paulo: Companhia das Letras, 1990.

Ford, Franklin L. *Political Murder from Tyrannicide to Terrorism.* Cambridge: Harvard University Press, 1985.

Freidel, Frank. *Franklin D. Roosevelt: A Rendezvous with Destiny.* New York: Little, Brown, 1990.

Goldman, Emma. *Living My Life.* 2 vols. New York: Dover Publications, 1970.

Gordon, David George. *The Compleat Cockroach.* Berkeley: Ten Speed Press, 1996.

Graham, Otis L. Jr., and Meghan R. Wander. *Franklin D. Roosevelt: His Life and Times.* New York: Da Capo Press, 1985.

Grun, Bernard. *The Timetables of History.* New York: Simon & Schuster, 1991.

Guérin, Daniel. *L'Anarchisme: de la doctrine à la practique.* Paris: Gallimard, 1987.

Guerrand, Roger-Henri. *Les Lieux. Histoire des commodités.* Paris: La Découverte, 1997.

Guilleminault, Gilbert. *Le Roman vrai de la III᷍ et de la IVᵉ République.* 2 vols. Paris: Robert Laffont, 1991.

Guilleminault, Gilbert and André Mahé. *L'Épopée de la révolte.* Paris: Denoël, 1963.

Henriques, Affonso. *Ascensão e queda de Getúlio Vargas.* 3 vols. Rio de Janeiro–São Paulo: Record, 1966.

Howard, Michael. *The Occult Conspiracy.* New York: MJF Books, 1989.

Hugo, Victor. *Les misérables.* Paris: Seuil, 1963.

Joyeux, Maurice. *Ce que je crois: réflexions sur l'anarchie.* Saint Denis: Le Vent du ch'min, 1984.

Kupferman, Fred. *Mata Hari: songes et mensonges.* Brussels: Éditions Complexe, 1982.

Lancastre, Maria José de. *Fernando Pessoa, uma fotobiografia.* Lisbon: Centro de Estudos Pessoanos, 1981.

Lentz, Harris M., III. *Assassinations and Executions: An Encyclopedia of Political Violence.* Jefferson, N.C.: McFarland, 1988.

Lessa, Orígenes. *Getúlio Vargas na literatura de cordel.* Rio de Janeiro: Editora Documentário, 1973.

Ludwig, Emil. *Juillet 1914.* Paris: Payot, 1929.

Machado, Carlos, and Paulo de Faria Pinho. *Memórias sem maquiagem.* São Paulo: Cultura, 1978.

Mackenzie, David. *Apis, the Congenital Conspirator.* New York: Columbia University Press, 1989.

Mackenzie, David. *The "Black Hand" on Trial: Salonika 1917.* New York: Columbia University Press, 1995.

McNeill, William H. *Plagues and Peoples.* New York: Anchor Books, 1976.

Magalhães, Jr. Raimundo. *O fabuloso Patrocínio Filho.* Rio de Janeiro: Civilização Brasileira, 1957.

Malcolm, Noel. *Bosnia: A Short History.* New York: New York University Press, 1994.

Mattos, Betty, and Alda Rosa Travassos. *Colombo cem anos.* Rio de Janeiro: Companhia Brasileira de Artes Gráficas, 1994.

Monestier, Martin. *Histoires et bizarreries sociales des excréments.* Paris: Cherche-Midi, 1997.

Morais, Fernando. *Olga.* São Paulo: Alfa-Ômega, 1989.

Myatt, Major Frederick. *Pistols & Revolvers.* London: Salamander Books, 1980.

Nataf, André. *La Vie quotidienne des anarchistes en France.* Paris: Hachette, 1986.

O Cruzeiro, August 13, 1955.

Oliveira, Júlio Amaral de. *Circo.* São Paulo: Biblioteca Eucatex de Cultura Brasileira, 1990.

Partner, Peter. *Templiers, francs-maçons et sociétés secrètes.* Paris: Pygmalion, 1992.

Peixoto, Alzira Vargas do Amaral. *Getúlio Vargas, meu pai.* Porto Alegre: Globo, 1960.

Peixoto, Celina Vargas do Amaral. *Getúlio Vargas—Diário.* 2 vols. São Paulo–Rio de Janeiro: Siciliano-Fundação Getúlio Vargas, 1995.

Peixoto, Paulo Matos. *Atentados politicos de César a Kennedy.* São Paulo: Paumape, 1990.

Pôrto, Agenor. *Da vida de um médico.* Rio de Janeiro: Irmãos Pongetti, 1961.

Prasteau, Jean. *La Vie merveilleuse du Casino de Paris.* Paris: Denoël, 1975.

Quinn, Susan. *Marie Curie, a Life.* New York: Addison Wesley and Simon & Schuster, 1995.

Rabaut, Jean. *Jaurès assassiné.* Brussels: Éditions Complexe, 1984.

Ramos, Graciliano. *Memórias do cárcere.* 20th ed. 2 vols. Rio de Janeiro–São Paulo: Record, 1985.

Rebérioux, Madeleine. *Jaurès. La parole et l'acte.* Paris: Gallimard, Découvertes Collection, 1994, p. 15.

Reouven, René. *Dictionnaire des assassins.* Paris: Denoël, 1986.

Richardson, John. *A Life of Picasso.* New York: Random House, 1996.

Robertson, Charles L. *The International Herald Tribune: The First Hundred Years.* New York: Columbia University Press, 1987.

Schevill, Ferdinand. *A History of the Balkans.* New York: Dorset Press, 1991.

Schirmann, Léon. *L'affaire Mata Hari: enquête sur une machination.* Paris: Taillandier, 1994.

Severiano, Jairo, and Zuza Himem de Mello. *A canção no tempo.* São Paulo: Editora 34, 1997.

Stevens, Serita Deborah, and Anne Klarner. *Deadly Doses.* Cincinnati: Writers Digest Books, 1990.

Taylor, Meadows. *Confessions of a Thug.* New Delhi: Asian Educational Services, 1988.

Torres, Antônio. *O circo no Brasil.* Rio de Janeiro: Funarte, 1998.

Tribuna da Imprensa 6, no. 1402 (August 1954).

Van Hartesveldt, Fred, ed. *The 1918–1919 Pandemic of Influenza: The Urban Impact in the Western World.* New York: Edwin Mellen Press, 1992.

Vankin, Jonathan, and John Whalen. *50 Greatest Conspiracies of All Time.* New York: Citadel Press, 1995.

Waagenaar, Sam. *Mata Hari ou la Danse macabre.* Paris: Fayard, 1985.

Wells, H. G. *The Outline of History.* London: George Newnes, 1920.

Wheelwright, Julie. *The Fatal Lover: Mata Hari and the Myth of Women in Espionage.* London: Collins and Brown, 1992.

Woodcock, George. *Anarchism and Anarchists.* Ontario: Quarry Press, 1992.

ABOUT THE AUTHOR

Jô Soares is one of Brazil's best-known and most-loved cultural figures. His hugely successful career in television, theater, and film has been supplemented over recent years by his entry into the world of books and journalism with the publication of three works of nonfiction as well as his internationally best-selling first novel, *A Samba for Sherlock.*

ABOUT THE TRANSLATOR

Clifford E. Landers is Professor of Political Science at New Jersey City University. In addition to his translation of Jô Soares' previous novel, *A Samba for Sherlock,* his translations from Brazilian Portuguese include the nineteenth-century romantic classic *Iracema,* by José de Alencar, novels by Rubem Fonseca, Jorge Amado, João Ubaldo Ribeiro, Patricia Melo, Chico Buarque, and Marcos Rey, and shorter fiction by Lima Barreto, Rachel de Queiroz, and Osman Lins.